Books by Fran Stewart:

Orange as Marmalade
Yellow as Legal Pads

Coming soon:

Green as a Garden Hose

Yellow as Legal Pads

Yellow as
Legal Pads

Fran Stewart

Yellow as Legal Pads

1st edition: © 2004 Fran Stewart

ISBN: 0-9749876-2-X

This is a work of fiction. Any resemblance to any person living or dead is purely coincidental.

This book was printed in the United States of America

To order additional copies of this book, contact:

Doggie in the Window Publications
PO Box 1565
Duluth GA 30096
www.DoggieintheWindow.biz

Dedicated to
Janet Bogle
who believes in me and in my books

and

in memory of
Ed Lowry (1946-2004)
my mostly cantankerous
often curmudgeonly
unfailingly generous
frequently infuriating
& deeply warm-hearted
friend

Acknowledgments/Gratitude

Biscuit McKee always writes a gratitude list at the end of each day. Five things for which she is grateful. Marmalade, as you will see, does the same. I've been using that process myself for seven or eight years, ever since I read *Simple Abundance* by Sarah Ban Breathnach. At the time I was working in an office, commuting long hours, and dreading work each day. I began to see that nothing associated with my job–except the fine women I toiled with–ever showed up on my gratitude lists. So I quit corporate life. And my writing eventually grew out of that shift. Thank you, Sarah Ban Breathnach. You are a woman I've never met, but your writing helped me enrich my life.

My gratitude list for this book has to include Nanette Littlestone, whom I met through the *Georgia Writers Association.* She was incredibly generous with her time, plowing through multiple versions of *Yellow* and offering advice that was succinct (and right!) At the same time, it was gentle. I appreciate you, Nanette.

I had great fun roaming through Happy's Antique Mall in Lilburn, Georgia, and interviewing Sharon Crouch and Jim Underhill. They set me straight on quite a few details about antiques in general and old trunks specifically. Any mistakes in this text are mine, though, not theirs.

One of my favorite people in the world is Anne Hammer, who in another lifetime years ago was a science teacher. She spent hours critiquing a chapter I'd had great fun writing. It was, as she carefully explained, riddled with mistakes. After we spoke, I had some more fun re-writing it. And then I junked almost the whole thing (in part because Nanette–see entry above–said it was boring and confusing). Oh well. Re-writing, revising, reevaluating. It's all part of a writer's life. I do appreciate you Anne. Your helpful spirit is indeed in this book. You are a good teacher.

My core of dear friends, Darlene Carter, Diana Alishouse, Kathi Moon, and Millie Woollen deserve my undying gratitude for reading the mishmosh I sent them and seeing a book inside it all. Diana, in particular, was meticulous in her dissection of *Yellow*, and yet kind in her commentary. And special thanks go to Darlene, who is my weekly MasterMind partner, for her honesty (ouch!) when she told me that *at least a little bit* of chronological order would truly help. (I tend to write books backwards and inside out.)

Stephanie Mooney taught me how to edit my web site. Now, if I'd just take the time to do what she taught me . . . I'd rather be writing, though. *Green as a Garden Hose* is calling me.

Finally, I'd like to thank the wonderful folks at Doggie in the Window Publications who guided me through the process of getting the second edition of *Orange as Marmalade* published, and who made it possible to put *Yellow as Legal Pads* out there.

This writing continues to be a work of love. Thank goodness.

Fran Stewart
at my new (to me) home on the side of
Hog Mountain, Georgia
August 2004

List of Characters:

Martinsville, Georgia:
Bisque "**Biscuit**" McKee, born 1947. Town librarian. Marries Bob Sheffield in 1996.
Bob Sheffield, born 1942. Officer of the Peace in Martinsville. *I call him Softfoot.*
Glaze McKee, younger sister to Biscuit. *Smellsweet.*
John & Ivy Martelson McKee, parents to Biscuit and Glaze. *Dreammaker and Sunset Lady.*
Larry Murphy, a barber
Margaret Ingalls, Monica Tarkington's only child, born 1956. Marries Sam Casperson in 1977.
Marmalade, Biscuit's cat. *Excuse me? I am not **her** cat. Widelap is **my** human.*
Myrtle Hoskins Snelling, reporter.
Pamela C. & Raymond L. Tarkington
 Mildred, their 1st daughter, born 1921.
 Married Peter Holvers of Atlanta in 1945 and Conrad Robeson in 1966.
Monica, Pam & Ray's 2nd daughter, born 1922.
 Married George Ingalls in 1955.
Melissa, their 3rd daughter (twin to James), born 1955.
 Owner of *Azalea House*, a bed & breakfast
Tom Parkman, owner of CT's, a restaurant. *Fishgiver is my name for him.*
Verity Marie, born 1992, Biscuit's grandchild

Atlanta, Georgia:
Gustav "The Old Man" Holvers.
 1. Married 1st wife in 1900
 Marcus, their 1st son, born 1901.
 Peter, their 2nd son, born 1902.
 Married Mildred Tarkington in 1945.
 2. Gustav married **Charlotte** McLeod upon death of 1st wife in 1905.
 Shirlene Holvers, born in 1907. Unmarried
 Her daughter **Sandy** Holvers, born in 1936.

Brenda Holvers, Mildred's only daughter, born 1946 in Atlanta.
Conrad Robeson, born 1925, brother to Estelle. Marries Mildred T.
Holvers in 1966.
Derry Murphy, an attorney with Scroop Grey & Cambridge.
Sister to Larry the barber.
Ernie Robeson, Mildred's only son, born 1967 in Atlanta.
Ernst B. Wilhelm III, a silk supplier
Estelle Robeson, born 1916. Conrad's older sister.
Married Thomas Placings in 1938.
Widowed Dec 7, 1941.
Secretary to Peter Holvers in Atlanta 1942 to 1965.
    Linda, her 1st daughter, front desk clerk, born 1940.
    Married Bull Finney in 1970, in Savannah.
    Diane, her 2nd daughter, a nurse, born 1941.
    Married Brando Williston in 1963, in Savannah.
Julius & **Hester** Robeson, grandparents to Linda & Diane

Savannah, Georgia:

Barry Murphy, owner of The River Landing, a hotel. Brother to
barber Larry & lawyer Derry.
Columbine "Colly" Sloan, a police officer
    Patch Sloan, her husband
    Brando Williston, her partner on the force, who married
    Diane Placings in 1963.
Horse and **Bunny** Munson, a troubled couple
Joan Fredericks. Married Russell Finney in 1947.
    "**Bull**" Finney - only son of Joan, born 1944.
    Adopted by Russell in 1949.
    Married Linda Placings in 1970.
Millie Cappell, general manager of The River Landing
Sally Whitehead, evening shift front desk clerk
Star, Joan's friend
Thin Woman
Woman with tape recorder

Chapter 1 - 1996

Sunday May 5, 1996 - Martinsville, Georgia

I slipped on my black dress, clipped my hair up on top of my head, and walked out of my lonely bedroom. Marmalade leaped onto the railing and walked with dainty grace beside me until I reached the top of the stairs. How does she do that without falling?

I am a cat. I know where my center is.

She hopped onto my shoulder, still with exquisite grace, and hitched a ride downstairs. "Guard the house while I'm gone," I told her. "And don't wake up your Aunt Glaze."

Of course I didn't bother to lock the door behind me. We don't do that in Martinsville.

A gray day. Appropriate, I supposed. I hoped it wouldn't rain. My granddaughter, Verity, old beyond her four years, had asked if there would be a limousine for the funeral. I told her I had decided against it. My green Buick was good enough for this.

When I reached Braetonburg, I pulled up in front of the old house I used to live in. There were several cars there already. I probably should have gotten here early, I thought, but this was the best I could do. It didn't seem fair to have driven home alone yesterday from my honeymoon and today be facing a funeral at nine o'clock in the morning.

As I walked up to the front door, I noticed that the ivy seemed to be getting ahead of Sally. Someday I'd volunteer to come back and help her dig some more of it out. Why did I ever plant that stuff to begin with?

"Mom, I'm so glad you're here." Sandra, the older of my daughters, was wearing black, too. It didn't suit her. Of course, my black didn't suit me, either. I looked like the undertaker instead of–of what? I wondered. Was there a title for this?

I could hear Sally, my younger daughter, the pregnant one, directing traffic in the kitchen. There would be food spread out on the big oak table. And the children would be milling around underfoot.

"Would you like to look at the body?" Sandra asked me.

There had been too much death recently, but this body I had to look at. "I suppose now is as good a time as any."

She led me into the living room, and there was the coffin in the center of the room. I nodded to the other women who were ranged about, some sitting, some standing. I noticed that Sally had moved the furniture around. I suppose that was her right now that she lived there and I didn't. But it was a bit disconcerting. My eyes were drawn back to the casket. The light wood was attractive, and the children had drawn designs on the sides and top. It was a true work of love. And Bob looked quite fetching like that, lying on top of the yellow silk lining.

Before I had time to think much about it, the pall bearers came into the room, closed the coffin, and gathered it up. Sally and Sandra stepped to either side of me, and we walked behind the casket, out of the living room, down the hallway, out the front door, and into the small field across the street.

The grave had already been dug, beneath the enormous oak that shadowed the ground that early May morning. We gathered around and waited for a moment in silence. Then Verity Marie, the oldest of my grandchildren, walked forward and threw some rose petals into the grave.

The pall bearers lowered the coffin.

As one of them began to scoop dirt onto the lid, Verity cried out. "Oh Mommy, can I look at him one more time?"

I reached forward and rested my hand on Verity's little shoulder as Sandra said, "Of course you can, dear." It is so moving, the anguish of children.

Sandra reached down into the grave and flipped open the lid of the cigar box. Verity picked up Bob, her goldfish who had died several days ago and who had been kept intact until I could return from my disastrous honeymoon. It was an honor to have the date of a funeral held up just for me.

"He's cold, Mommy," she said.

"Yes, dear. That's because he's been in the freezer. Let's tuck him in the nice warm earth, shall we?"

So, on a gray Sunday, eight days after my wedding to Bob Sheffield, we buried his namesake, Bob the Goldfish. Then we returned to the old house and had vanilla ice cream and chocolate cake. Was it only yesterday that I had come home from my honeymoon in Savannah without Bob my husband?

* * * * * *

The return home yesterday, Saturday May 4th, one week after my wedding, had been a simple affair. Get in the Buick and drive, and drive, and drive, from Savannah in southeastern Georgia to Martinsville, my little town in northeast Georgia. As I drove the green Buick up Beechnut Lane, I took a moment to look at the comfortable old gray house that Marmalade and I had moved into just five weeks ago, a month before my wedding to Bob. Its wide porch wraps around three sides, shading the rooms from the summer heat and glare. The dormer windows on the second floor give the house a welcoming look, as if happy family members are watching from them and waiting for our return.

I am waiting for you. I know you will be here soon.

The house is unusual, even for Martinsville, where no two houses are the same. There is a row of tiny windows set high under the eaves, like freckles along the hairline of the steeply pitched roof. They let a great deal of light into the attic, which is full of boxes and trunks, lamps and hobby horses, hatboxes and rocking chairs, the assorted detritus of generations of inhabitants. Elizabeth Hoskins, who sold us the house, said that nobody had ever gotten around to clearing it out. I took one look up there and decided that it would have to wait till well after the honeymoon.

Already I loved the place and thought of it as home. I had missed its comforting presence for the past week. Well, that's not exactly true. There were quite a few moments when the house was the last thing on my mind. It was, after all, our honeymoon. Even marred by the murder and all my anguish, I had to admit that Savannah had been a lovely city, but the memories were still raw, still painful.

The wide front door, with its beveled glass and its lace curtains, opened before I even stopped at the curb, and Marmalade came racing down the walkway, past the dilapidated but freshly painted mailbox, and launched herself at me as I was trying to step from the car.

She is the most unusual cat I've ever known. Right from the start she was demonstrative of her affection. She started by bringing me dead mice, but soon she graduated to hugs and purr sessions.

For a moment it was a hopeless tangle of orange and white tabby cat, me, my purse, and the yellow scarf that had been draped around my shoulders a minute before. Oh well. I gave myself up to adoration and buried my face in the incredibly soft fur. "I missed you, Marmy. . . ." I felt the purr before I heard it.

I missed you, too, Widelap, but my thoughts were with you all the time.

I no longer think it's silly to talk to my cat. She always purrs back at me, so it feels like a real conversation. I pulled away a bit and looked into her golden eyes. "Did Glaze take good care of you?"

Yes, we had long conversations, and she read me bedtime stories. Her books are not interesting, but I like her voice. Fishgiver was here a lot, too, and he brought me good food, like salmon and chicken.

Marmalade, who was now purring her little heart out, seemed to have put on some weight. I could feel the beginning of a pouch underneath her. I knew she wasn't pregnant, since I'd had her spayed shortly after she wandered into the library last year and adopted me. I wondered if Glaze had been overfeeding her. More likely Tom had been bringing salmon from his restaurant for the "furball," which is what he called Marmy.

As if summoned by my thoughts–or more likely by Marmalade's antics–my gorgeous, silver-haired younger sister Glaze, who had come to Martinsville from Philadelphia three weeks ago to help me get the house ready for the wedding, sauntered down the walkway, hardly limping at all. The ankle she had sprained just before the wedding seemed to be much better. "No need for me to hurry," she said with a smile. "The welcoming committee seems to have you tied up." Once I managed to untangle my scarf and set Marmalade down, she enveloped me in a big sisterly embrace. Her favorite vanilla perfume wafted around both of us, bringing cookies to my mind.

She always smells sweet.

"Let me grab my suitcase, and then I could use some iced tea."

Smellsweet did not make any.

Glaze grimaced. "I forgot to make some."

"No iced tea?" I said. "After all I've been through, you don't have any iced tea for me?"

"Quit wrinkling your eyebrows at me. I've lived away from Georgia too long to remember iced tea."

There's some nice chicken in the fridge.

I stepped around Marmalade, placed my hands on my hips, and fixed my middle-aged sister with a stare. "Just because you've been living out of state all this time, that's no excuse. Didn't our mama teach you right, young lady?"

To be honest, though, our mother had been the last person on earth ever to think about glasses of iced tea, that southern staple of gracious living. Mom was—and still is—a potter. Her hands are usually in clay at the pottery shop that fills a big corner of the backyard at the old house in Braetonburg, a few miles up the valley from here. She won't stand for having easily-broken glasses around. And she can't abide plastic. Mugs were her stock in trade, so we had hot tea year-round as we were growing up.

Now, however, iced tea sounded wonderful, mostly because it wasn't available. Why do I so often long for something I don't have?

You have me. And there is some chicken in the fridge.

Guess I should be grateful for what I do have. I'm glad I write a gratitude list each night. It helps me remember how lucky I am.

Glaze appeased me with a welcome suggestion. "I have some fresh orange juice, if you're interested."

I did a quick mental computation. "It's been four hours since lunch, so juice sounds great." I always wait four hours after eating carbohydrates or proteins before I eat fruit in any form. Or I eat the fruit half-an-hour *before* carbs and proteins. It's one of those strange ideas that I'm convinced works wonders.

I stick to cat food, treats, and mice. And chicken.

I even had Bob eating that way before . . . No. No, I didn't want to think about that. Not now.

You will find joy again, Widelap.

I had to step over Marmalade again as I linked arms with Glaze and started up the stairs onto the wide porch. "Did you have a good stay here?" I asked her.

"Yes. I did have a good time, except for worrying about you. House-sitting is a breeze. Marmalade and I got along really well."

"You didn't have any trouble getting around?" I had been somewhat concerned because of her sprained ankle, but it must have healed quickly.

"Not a bit of a problem. Of course, Tom helped out some the first few days."

He has been here every day, bringing me good food from his restaurant.

Tom Parkman, Bob's closest friend, owned CT's, the best restaurant in Keagan County, Georgia. He was fascinated with Glaze right from the moment they met, almost two weeks ago. I could easily imagine how willing he'd been to help. I wondered how much time . . . Don't go there, Biscuit, I thought. None of your business.

I could tell you everything that went on, if only you would listen to me.

Marmalade was certainly underfoot a lot. Probably just happy to see me home. It occurred to me that she'd make a good snitch, if only she could talk.

Mouse-droppings! Some day you will learn to listen to me.

I stepped over Marmalade again and crossed over the wide planks of oak flooring to set my purse down on the lovely old oak drop-leaf table that graces the big entranceway. My first mother-in-law gave it to me as a wedding gift, twenty-some-odd years ago.

Glaze walked up beside me. "By the way," she said, "I'm not heading home tomorrow. I'll stay as long as you need me to be here for you."

Bless her heart, I thought. I ran my hand over the table's beautifully-grained wood. I had been so looking forward to coming home with my husband. "Oh, Glaze," I said, "how am I ever going to deal with this?"

By the time we got out the big red-striped glasses and poured the freshly-squeezed orange juice, my despair had subsided somewhat. I gave Marmalade a little nibble of some chicken I saw on the top shelf of the fridge. Tom must have been coming by rather often with treats. Oh well, I could start her on a diet tomorrow.

No thank you.

Glaze suggested that we sit out on the verandah. That was what Elizabeth Hoskins, the widow who sold us the house, insisted we should call the huge covered porch. We gravitated around to the left, where the swing is, on the shady east side of the house. We could hear the birds chirping as they flew in and out of the Lady Banks Rose that clambers all over the back corner of the porch–verandah. Its big yellow blooms should be popping out within a month. I can't wait. Marmalade hopped up on the swing between Glaze and me, and we rocked gently for several minutes in silence.

Glaze took a deep breath and set her orange juice glass down on the floor next to the swing. I was going to have to get some little tables. "Biscuit," she said, "you're going to be better off if you talk this through. So, I want you to tell me. Other than the murder, how was your visit to Savannah?"

I finally managed a relatively coherent story. She knew some of it already, of course, but the sun went down and the mosquitoes came out before I got it all told. Glaze was right. It felt healing somehow to talk about it.

That night, Glaze was planning to sleep on the couch in the living room, since there wasn't a guest room. I couldn't face sharing my bed with my sister, when I had so looked forward to having Bob, my husband, there with me. As I walked up the stairs to my lonely bed . . .

I will be there with you and will keep you safe.

. . . I wondered idly what Glaze had thought of the wedding. There hadn't been time to ask.

My Gratitude List for Saturday May 4th

Five things for which I am grateful:
    1. Orange juice
    2. A safe trip home
    3. Home itself
    4. Glaze
    5. Marmalade

my gratitude list:
    Widelap and Smellsweet
    naps
    bird-watching from the window
    the swing
    being patted gently (and hugged)

As Glaze walked into the living room to make up her bed on the couch—and quite a comfortable couch it is, she thought—she was thinking back to just the week before when she had witnessed her sister's marriage on the 27th of April.

She paused as she spread the bottom sheet over the fat cushions of the couch and laughed to herself. The wedding had been a real doozy. She'd heard some horrified snickers when she walked into the sanctuary that Saturday, limped rather, from the pastor's cubbyhole to stand beside Bob Sheffield. She was holding the ring on a little pillow that she and her sister Biscuit had made on a last minute impulse, from some yellow chintz material that was leftover from the kitchen curtains they had sewed earlier in the week.

Those snickers were nothing compared to the gasps and then laughs as Tom Parkman, Bob's best friend, stepped down the aisle, carrying the bridesmaid flowers aloft, like a torch. As he got closer, Glaze could see a mischievous light twinkling in his dark brown eyes. He winked at her as he stepped aside and turned to look toward the back of the church where Biscuit McKee was just appearing, with Dad.

Glaze thought her sister, named Bisque by their mother the potter, but nicknamed Biscuit early on, looked stunning. For a forty-nine-year-old widow, she was in pretty good shape. Must be all the gardening she did. That and running up and down the library stairs all day at work.

As Biscuit leaned close to say something to their dad before they started down the aisle, Glaze glanced over at her mother. Ivy Martelson McKee had strong features to match her strong potter's hands. Her hair, still an ash brown after seventy-four years of vibrant living, was sprinkled with gray, rather like Biscuit's.

She and Dad had driven to Martinsville on Thursday from their home in nearby Braetonburg to spend two days with their daughters before the wedding. Glaze had driven down to Georgia last week from Philadelphia, just in time to help her sister sew curtains for her new house, where the whole family would gather after the reception. I'm glad Mom and Dad didn't get here earlier, Glaze thought. If they had, they would have been involved in some real unpleasantness—a break-in, two arrests, and the solving of a year-old murder.

Other than that, it had been a relaxing week. She glanced over at Tom's profile. Nope. Don't go there yet, girl, she instructed herself. After all, she still had time. Only forty-four and never married, she lived in a lovely Philadelphia town house with a roommate who was a midwife-apprentice. Glaze's life was good finally, despite a rocky beginning with years of undiagnosed bipolar disorder. It was called manic-depression back then. No more of that now, thanks to counseling, good nutrition (in addition to the milkshakes she loved) and the right medications. No need to rush things, she mused as she brought her attention back to Biscuit.

Thank goodness this late April Saturday wasn't too hot. Even the summers in this deep valley in northeastern Georgia were relatively mild. The whole of Keagan County, the smallest county in the state, was made up of lovely rolling hills with a few deep valleys and quiet rivers.

It's a rather quaint area, Glaze thought. Her home town of Braetonburg had a lot of old-fashioned ways, with its town band and the nosy neighbors, but Martinsville had Braetonburg beat big time. She recalled the mandate in the Martinsville town charter that specified the town had to maintain *an officer of the peace*, the position Bob had held for years. And there had to be a town jail, too. Biscuit had laughed several days ago when she'd told Glaze that the jail in the little City Hall was one room that could be locked. All those silly requirements were probably based on the early settlers' fears about brigands and thieves, although who on earth could even find little Martinsville, tucked away in a narrow dead-end valley like this? Glaze doubted the rest of the state had even heard about Keagan County, much less Martinsville.

The Old Church, which had been rebuilt after a fire 150 years ago, had wonderful cross ventilation, for which Glaze was thankful. It was augmented by some overhead fans. Their installation had caused months of squabbling in the little town three years ago, according to Bob. Once installed, however, they had been thoroughly appreciated. And used a lot

Today someone had left the front door open for even more ventilation, and Glaze chuckled as she noticed the late arrival of the final guest, who paused in the open doorway, backlit by the late morning sun, glanced around, walked through the short foyer and was momentarily lost to view as she disappeared behind Dad's gray-suited legs and Biscuit's simple white lace-trimmed ankle-length frock. Annie McGill, who owned an herb shop in town, had made the lace to give to Biscuit at the shower the town women held for their well-liked librarian. And Biscuit had stitched it lovingly onto her dress.

The late visitor didn't seem at all embarrassed. She simply wove her way around the two people who had already started walking down the aisle, stepped in front of them, and preceded them along the well-worn carpeting. Glaze could see Biscuit trying to hold in a laugh, but finally giving way to it. Leave it to Marmalade to insist on being included in the ceremony.

Her ringed tail held aloft in dignity, Marmalade escorted the bride and her father to the front of the church and stepped up beside Reverend Pursey, whose good nature had been tried already by having Glaze and Tom switch roles—necessary because Glaze's bandaged ankle kept her from being able to walk comfortably in front of her sister. The patient minister had sighed a bit, but finally agreed.

Now, the good Pastor barely ruffled his surplice as the dignified cat turned to face the bride and then sat, purring, with her tail curled tidily around her feet and gazing up at Biscuit as if to say, 'What next?'

What happens now, Widelap? It is nice to have all my favorite humans here: Softfoot and Smellsweet, Dreammaker and Sunsetlady, and Fishgiver. This is obviously an important ritual because I can smell the happy tears getting started. I would have been here sooner, but I detoured over to the place where you plant the bodies, to be sure it was quiet there. Now we are all in place, so we can start. Nice flowers, by the way.

Glaze noticed that Biscuit glanced down at the loudly-vibrating, regal cat several times before she managed to focus on the minister.

"Dearly Beloved . . ." Reverend Pursey's deep rumbling voice drowned out Marmalade's insistent purr as he began the familiar words. Biscuit and Bob had been engaged for over six months, and had spent part of that time, when they weren't busy catching criminals, writing their own wedding ceremony. It was obvious to Glaze that they had wanted enough of the old-fashioned wording to satisfy the more orthodox members of the congregation. But there were some changes that Glaze particularly liked.

"Who accompanies this woman to do her honor today?" Dad raised his hand, kissed Biscuit's cheek, and turned to join his smiling wife. Biscuit's two daughters and their families sat in the second pew. Her son, who had flown in from Alaska for the ceremony, sat next to his grandmother.

"I, Robert, joyfully take you, Bisque, to be my lawful wedded wife. I promise you my loyalty. I promise to laugh with you each day and love you to the best of my ability. I promise that if anything unlike love comes between us, I will seek the Higher Path of greatest good for both of us, the path of compassion and communication. I promise to be worthy of your trust. As a symbol of my vow I give you this ring, round as the circle of time, and never-ending. "

Bob smiled at Biscuit as he slipped the ring on her finger, then glanced down toward Marmalade, who had stepped between the two of them.

I, Marmalade, promise to remain true to both of you for my lifetime. I promise to protect you to the best of my ability. . . .

Biscuit paused a moment before starting her vows. Marmalade was making a sing-song racket, much to the amusement of the entire gathering.

. . . I promise to comfort you when you feel pain, to see your goodness when you forget how good you are. I walk the Higher Path at all times, and I promise to remind you of it often. I promise to be worthy of your trust. I also promise to understand your lack of understanding.

The cat stopped her noise and looked back and forth, almost as if she could follow what they were saying.

"I, Bisque, joyfully take you, Robert, to be my lawful wedded husband. I promise you my loyalty. I promise to laugh with you each day . . ."

Glaze noticed that Tom held Biscuit's bouquet of ivy, oat grass, daisies, dianthus sprigs, and euonymous without a trace of embarrassment. A man had to be very sure of himself to volunteer to be the bridesmaid. And she was glad he'd done that. Her ankle was beginning to throb again. I'll think of something happy to take my mind off it, Glaze thought, as her eyes wandered over Biscuit's bouquet.

The two sisters had gotten up early that morning to mosey (and limp) around the big back yard. They had been joined by Biscuit's close friend, Melissa Tarkington, who owned *Azalea House,* the bed and breakfast where Biscuit had lived her first year in Martinsville. Gathering the blossoms and the greenery, even collecting some structurally interesting weeds from the back fence, the three women had laughed a lot and cried a little. The center blossom of the bouquet was an enormous unopened floret of Joe Pye Weed. "It's lovely," Biscuit had said, "when you don't think of it as a weed. If there weren't so many of these springing up along roadsides, we'd have to pay a fortune to buy it in a flower shop."

Glaze brought her thoughts back in time to hear the rest of the ceremony. After the kiss, there was a round of applause as Marmalade stepped forward, placed an inquiring paw on Biscuit's knee, and received an okay as Biscuit nodded, patted her upper chest, and said, "Hup!" With a graceful bound the tabby leaped into Biscuit's arms, where she was squashed a bit between Biscuit . . .

Widelap

. . . and Bob . . .

Softfoot

. . . as they kissed one more time. Then the three of them turned and walked up the aisle and into the sunshine, with Glaze, leaning on Tom's arm, hobbling behind them. Tom was still carrying both bouquets, since Biscuit's right arm was filled with cat.

Yes. Of course.

After the reception, Bob and Biscuit left for their honeymoon, and Glaze eventually settled into the big bed upstairs with Marmalade, who spent a long time purring before they both finally drifted into a deep and welcome sleep.

my gratitude list for Saturday

my humans, especially Widelap, who is
*   forgetting to write in her journal tonight*
a quiet morning with flowers and ribbons
the sweet ritual in the old building
laughter
the salmon that Fishgiver gives me

* * * * * *

From the *Keagan County Record*
Wednesday, May 1, 1996

It is with great delight that we announce that this issue of the *Record* will feature a brief history of Myrtle Hoskins Snelling, one our most-loved reporters. Over the past fifty-one years, Myrtle has never missed a deadline. And she made the one this week on time, too. In honor of Myrtle's seventieth birthday, this special issue reprints some of the best of her articles over the years.

Myrtle's Musings from Martinsville began in 1945 when nineteen-year-old Myrtle Hoskins came to our offices with three sample columns. In the first one, she reported that an entire family was saved when a pregnant mother was rescued from a tree and adopted, along with all her kittens born that afternoon. Her second sample column told of the wedding of Martinsville's own Mildred Tarkington to Atlanta's most eligible bachelor, Peter Holvers. Finally there was a piece about the renovation of the old Millicent Mansion, one of the largest houses in Martinsville. We saw right away that her column would soon become a favorite. Due to the timely nature of the second sample, we ran the wedding report as the first of *Myrtle's Musings.*

We are honored to be able to share with you some of the best of Myrtle's Musings, the most recent of which covers the marriage last Saturday of Martinsville's Librarian Biscuit McKee and Officer of the Peace Bob Sheffield, who is, we are sorry to report, in critical condition in a hospital north of Savannah. Please add him to your prayer list.

But, as Myrtle always says, "On a happier note . . ." you will find her column in its usual place on page three, surrounded in this issue by a random selection of her columns gleaned from the past half-century.

There will be an open house today from 10:00 to 3:00 at the Snellings' home on Third Street in Martinsville. All are welcome to drop by and offer congratulations. The open house will be hosted by Myrtle's husband Frank, owner of the Snelling Frame Shop in Martinsville, and her aunt Pamela C. Tarkington, who says she has "read every single issue of the *Record* from cover to cover for the past eighty years." Myrtle will *(continued on back page of this section)*

Chapter 2

Tuesday, April 30, 1996 - 4:30 a.m. - Savannah

Mrs. Sheffield?" The police officer who called my name so softly sounded like she didn't want to startle me. The waiting room for the intensive care unit at the Guildencrantz Memorial Hospital north of Savannah was surprisingly empty. In fact, I was the only occupant. I'd been here for two hours already, waiting to hear about Bob's condition. They gave me updates, but nobody said what I wanted to hear. That he was awake and alert. And calling for me. Me. His wife of almost three days. Married last Saturday in Martinsville, Georgia. Here in Savannah . . .

I am with you in my thoughts.

. . . for our honeymoon.

It was a lovely wedding.

I had a sudden inexplicably happy memory of Marmalade's part in the ceremony. How can I feel happy at a time like this? I wish she were here now. She's such a good cat.

Thank you.

"Mrs. Sheffield?"

"Yes, but my name is Bisque McKee. We were married last Saturday, but I kept my maiden name."

Officer C. Sloan–I could see the name badge above her uniform shirt pocket–paused over her notebook. "I'm Officer Sloan, part of a special investigations team. I'm sorry about your husband bein' poisoned, but I need to ask you some questions about yesterday mornin'."

"You mean last night, don't you?"

"No. I'm talkin' about yesterday about three in the mornin'." Officer Sloan sat down on the blue chair across from me. "I've been told," she said, "that you were the one who found Margaret Casperson."

"Yes–that is, Bob–my husband–and I found her. Well, we didn't exactly find her; she fell against our door. Why do you need to ask about her? Is something wrong?"

"Could you tell me what happened from your point of view?"

"We were asleep. She woke us up, beating against the wall."

She looked up from her notebook. "Do you mean against the door?"

"No, Ma'am. Before that, we heard her–or someone–pounding the wall right above our heads and calling for help." I paused, re-membering the hideous noise coming through the thin wall and the jolt of adrenaline that had catapulted me out of bed. The bed I shared with Bob. Oh God, please let him be okay. Please.

Take a breath, Widelap.

"What happened next?" Officer Sloan prompted.

I took a deep breath and said, "I didn't even know she was stay-ing in the next room."

"Why would you expect to know who was in the next room?" she asked in a slow drawl.

"Bob and I know her. She's from Martinsville, where we live." As I answered her, I wondered what the letter on her name tag stood for. *C. Sloan.* Catherine, probably.

"Had you seen her earlier in the day?"

"Yes. She was walking through the lobby as we were checking in and came over to talk."

"What did you talk about?"

"Nothing much. She said she was here for a brief visit. I know she goes on a lot of antique-buying trips."

"Did she say anything else?"

Yes she did.

"Not really. As soon as we checked in, we came right up to our room."

"You said you were on your honeymoon?"

Something in the tone of Officer Sloan's voice made me stop and look at her. Really look at her. There was a deep compassion in her eyes. This was a woman who understood how sweet a honey-moon could be. This was a woman who loved her man. I could tell as easily as if she had a tattoo blazoned across her forehead that said *I love my husband.* "Yes, that's right," I said, knowing that the smile I felt inside me was coloring my words.

For a few moments, neither of us moved. "I'm really sorry that your husband got hurt," she finally said, and I felt somehow better. Maybe her name is Cora. That's a compassionate-sounding name. Or Charity.

"What did you do when you heard the noise?" she asked, shifting back to an official-sounding voice and resuming the interview.

"I threw on a hotel bathrobe. Bob was almost at the door when we heard her fall against it." I bet her name is Casey. That would fit her.

"Yes?"

"We could hear her throwing up even before we opened the door. Thank goodness I've raised three children; otherwise I don't think I could have made it through the next hour."

Officer Sloan looked at me for what felt like a long time. She must not have children herself, although I could see a wedding ring. She was left-handed. That's supposed to be an indication of a creative mind. Maybe her name is Chloe. Or Clarissa.

"What else?"

"She was crying and babbling."

"Could you tell what she was sayin'?"

"Not really. It didn't make any sense. She said something about colors."

Officer Sloan took a deep breath. Good for her. Breathing deeply is so important. "Can you remember her exact words?" she asked in a measured drawl. I think she might have been getting a tiny bit impatient with me, so I tried to be more specific.

"She mentioned pink and violet."

"Did she say anything else?"

"Something about her cousin."

Officer Sloan stopped writing for a moment. "She was cussin'?"

"No, cousin. Cousin. She seemed pretty anxious about it."

"Did she say who this cousin was?"

"Oh, I forgot to tell you that she mentioned she was here to visit her cousin Brenda."

"She said all that while she was throwin' up?" I noticed she wasn't writing anything down at this point.

"No, Ma'am," I told her. "She told me about Brenda in the lobby when we checked in."

I am glad you remembered that.

Officer Sloan tilted her head and looked at me. "Her cousin Brenda?"

"Yes, let's see, that would be her Aunt Mildred's daughter."

She was back to her writing again. "Do you know this Brenda?"

"No. Bob knew about her, but he told me she hadn't been to Martinsville since she was a little girl. Mildred, her mother, lives in Atlanta somewhere."

"Atlanta." It wasn't a question. Officer Sloan seemed to be speaking what she was writing in her black police notebook. "Do you know Brenda's last name?"

"No Ma'am. It used to be Holvers . . ."

Officer Sloan stopped writing. "Like in underwear?"

"Right. But I heard she changed it. Her Aunt Melissa, who owns the bed & breakfast where I stayed last year, said Brenda didn't like people associating her with lingerie." Maybe C stood for Christine. Or Connie.

Shaking her head, Officer Sloan pursed her mouth. Slowly her expression spread out into a rueful grin. She glanced down at her notebook. "Did she mention Brenda's new last name?"

"No Ma'am." Or Carmen. She certainly looked exotic enough, with her honey-brown skin and her huge eyes. In this light they looked like a couple of caramel drops.

"Is this cousin older or younger than Mrs. Casperson?"

"I'm pretty sure she's older. Sam, that's Margaret's husband, would know. Bob . . ." my Bob. I could feel fear welling up, but I ignored it. "Bob tried to call him when she was taken off in the ambulance last night. I mean Sunday night, or rather, Monday morning. . . ."

Slow down, Widelap.

This was ridiculous. I was babbling. I took another breath and tried again. "Bob called Sam's house, but there was no answer. Bob thought Sam might have gone fishing, so he called Ernie."

"Who is Ernie?"

"Ernie Robeson." Like so many southern women, and women everywhere else, for that matter, I had a tendency to collect genealogical information in a table I carried around in my head. I'd met Ernie once at Sam and Margaret's house, and of course Margaret had given me the complete story, but I didn't know him well. "Oh, let me see. He would be Mildred's son by her second husband."

"So he'd be this Brenda's brother?"

Claire. That must be her name. Claire means *brilliant*. I wondered if she'd drawn one of those little charts with *whose-kid-is-whose* in her notebook, but as I tried to peek, she turned slightly, and I couldn't see what she was writing.

"Yes, I suppose he is her brother. Well, her half-brother. But she was pretty well grown by the time he was born. He's quite close to Margaret and her husband, though."

"We called the Martinsville Police Station, but they said the town officer of the peace was on vacation."

That would be Bob, my Bob, she was talking about without even knowing it.

I explained the situation. She had the grace to look a bit embarrassed at not having caught the connection. I was frankly surprised that whoever had answered the phone in City Hall hadn't given her a whole report on the wedding, and I told her so.

Perhaps her name was Cynthia. I wondered if she had a good sense of humor. Bob always said a good cop had to be level-headed, with enough humor to stop his–or in this case her–heart from breaking.

"Did she say where this cousin Brenda lives now?"

"Well, when I saw her she was on her way out of the hotel to meet Brenda, so she must live in this area, but no Ma'am, she didn't say where." People from the North don't always understand the importance of the words Ma'am and Sir in polite conversation. They teach their children to say *yes, please* and *no, thank you*, but we learned from the cradle to say *yes please, Ma'am* and *no thank you, Sir.*

My dad, who was brought up in Connecticut and came to Georgia straight out of college with a degree in music education, tried only once to tell Mom that those extra words were unnecessary, since the politeness of the exchange had already been established with the please or the thank you. The family legend (started by my Auntie Blue who was sitting there at the time and heard it all) has it that my mother looked up from the tall vase she was glazing and said, "John, next thing you'll be telling me is that those couple of extra things I did last night were unnecessary, since the basic premise had already been conveyed." Dad never objected to Ma'am or Sir again, and he was rigorous about insisting that my sister Glaze and I use the terms.

Of course, in this case it did seem a little silly, since Officer C. Sloan looked to be about the age of Sally, my younger daughter, the one who now lives with her husband in my old house in Braetonburg. Officer Sloan, however, was a cop, so maybe the extra respect would be appreciated.

"Ms. McKee? Did she say anything else that you can remember?"

"No Ma'am. She really was incoherent."

"Any other words you recognized?"

"Well," I said, thinking back to the chaos and the fear, "the only thing I remember is that right before she passed out, she grabbed my arm and said something about her father. I can't remember exactly what she said, but she did say *my father*."

"Her father?"

"Or maybe she said *the father* or *her father* or something like that."

"Do you know her father?"

"Yes, Ma'am. That would be George Ingalls. I know him because he's the town council member who heads the library committee." There wasn't much else I could tell her.

"Would you have a number where we could reach him? He might know how to contact Mr. Casperson."

"But . . ." Her question surprised me. ". . . he's in Margaret's room. Sam is. Didn't you know? Ernie found him fishing at dawn and drove him here. Bob and I saw them when they arrived yesterday afternoon."

Officer Sloan looked as if there were several things she would have liked to say. Instead, she folded up her notebook, thanked me, and turned to leave. I had a feeling somebody was going to get an earful for not having told her that Sam was here.

The nurse came back in just then to give me a report on Bob.

I am so sorry you are worried, Widelap.

I would have given anything to have Marmalade purring in my arms right then.

I would be there if I could.

"Nothing much has changed," the nurse, a blond woman with square shoulders, told me. "We're cautiously hopeful, though, since his vital signs haven't gotten any worse." Cold comfort indeed. My Bob wasn't talking or moving. It was 4:30 in the morning and I was all alone with cold feet in a hospital waiting room, and I had grumped at my husband yesterday about something as inconsequential as leaving his socks on the floor. What a stupid thing to do.

As I stood there close to despair, the hotel's general manager walked in. I couldn't for the life of me remember her name, which was ridiculous since I'd already met her several times. The first time was over Margaret's body in the hotel hallway. And again in the hospital lobby and finally next to that unfortunate dead man on the River Walk a few hours ago. I felt happy to see her now, even if I couldn't recall her name. Human connection was important right then. Maybe it was only that I'd had two nights of interrupted sleep. And each time it had involved women screaming. That was getting real old real fast.

"Mrs. Sheffield, I'm so sorry about what happened."

"Thank you, but please call me Biscuit. Everyone else does." Except Officer C. Sloan. "And my last name is McKee. I kept my maiden name."

"Sorry for the mistake. You can call me Millie."

Even with my concern over Bob, I was interested in taking a closer look at this efficient and slightly intimidating woman. Although it was a ghastly hour of the morning, she was elegant in light gray dress slacks with a dark yellow blouse and a gray checked blazer. And here I was still in my nightgown and the hotel bathrobe that I'd thrown on when I first heard the screams from outside by the river. Thank goodness I had slippers on, but my feet were cold. Very cold.

I was surprised to notice that she was about my height, a little over five and a half feet. She looked tall. Maybe it was because of her professionalism. Maybe it was her slender build. Maybe it was the cut of her clothes. Oh well, this was hardly the time to be embarrassed by my lack of fashion sense. She was blessedly direct, though.

"You must be uncomfortable in that bathrobe, Biscuit. Would you like me to run you back to the hotel so you can change?"

"No. No, thank you. I don't want to leave Bob, in case he . . . in case . . ."

"In case he gets better and can talk to you. Of course you don't want to leave. Would you let me go into your hotel room and bring something for you to change into?"

What a dear woman she was. I gave her some rather vague instructions about where I'd put underwear and slacks, and asked her to get me a shirt and a sweater. And a comb. And some shoes and socks. And my purse. I fished the room key out of my bathrobe pocket. I must have grabbed it as I ran for the door last night. "Would you bring my journal, too? It's on the table beside the bed. It looks like I may be here for awhile, so I might as well write."

Reaching for the key, Millie said, "You must have a lot to write about. As I was getting off the elevator, that police woman was just getting on. She probably had a lot to ask you about tonight."

"Not really. She was more interested in yesterday."

"Yesterday?"

"Yes. When Margaret Casperson fell against our door, she was trying to tell us something, and Officer Sloan wanted to know about it."

Millie seemed quite concerned. I could see a crease deepening between her eyebrows. Of course she'd be concerned. It had happened in her hotel. They must be on the alert all the time to keep lawsuits from happening. Maybe she had come here to find out about that. Maybe she wasn't so worried about Bob and me, or Margaret either. Of course. This was a business trip. At five o'clock in the morning? I didn't care. There was a warm-blooded human being in front of me. Someone who was going to bring me my socks.

"What did she say?" she asked me.

I thought I would put her mind at ease. "She didn't say anything about the hotel. It was just ramblings. Babbling, really. Some colors, pink and whatever. A few words here and there. She did say something about her father, but I can't remember offhand what it was." Here came the square nurse again, with her head looking like a box piled on top of her shoulders. That sounds unkind. I don't mean it that way. I turned away from Millie.

"You can go in to see him for five minutes," the nurse said. "He's still not responsive, but I know how upset you are. Five minutes, though. That's all." Bless her heart, she seemed to be telling me as gently as she could, but it sounded like a horrible warning to expect the worst. I noticed her name tag. D. Williston, R.N. it said. I wondered what the D stood for.

As I turned toward the heavy swinging door, I heard Millie ask the nurse if she could see Margaret Casperson. "She's a guest at the hotel," she was saying, "and I'm deeply concerned about her."

"You can't see her. You're not next of kin." Why did I have the feeling the nurse had taken a dislike to her when Millie was trying to be so helpful?

As anxious as I was to get to Bob's side, I paused to tell the nurse that Bob and I were from the same town as Margaret. "I hope she'll soon be over this illness," I said.

"We'll see," said Nurse Williston. "We'll see."

We left Millie standing there with my hotel key in her hand.

* * * * * *

Jottings from the personal notebook of
Colly Sloan:

tues 4-30-96

this investigatin is a challenge for someone
who's always been a beat cop, but brando thinks
it'll work. hope he's right. we're askin all these
questions, but doggone it, somethin's missin here.

it was real obvious at my party last saturday
that linda can't stand that millie cappell. I wonder why? note: ask brando to see if diane knows
why.

maybe I should have confronted her this
mornin when I left biscuit—seems like a nice lady—
and saw millie drinkin from the water fountain
right outside the waitin room. but she was all
spruced up lookin like a model or somethin. in
the middle of the night for criminey sakes—and
it didn't seem very professional for me to go up
to her in my uniform and say why doesn't linda
like you, so i let it be, but it bothers me.

much as i'm sorry finney's dead—and I'm
goin to catch me that murderer for sure—I still
think somethin's fishy with him and with
margaret. wish biscuit could remember more.
need to ask questions that will jog her memory,
but what are those questions?

* * * * * *

I could see Bob's face from the doorway. He looked entirely too
still, entirely too like a statue. I thought back to the dead body I'd
found last year . . .

I found it.

. . . and tried to blot out my memory of that alabaster face. And
I refused to think about the contorted face of that man who had been
murdered on the River Walk just a few hours ago. No, I would con-
centrate on Bob being alive. He was. And he would soon be back to
normal. He looked all blurry somehow. I wiped ineffectively at the
tears streaming down my face, and picked up his hand—the one that

didn't have any tubes running in and out of it. I could have sworn his grip tightened a hair. I hoped that wasn't just my wishful thinking. The square-shouldered nurse murmured a reminder that I had only five minutes, and left the room. I stood there beside his bed and thought about how much I loved him and how glad I was that we'd gotten married. It was a lovely wedding, too.

As I reached forward to smooth a strand of his wavy black hair back from his forehead, I found it hard to believe that it had been not quite two days since we'd arrived in Savannah. I could see myself looking around the River Landing Hotel bridal suite when I walked into it on Sunday afternoon. I had dropped my small tapestry bag onto the luggage rack that nestled near a tall mirrored wardrobe. Then I started to plop my purse on a graceful table that was backing a yellow-cushioned loveseat. Nice little grouping, facing the fireplace like that. No, not on the table. I shifted it onto the dresser near the bed. It would have been a shame to disturb the table's arrangement of one lovely glass dish filled with fruit, and a leaded crystal vase holding a bit of greenery and three yellow dahlias. The dahlias were beginning to brown around the edges. Hmm. I thought cut dahlias lasted a long time. Ah well, between the vase and the fruit there was a substantial lamp, tall and heavy and yet somehow elegant. Of course it was elegant. It must have cost as much as my yearly stipend as a librarian.

Kicking off my shoes with a big sigh, I sank my toes into the lush carpet. None of that dark-patterned heavy-wear movie-house carpeting for this place. No, this was a deep-piled cloud of soft peach that must have driven the housekeeping staff nuts, but it calmed my eyes as well as my sore feet. Too long in the car, even though we stopped often for stretch-breaks.

I will teach you how to really stretch.

I wandered out onto the wide balcony, and started to weave my way past a wrought iron table, topped with blue and white tiles, that sat between two cushioned chairs. I stopped, though, when I noticed a damselfly perched in the center of the little table, his iridescent body and wings flashing blue lights as he fanned them slowly in the sun. The females are brown; only the males have bright colors. Seems backwards, but I suppose bugs know what they're doing. What a great place for morning tea, I thought. As the damselfly lifted off, I walked to the railing and looked down onto the spacious flagstone patio three floors below. I was pleasantly surprised to see a masterpiece in stonework. The patio in back of the River Landing had wide slabs of reddish-brown flagstone interspersed with bricks in a her-ringbone array. Looking down on it as I leaned my elbows on the iron railing, I could see the overall pattern, a brickwork circle, from which five brick paths branched out, like spokes of a wheel. Be-tween those spokes were the wide paving stones. It was intricate, but didn't look fussy.

I saw climbing roses off to one side of the hotel, close to the parking lot where we'd parked my old Buick. Savannah is so much farther south than Martinsville. It's hard to believe, though, the dif-ference in bloom time. My roses at home wouldn't open for another month, and here was a whole arbor covered with enormous yellow blossoms that brightened that entire corner. I could imagine how beautiful they'd be in the evening. There was a woman dressed all in black sitting on a bench tucked underneath the curve of the rose arbor. I bet it smelled delicious under there.

Even though it was already the last of April, the late morning air of Savannah had a bit of a chill in it, probably because of the turbulent-looking storm clouds I could see blowing toward the city from the southeast, where they were trying to obscure the sun. I was glad that I'd brought my cardigan with me. "This view," I told Bob as he walked up behind me, "is magnificent, and listen to all those birds singing."

Wrapping his warm arms around me, he whispered, "I'm so glad you approve, Ms. McKee."

I'd been born Bisque McKee, had kept my name through my first marriage of almost twenty years to Solomon Brandy, simply because the thought of being called Biscuit Brandy was, well, unac-ceptable. Most married women in small towns in our part of the country wouldn't have considered keeping their maiden names, at least not twenty-some-odd years ago. But Sol didn't mind, and three kids later, when he died after a severe but blessedly short illness, the last thing he said to me was, "I love you, Biscuit McKee."

My marriage to Bob Sheffield, the Martinsville officer of the peace, seemed destined to be equally happy, if not more so. I had, however, chosen to keep the name I was born with forty-nine years ago.

Bob nuzzled my ear gently. "Are you planning to stay out here a long time?" he asked.

"Maybe not, now that you mention it. Just look at that dramatic patio."

"Right," he said.

I love it the way some people can turn that word into three syllables. "And look at that beautifully designed stone wall."

"Uh-huh," he said, tightening his arms a bit.

"And look at those enormous climbing roses."

"I don't see any roses," he said.

"You're not looking," I reminded him.

He pulled back a bit, peered over the balcony railing to the patio, and repeated, "I don't see any roses."

"They're over there." I had to point with my nose, since my arms were thoroughly wrapped up from behind. It felt lovely. "On that big arbor," I added in what I hoped was a helpful tone of voice, although it sounded more like a puddle of melted ice cream.

"Why don't you plant some roses when we get home," he asked me as he did something deliciously disturbing with the back of my neck.

"Not a chance," I managed to say. "Roses take too many insecticides and poisons, although if I had to use them, I'd use dish soap or nicotine."

He stopped what he was doing, and turned me around so I was facing him. "Nicotine?" he asked. "Dish soap?"

"Yes. Dish soap disrupts their body chemistry somehow or other, and nicotine is one of the oldest known insecticides. It'll kill bugs in a heartbeat."

"Sounds dangerous."

"Sure is, especially if you're a bug."

Bob freed one hand and ran his fingers through his silver-sprinkled black hair, then carefully removed the big clip from the top of my head, letting my longish ash-brown and gray waves tumble around my shoulders.

I've always enjoyed having hair that was long enough to hold with a single clip, probably due to the TV show called *Guess My Secret* I watched as a kid. Once on the show, there was a woman whose secret was that her elaborately-coifed hair was held up by a single bobby pin. I still can see her reaching up after they'd guessed her secret–and I remember thinking that they must have had some hints beforehand to guess that one–and removing one pin. Her action was followed by a marvelous tumble of tresses that cascaded almost to the floor.

My hair tumbled only to my shoulder blades, but that was enough to make both Bob and me happy.

My Gratitude List for Saturday, April 27, 1996

(written Sunday morning because I didn't even think about it last night!)

    Five things for which I am grateful:

        1. Bob, my dear husband
        2. Our lovely wedding yesterday
        3. My sister who is house-sitting
        4. A safe journey
        5. My wedding night – wow!

Tuesday, April 30, 1996   5:00 a.m.

"Bob, if you can hear me–and I have to believe that at some level you *can* hear me– please, please come back. Please get over this. We haven't had enough time together. Bob, I want to grow old with you. I . . ." Words failed me at that point. I wasn't sure whether I'd been talking out loud or only in my mind, but Bob just lay there. I kept holding his hand, willing him to wake up, knowing that if I kept trying long enough, I could make him come back to me. He had been so vibrant, so alive yesterday when I'd opened my stupid mouth . . .

I couldn't believe it. Those were socks on the floor. We hadn't even been playing around, either. No excuse. "Bob, are these your socks on the floor?"

He said something that sounded like "Ooo elth wouo ey bog to, seetie?"

"Are you going to pick them up?"

He took the toothbrush out of his mouth. "Am I going to pick them up?"

"Yes, are you going to pick them up?"

"Why are you asking if I'm going to pick them up?"

We were getting nowhere. "I just want to know if you're going to pick them up."

He finished with his teeth and started combing his hair. "No."

We were still getting nowhere in a hurry. "Why not?" Was I really asking this question on our honeymoon? What happened to moonlight and roses?

Bob sauntered out of the bathroom looking damp and, I had to admit, wonderfully manly. He has this curly hair right in the center of his chest that . . .

"Biscuit, why are you asking me about socks?"

"Because they shouldn't be on the floor."

"They are *my* socks."

"And you dropped them on the floor."

"You're very welcome to kick them out of your way."

"I will not, will not, will not pick up your socks, Bob Sheffield!"

"Nobody asked you to." He reached for my hand, but I was a little too irritated with him. Come to think of it, I was feeling extremely pissed off at him.

"Then why don't *you* pick them up?" I was actually clenching my hands. Why wouldn't he just pick up the blinkin' socks and get it over with? I know that red is not my best color when it's covering my face.

"Biscuit, I will not pick up my socks. I've left my socks on the floor off and on for fifty some-odd years, and I can't see why I should change my ways now."

"Because you're married to me now, and I don't like to see dirty laundry on the floor, and I absolutely refuse to encourage such behavior. I never did with my kids and I won't with you."

Bob's voice dropped half an octave. "I am not one of your kids."

"Don't you try logic on me, you ungrateful anthropoid. Socks do not belong on the floor. Didn't your mama teach you right?"

"We can leave my mother out of this." He stopped reaching for my hand and folded his arms across his chest. His manly chest. Phooey. What was I doing? So, I did the only thing that made any sense at that precise moment. I burst into tears.

* * * * * *

A different nurse bustled in, interrupting my train of thought. "I have to check his IV line now. Would you mind going back to the waiting room? I'll come get you in about an hour." She stopped on her way to the far side of the hospital bed and looked at me over her shoulder. "You might want to go down to the cafeteria. The food service is closed now, but there are some vending machines."

"No, I'll sit in the waiting room. I don't have my purse, anyway. And I'm not hungry." And my feet are cold, I thought. And I don't want to leave Bob.

Twenty minutes later I was still cold and still miserable, and I decided to wake up my sister. It was practically dawn, so maybe she'd be up. No, she wouldn't, but what else were sisters for? But I waited until almost 8:00 before I called Martinsville.

7:45 a.m.

"Glaze, I'm so sorry to call you this early. But I'm glad you weren't in the shower. I didn't want to leave this on the answering machine. Can you stay a few days longer . . ."

"This isn't too early. I've just made coffee." My sister's voice sounded so sane, so normal. She went on in a bantering tone, "Having a great time on our honeymoon, are we?"

"No, sis. I'm serious. Bob's in the hospital. . . ."

I tried to tell her, but she will not listen to me.

"There's been a murder . . ."

"Not Bob?" she practically hollered at me.

I hastened to reassure her. "No, but he tried to revive the guy and got some of the same poison in him as the dead guy . . ."

"Another one?"

". . . and we seem to be witnesses of some sort, since we found the body."

"Why didn't you call me sooner?"

"I didn't want to wake you up too . . ."

"What on earth," she interrupted me, "does that have to do with anything?"

She was right. I wish I had called her instead of sitting here feeling sorry for myself and angry at the whole situation. Not that she could have done anything about it, but talking helped.

"Are you going to make a habit of this?" she asked.

Please do not.

"Of what?"

"Finding dead people."

Her question was a reasonable one, even if unwelcome. I'd found that body on the library stairs last year . . .

No. I am the one who found it.

Well, to be perfectly honest, Marmalade is the one who found it. But I was the one who had to call the police station . . .

I am going to have to learn to dial a telephone.

 . . . and it's a good thing I did, because that was the way I met Bob, the town cop, who now is my wonderful–but comatose–husband.

"Biscuit? Did we lose the connection, or are you day-dreaming again?"

"Sorry." What was I doing, wool-gathering at a time like this?

You were thinking about Softfoot.

"Are you still in Savannah? Do you need me to drive down there to help?"

Do you need me to come also?

"Oh, I wish you were here. But no. I need you to stay there and take care of Marmalade. I was wondering if it would be possible for you to stay a few extra days, just in case we're delayed much longer? Hopefully, Bob will be out of the hospital soon." I didn't want to tell her he wasn't responding. How would I ever deal with that? "I know you already took some time off to come down for the wedding," I went on, "so this seems like a terrible imposition."

No, it is not. She loves you. Anyway, Fishgiver is visiting her every day.

"Nonsense," Glaze told me, with what sounded like real enthusiasm. "I'm happy to help out. I just hope Bob will be okay. At any rate, my ankle isn't quite up to snuff yet, so I'd love to postpone the drive back to Philly."

Yesterday Glaze and Tom Parkman had disagreed about something. I knew a little about it from a phone conversation we'd had when I called to check on Marmalade, so now I wondered idly if she had patched up her disagreement with him. If so, that might be part of the reason she was so happy to delay her leaving. "Are you sure you can stay longer?" I asked her. "What about work?" There was a long, long pause. "Glaze? Are you still there?"

"Oh. Work? Don't worry. That'll be okay. I have a lot of vacation time saved up."

She is not telling you the truth, Widelap.

Why did I not believe my sister? She sounded a little too bright. A wee bit artificial. But I let it pass. For now.

"So, tell me what's happened to Bob. Is he okay?"

"Yes. He's going to be fine. He's having a little reaction to the poison." A little reaction. Right. He's comatose, but his vital signs are stable.

Keep trusting, Widelap. Softfoot wants to be well.

"What about this murder? What's going on there?"

"Some jogger killed a man and then mugged the man's wife."

"Since when do joggers kill people?"

Good question.

"Good question. I don't know any more than that. They haven't caught the guy yet. I'm just sitting here in the hospital waiting room. Waiting." I gave her the number, just in case. "In the meantime, would you call Reverend Pursey and tell him I won't be able to supply the flowers for the church service next week? Or, better yet, call Sadie and ask her to fill in for me."

"Are there that many yellow flowers blooming this time of year?"

Looselaces can always find yellow flowers.

Dear old Sadie Masters, one of the elderly volunteers at the Martinsville library, who wandered around with her tennis shoes untied most of the time, didn't know that any color other than yellow existed. Her house, her furniture, her garden, her clothes, even her car, for goodness sakes. There had to be a reason. I didn't think she was actively crazy. "Don't worry. She'll find some. Now, I need to get going. If you need anything . . . " Was I going to say this? Yes, I was. ". . . you can always call Tom."

She does not have to call him. He came for breakfast and brought her some flowers. He is sitting here at the big table right now. She made some very bad coffee for him. He does not like it, but he is smiling anyway.

"Uh, thanks for the suggestion. That's all fine now."

As we said our goodbyes I wondered if Tom might be listening to her side of the conversation. I wondered where they were. We had phones in the kitchen, the living room, and upstairs. In the bedroom. Hmmm.

Glaze called me back about twenty minutes later. "Tell me the truth, sis. How's Bob? And what's really going on?"

What indeed? Margaret unconscious and it must have been something awful because that cop was here questioning me about it, and some man murdered and Bob in horrible shape because of it. It's my honeymoon and I feel lousy. And lonely. And angry. And she asks me what's going on? So I told her. And felt better for the telling.

Chapter 3

At 8:45 I was still sitting in the hospital waiting room, although this time I was comfortably dressed in a pair of navy slacks and my light yellow polo shirt, delivered a short time ago by that sweet Millie. She'd brought some hotel soap, a little tube of toothpaste, and a new toothbrush. She even had a washcloth for me in a plastic bag. The phone rang, and the volunteer who was sitting at the little desk answered. She punched a couple of buttons, then motioned me to pick up the white phone on the magazine-strewn table next to my chair. It was Glaze, sounding concerned but bright, as if she were determined not to send any more gloom and doom my way.

"Okay, sis," she said when I answered. "It's me again with long-distance girl-talk therapy. You need to take your mind off what's going on there. I assume Bob is still holding on, right?"

"Yes," I told her. "I would have called you right away if there'd been a change."

"All right. Good. Now, blow your nose and then you start telling me about what all you've been doing for the past three days. Not the yucky part. I want to hear all the happy details."

So I sat there, with the hospital noises going on around me, and I told her about arriving at the River Landing Hotel. Was it only yesterday? I left out a lot of the details. Some of them were none of her business, after all.

"You wouldn't have believed it, Glaze. There I stood yelling at him about *socks*."

"Were you really yelling? I thought you two were lovebirds."

That is not a good description. You should hear what birds say to each other. They squabble a lot.

"Maybe not yelling exactly, but all of a sudden I turned into this monster when I saw him dump his socks on the carpet and walk into the bathroom."

"You got it worked out, though, didn't you?"

Yes.

How on earth do I answer that one? We did work it out, but it took more than just his arms going around me while I was crying. I guess I had thought–talk about naive–that we would always get along and be in tune with each other. Not that it was always that way with Sol, my first husband, who died after our kids were pretty well grown. In twenty-some years, though, Sol and I never really had any arguments. Come to think of it, Sol and I had pretty much stopped talking, other than to discuss the kids or the yard, or his music students. What on earth was I thinking? My first marriage was a happy one. It was.

After I cried on his shoulder a while, Bob indicated pretty clearly that he thought he knew a way to smooth this over. I didn't particularly feel like a romp in the hay, though. How to tell him that I loved him but didn't want to love him right then?

"Bob, I'd feel a lot better if we could just take a walk along the river bank for a while. Would that be okay with you?"

He stepped back from me, but kept his hands on my shoulders. "Woman, are you telling me no?"

"No. Well, yes, I guess I am, but only for now, until I can get my frazzle put back together."

"Your what?"

"My frazzle. My scattered thoughts. My tummy in an uproar. My . . ."

Your anger?

"Your anger?"

"Oh, phooey, Bob. I don't want to be angry at you." The carpet right next to my left foot had been pulled a bit, as if a cat had scratched it.

Why are you looking at the carpet?

"But you *do* feel angry at me."

I had no practice dealing with this sort of thing. Why did this have to happen on our honeymoon, for goodness sake? Why did he have to be looking so directly at me? Marmalade is much easier to deal with.

Of course I am. I do not have socks.

Bob slipped his hand under my chin and stroked it gently. "Biscuit, I haven't told you a lot about my first marriage."

I knew that he'd been married for several unfortunate years way back when, but he'd never given me many details. I wasn't sure I wanted to hear about wife number one right then.

He let go of me and scratched at his own chin. It wasn't anywhere near five o'clock, but he already had a distinct shadow on his upper lip and along his jaw. He needed a shave. Why did I marry someone so hairy? "Let's walk along the river," he said, "and I'll tell you something about what happened. It had to do with anger. I learned a big lesson from it. A lesson I don't want to repeat."

I grabbed some outside clothes and stalked into the bathroom, closing the door behind me. I even locked it. I didn't want to change my shirt with him looking at me. I didn't want to think that only half an hour before we'd been so comfortable together. My face in the mirror looked resentful. No. It looked petulant, like a little kid who didn't get a new toy when she wanted it, and who was ready to throw a tantrum. I was glad, for that moment, that Marmalade wasn't anywhere nearby, because I didn't want my cat to be worried about her two people.

Too late.

When I came out into the room, with my face feeling cool from the cold water splashing I'd given it, Bob was dressed in a soft blue shirt and his tan chinos. Sandals on his bare feet. He'd left his watch on the bedside table. I ignored my purse, stuffed a couple of tissues in my pants pocket, and turned toward the door.

"Bisque." His voice sounded calm, but was deeper pitched than usual.

"Yes?" I didn't look at him.

"Bisque, I know you're feeling really angry about this situation. I think it's okay for us to feel some anger once in a while at each other. But will you hold my hand as we go out for our walk? I think that might help us remember what we promised. Remember? When anything unlike love comes up," he quoted, "I pledge that I will seek the Higher Path of greatest good for both of us, the path of compassion and communication. I promise to be worthy of your trust."

I took a deep breath, stepped over his socks, and reached out to take his hand. Maybe this wouldn't be so hard after all.

"You got it worked out, though, didn't you?" Glaze asked again.

I brought my wandering thoughts back to the ICU waiting room and looked idly at the volunteer, who appeared to be trying not to listen. Or to look like she wasn't listening. What the heck. "Yes," I said. "We got it worked out. . . ."

There had been long stone benches set at intervals along the river wall. Each bench had a big round concrete tub next to it, filled with a luscious assortment of plants with various interesting textures, including some of the oleander that seems to grow everywhere around here. Why so much oleander? It's really poisonous. I read a while back about some kids who died when they roasted marshmallows on oleander sticks.

Bob and I chose a bench at random. I kept thinking about oleander. Some part of me knew that my mind was looking for any other subject than what was coming, but I kept on mind-meandering anyway. Next to the oleander, there was a spider centered on her web that stretched from a dwarf spirea to a little mound of oatgrass. I like spiders. They eat a lot of bugs.

Behind the web there were some sad-looking daffodils that had long since finished blooming. They need to get their landscape person busy. While they're at it, they ought to figure out who this gardener is who keeps planting all these deadly shrubs and vines. I'd never seen such a collection in one place. The hotel was surrounded with azaleas, covered in pink and red blossoms. I'd seen yew hedges, and castor bean plants with their enormous leaves. There were yellow-flowered Carolina jessamine vines and rhododendron bushes everywhere. The place was positively blooming with danger.

I sat down in the middle of the bench, still not quite sure I wanted to hear whatever he was going to say. Bob stepped past me and settled in on my right, near the huge oleander bush that overhung the path and the stone wall. I'd read enough sales manuals the year I worked for the marketing firm in Boston to see the sense in his move. I wondered if he knew what he was doing or if it was simply instinct on his part. You see, if you want to sell somebody something–whether it's a piece of merchandise or an idea–sit on their right. That side is the most open to persuasion. It's the least defensive side psychologically. That's why the old-fashioned Victorian love-seats are supposed to be shaped like an S instead of a backwards S. That way BOTH people have their right sides toward each other. People can set up their offices or their living rooms to be win/win or to be I win/you lose.

"Biscuit? Are you here with me?"

I am here for both of you.

Was I? Did I want to be persuaded? Well, I wanted his socks off the floor, and I didn't want to pick them up myself. I came close to getting up and moving around to *his* right, but decided that would be somewhat juvenile. I knew, though, that there was nothing he could say to me–nothing that would change my mind about the socks. "Okay. I'm listening."

Not really.

Sort of.

Bob reached out to take my hand, resting it on his knee. "You know I was married once before."

"Yes."

"But you don't know why we divorced."

I do not know either.

"You said the two of you were incompatible."

"That's right, but there's more to it than that."

There usually is with you humans.

Oh my gosh. What was I about to learn? Was there some sort of disease involved? Did he have a violent temper that came out only *after* marriage? I leaned back and took a good long look at this man I had married. I'd known him almost exactly one year. He had more common sense than any man I'd ever known. He had a gentle voice, and his silver-sprinkled black hair formed an unruly arc across his forehead. In fact, if he hadn't had such a crooked nose from an old baseball injury when he was a kid, he would have been almost too handsome. Maybe there's something wrong with him, though. I knew this was too good to last.

"Biscuit, you did it again. You faded out on me."

And you are making up all this fear-thought.

"I'm sorry, Bob. I'm sitting here wondering if you're an ax murderer or something. But your glasses sit crooked on your nose, so you can't be."

"You are making no sense whatsoever, woman."

At least he was calling me woman again. That was something he'd started doing in private a couple of months ago. Someone who didn't know the two of us might think it sounded proprietary, like a cave man, but it was always said with humor and a sweetness that was hard to resist. Come to think of it, he was a very sweet man. And I was acting like an idiot. "Okay, I concede you're not a murderer."

He straightened his back ever so slightly, and turned to watch a biker glide past us at a leisurely pace. I noticed the furrow on his forehead deepen a bit. "Actually," he said, "I am."

The undercurrent along this stretch of the river caused a low-pitched hum. From where I sat, it sounded like a bee hive or distant thunder. The clouds were moving in, and one crossed in front of the sun. We were married. We'd made sweet happy love several times each day. We were still holding hands. I didn't like what I had heard.

"Would you like to explain that statement?" I asked him.

"No, I wouldn't like to, but I have to. I should have told you earlier, but there never seemed to be the right time."

"And you figured you'd marry me first before you admitted killing somebody? And you a cop? How did you get away with it? At least tell me it was self-defense."

"I may deserve this tirade, but I wish you'd let me explain."

"And what on earth does this have to do with socks? You said it was something about socks!" Lord, did he kill off his first wife because she nagged him about dirty laundry? What had I gotten myself into? "Who else knows about this?"

"My mom, and Ilona." Bob's sister, who lives in Athens, has some physical challenges. She uses a wheel chair for mobility, and is a feisty soul whom I like a whole lot. How could she know about this and still claim him as her brother?

"Please explain right now, before I go nuts wondering what's going on."

Give him a chance, Widelap.

Bob shifted his position on the hard bench and grasped my hand even more firmly. A couple strolled by, arms entwined around each other's waist, her head leaning against his shoulder. It looked extremely uncomfortable to me. Of course, when Sol and I were first married, I used to sit beside him in his big recliner, with my head all skewed out of kilter so I could snuggle on his shoulder. I thought that was how to show closeness. Boy was I dumb. All I got out of it was an aching neck. And Sol finally admitted that his fingers went numb whenever I was leaning on his arm like that. As the couple passed us, I took a deep breath, and noticed that Bob was doing the same thing.

"I married Sheila shortly after I got back from Viet Nam. . . ."

That was it, this was a war confession. He'd killed people over there and now he was feeling guilty about it. Maybe we could get him some help through the VA hospital in Atlanta.

"Did you talk to Nathan about it?" Nathan Young is our doctor in Martinsville who combines western medicine with holistic practices such as herbal therapies and nutritional counseling. He's even studying acupuncture. Maybe acupuncture could help Post Traumatic Stress Syndrome.

"Nathan? Why would I talk to Nathan?"

"He could help you with it."

"With what?"

"With your Post Traumatic Stress Syndrome."

Bob twisted around so he was facing me directly. Taking my shoulders in both his hands, he started to say something, changed his mind, paused. Then he burst out laughing.

"Here I am," he said, "trying to admit to you something that is very painful to me. Something that I haven't shared with anyone except my mother and my sister. Something that you need to know. And you are inventing scenarios right and left without giving me a chance to explain. What am I going to do with you?"

"You are going to explain what the heck you're talking about. How dare you tell me you're a murderer, and then laugh about it?" Nathan is going to have to check my blood pressure when I get home. If I ever get there. If my husband doesn't do me in, first.

You two should start this conversation over again.

This will not do. I wish we could start over again. "Bob, I'm going to take a deep breath. I want you to do the same. Then, please, tell me what's going on."

"Sheila accused me of killing our baby." His voice was flat. His eyes had gone a dark gray. He kept looking at me.

Killing . . . a baby? Killing a . . . baby? Killing a baby. The phrase sounded like a gong, like a mantra in my head. When Sally, my second child, was born, she had a light layer of peach fuzz all over her head. It took almost three years before it grew to any length at all. And then one day Sandra, her long-haired older sister, took the forbidden scissors and chopped half of Sally's sweet little curls right down to the scalp. I remember thinking at the time that I could have willingly flushed Sandra down the drain for having done that. Why did I ever carry that kind of anger within myself over something as inconsequential as a child's haircut? Sandra is my daughter. Sandra is the mother now of Verity Marie, my oldest grandchild. Now that I am married to Bob Sheffield, he is Sandra's father. He is Verity's grandfather.

"Biscuit?"

"Hmmm?"

"Biscuit, talk to me."

"No, Bob Sheffield, you talk to me. What do you mean you killed a baby? You tell me why you haven't told me this before. Tell me why you even married me."

"Why are you assuming that her accusation was true?"

"Because you just told me you were a murderer. And because you're pussy-footin' around about this whole thing. Tell me what happened." The entwined couple was walking past us again, going in the opposite direction. They veered to the far side of the walkway. I suppose my voice was a little loud. . . .

You have been shouting.

. . .The two of them averted their eyes as I glared at them.

"Settle down . . ."

"You want me to SETTLE DOWN?"

Yes. Settle down.

". . . and I'll explain."

I crossed my arms. This was turning out worse than I thought. It would have been much easier if he'd had a disease.

On the other end of the phone line, I could almost hear Glaze shaking her head. "It must be quite a story," she said, "if it's taking you this long to figure out what to say about it."

I thought again of Marmalade, wishing she were in my lap. How does she manage to stay trim when all she does is sleep in people's laps? . . .

I fought a bad man two weeks ago and I have been very busy here for the past two days.

"Oh, it's pretty simple," I told her. "Bob agreed to pick up his socks within two hours of dropping them on the floor, and I agreed to stop leaving long hairs on the soap in the bathtub."

Even though Glaze and I hadn't spent much time together since childhood, I knew she could tell I was lying. Not lying, exactly, because that *was* what we had finally agreed on, but there are simply some parts of this story that are better not said.

We had both cried about it when Bob managed to tell me what had happened. When I finally uncrossed my arms and was willing to listen.

"We'd been married almost six years," he told me, "when Sheila came home one day and told me she was pregnant. I thought she was teasing at first, because of the way she was laughing. But she wasn't teasing. She was just happy. She was sick a lot, but she said that was normal for the first part of being pregnant. But then she kept on being sick, even when she was four and five months along. I didn't think anybody could be that sick."

Bob stopped for a moment to watch a white-haired fisherman amble past us. "Didn't catch a thing," the old man called out. "But I had a great time trying." Bob and I both nodded mechanically, as if we were interested in his fishing stories.

Once the man passed beyond earshot, Bob continued. "We were living in Atlanta. There was a big flu outbreak that year. Sheila woke up one morning throwing up much worse than ever. Of course, we both thought she'd caught the bug. I went on to work, and she called in sick. About ten o'clock I was in a big meeting. She called and insisted the company secretary get me on the line. 'I'm really sick,' she told me. 'I need to go to the doctor.'"

Bob had taken my hand again, but he let go of it and passed his hand over his face, as if he were wiping off sweat. The oleander beyond his shoulder was nodding in the breeze that had sprung up.

"The meeting was an important one to me. There would have been a big promotion if I had been able to convince the managers to vote for my proposition. I told Sheila I'd be home as soon as the meeting was over."

Bob was quiet for such a long time I thought he might have forgotten where he was, but he finally reached over and took my hand again.

"When I got home, about eleven-thirty, she was lying on the floor next to the phone. There was blood spreading out around her. I thought she'd been attacked. She was almost unconscious, but she managed to tell me that she had tried to call me again. I never got that call. By the time I got her to the hospital it was way too late to save the baby. The doctor told us that there was a reason for the miscarriage and that nothing would have saved the baby anyway, but Sheila always thought differently."

"And what about you? What did you think?"

Bob stood up, walked behind the bench to peer over the stone wall. I sat for a while, then joined him. The water looked peaceful. I looked up river and down river, and then I inspected the stone wall we were leaning against. There must have been two dozen spindly-looking daddy longleg spiders traipsing up and down the river side of the wall. They didn't seem to be headed anywhere in particular. Just roaming around with nothing to do.

He finally answered me.

"What did I think? I think I killed our baby. I think I should have taken her to the hospital the first time she called. I think I should have been more concerned. I think I should have been able to . . ." His voice, which had risen at first, tapered off to nothing.

"Oh, Bob. I . . . I don't know what to . . . I'm so sorry." What a lame thing to say.

"Sheila never did forgive me. And I never forgave myself. She was in the hospital for two more weeks. Kept bleeding. We almost lost her several times. She wouldn't talk to me. She shut me out of her mind. She never talked about her anger, never told me how betrayed she felt. But when it was time for her to come home, she called her sister to come get her. A couple of months later she mailed me divorce papers to sign. There was a note that said the divorce would take only thirty days, since there were no children involved. No . . . children . . . involved."

We must have stood there for half an hour, watching the river surge past us. There didn't seem to be a lot to say. I asked him if Tom knew about it. Tom, who had been Bob's best man for his first wedding, and who had been my bridesmaid for this one.

"No. I couldn't tell him. He knew Sheila, of course; he knew she'd lost the baby. He knew she was upset about it. But, no, I never told him."

"Don't you think it would have helped to talk to somebody about it?"

"I talked to my mom about it. She loved Sheila a lot, and was so sad about the divorce, but I think she understood. She told me she'd lost a baby before I was born. I never knew that. She said it would kill me inside if I didn't talk about it, and she got me to go see a counselor."

"Did that help?"

"It was painful as hell, but I suppose it did help me. He tried to get me to see that it wasn't my fault, but I used to wake up at night thinking I heard Sheila calling out to me. And then I started thinking I was hearing the baby. It was a boy. Tommy, we would have named him."

"When did the nightmares stop?"

"They didn't completely. I still wake myself up sometimes, wondering if I could have done something differently." Bob turned away from the river and leaned his elbows back on the stone parapet. The palm tree in front of us had lost a frond that was beginning to shrivel. It looked out of place lying in the lush grass near the base of the trunk.

I didn't understand how Bob could have avoided telling Tom. I guess that's the difference between men and women. We tell our friends sad things to lighten the load. Men shoulder their loads separately.

"Does your brother know about this?"

"He knows about the miscarriage, of course, but he doesn't know that Sheila accused me of murder. He's not the kind that would care, anyway."

"Not care about his own brother?"

"Biscuit, did you notice he didn't drive up for the wedding? We're business partners, but he doesn't give a shit about me otherwise."

Finally, we simply turned and walked back to the River Landing. We skipped lunch and sat on the patio for a couple of hours. We figured out a compromise on the socks issue, which didn't seem to matter much anymore. We ate dinner silently. It took a long time to get to sleep that night, but we lay in bed curled together like a turtle and a shell, although which of us was which, we couldn't have said.

my gratitude list for Sunday

> *Smellsweet, who hugs me gently*
> *happy humans*
> *red dogs who are polite to me*
> *Widelap and Softfoot, who talk to each other*
> *the chicken Fishgiver gives me*

Monday April 29, 1996 – Savannah

The next morning, for the second time in my life, I woke up next to Bob Sheffield. I was lying on my left side, of course, since that's the way the digestive tract works most efficiently. It has to do with the way gravity assists the natural flow of bodily fluids. Why on earth do I think of such things at a time like this?

I could feel the warmth from Bob's body curved around my back. The early morning sunlight was yellowing the white ceiling of the bridal suite, and I could see little motes of dust rising through the sunbeams. The sun's warmth was setting up a convection current. Bob must have been setting up his own convection current, for I found myself turning over to find his blue-gray eyes awake and twinkling as he said, "Are you ready for . . ."

"Again?"

"I was going to say a stroll alongside the river, Woman."

"Maybe a quick hug first. Or a long hug, as the case may be."

I would enjoy having my ears scratched right now. Maybe I will walk across Smellsweet to wake her up.

"I think I could manage a long hug. Then a walk. I need a little exercise before breakfast."

That sounded great. I needed a walk to clear my brain a bit from the emotional upheaval of our talk yesterday, to say nothing of the lack of sleep because of Margaret Casperson's illness during the wee small hours. Thank goodness we'd gotten back to bed within an hour or so.

We hugged and stretched and dressed and left the room.

Crossing the patio quickly, we headed along one of the paths that led down to the combination bike path and walking trail along the river.

The Savannah River is deceptively gentle-looking. The River Landing Hotel, surrounded by a large park, sits out on a promontory formed by a wide bend where the river loops back on itself.

We met several late-morning joggers as we strolled along. Our pace wouldn't count as exercise, but we were enjoying ourselves, saying hello to people who passed us. Bob paused to speak to yesterday's white-haired fisherman, and I continued on, expecting Bob to catch up with me in a moment or two. When he didn't, I turned around and saw him apparently engrossed in conversation. Fishermen amaze me. They can talk about lures and baits and lines all day long. Bob was an expert at tying flies. He'd even named one of his best flies for me–the "Bisque Whisk." I loved its feathery softness and the way it rotated through the air. He should make a larger version– minus the hook, of course–as a cat toy for Marmalade.

I would enjoy that.

I spent a few moments thinking about Marmalade before I walked back to join the two men. I was just in time to hear Bob ask if swimmers ever interfered with the fishing.

"No, you wouldn't want to swim in that. At least, not along here."

"Why not? The water looks pretty calm."

The fisherman reached up to scratch at his bushy mustache and to wave away an insistent mosquito. I wish Bob would grow a mustache. I think he'd look quite distinguished. "Mighty strong undertow along here," the man drawled as he turned to look across the water.

As we walked away, I asked Bob if he thought the water was really dangerous.

"He was just trying to make it sound dramatic," Bob said. He looped his arm over my shoulders. "Let's stick to the hotel pool, though, shall we, just in case?"

Please take good care of yourselves. I want you to return home to me.

The rest of the stroll was equally uneventful. The black-garbed woman I'd seen yesterday passed us. I noticed she was carrying what looked like a tape recorder. I smiled at her, but she didn't respond. She seemed to be wrapped up in a world of her own. A little farther down the path we saw some lizards that Marmalade could have enjoyed investigating. Why was I thinking about my cat during my honeymoon? We returned in time for a leisurely breakfast in the hotel's homey dining room, then went upstairs to change for a quick swim in the pool. We got diverted, however, and finally decided that the swimming pool wasn't on our agenda that morning.

Gratitude List for Sunday, April 28, 1996 (written Monday morning because I forgot again!)

    1. Life itself – and safety and good health
    2. The talk with Bob about the baby
    3. Learning to trust
    4. Silence when it feels right
    5. My memories of Marmalade that bring me joy

Thank you.

Later, Bob propped himself up against the headboard and said, "It's really too bad we had to start our honeymoon with Margaret's collapse."

"We didn't *start* it with that. We started it with a party for the whole town, a family reception, a long car trip, dinner a little way south of Augusta, an absolutely lovely stroll around the courthouse square in that funny little town you found off Highway 17, a wedding night that was . . ." I paused, unable to think of adequate words. Delightful? Wondrous? Comforting? Fun? Exhilarating? Exhausting?

"Yes?" Bob prompted with a merry smile.

"You know perfectly well what Saturday night was like." I smiled at my husband of almost two days and continued my litany. "Sunday morning, after a leisurely breakfast and . . ."

"Yes?" he asked again. His eyes really do twinkle at times.

"Anyway, we did manage to drive here to Savannah, despite a twelve-mile scenic detour at the end while we looked for this hotel. Then we had an elevator ride up three stories. We came in here and . . ."

"Yes?" he questioned helpfully.

"As I was saying before I was almost diverted from my train of thought, we had a lovely day . . ."

"Yes, we did."

. . . and a lovely evening . . ." Bob's hand was inching its way in a delicious curve. ". . . and a beautiful night . . . Quit it, Robert." I was trying very hard not to giggle. It seemed inappropriate at my age. I giggled anyway. "I can't think straight, Bob." Of course, who cares whether or not I can think straight at a time like this?

That beautiful night I'd been describing, though, had been interrupted shortly before three o'clock, by someone pounding on the wall of the room next door. I thought at first it was some over-enthusiastic couple. How dare they be having a good time when Bob and I had taken such a long time to get to sleep? Then we heard a woman in the hallway calling for help. By the time I threw on a robe, Bob had already opened the door. Thank goodness he'd thrown on his undershorts. The woman was on the floor, gasping and choking. I yelled for help as Bob turned her on her side so she wouldn't choke, and supported her head. She didn't look very good. Other guests, in various stages of night-dress, were collecting around the periphery, offering stunned commentary. Someone ran off to call the front desk and demand an ambulance.

Of course, even with her face distorted in fear and pain, I recognized Margaret immediately. Sweet Margaret Casperson. She must have had the room next to ours. I'd seen her many times in the Martinsville library. And, of course, I'd spoken with her yesterday when we arrived at the River Landing. For a moment, as she lay there, she tried to tell us something. She was obviously delirious, spouting something about colors. And she said something like "He's my father." There was more, but I wasn't sure what she was saying.

Then we all watched Margaret lapse into unconsciousness even as the ambulance crew was scrambling out of the elevator, followed by a worried-looking woman who turned out to be the hotel's general manager. I gave the medics Margaret's name, answered some quick questions, and watched them load up her inert form.

Once the ambulance crew was gone, the manager turned to me. "The front desk called me. Luckily I live nearby. Could I use your room phone for a moment to call the hotel owner?"

"Sure," I said. "Barry's an old friend of my husband's from Martinsville."

I walked with her into our room and showed her where the phone was. As she was placing the call, I realized how silly that had been of me. Of course she knew where the phone was. This was her hotel. I quite frankly eavesdropped on her conversation. When she hung up, she turned to me and said, "Thank you for trying to help poor Mrs. Casperson."

"That's quite all right. I wish we could have done more."

"Did she say anything about what was wrong?"

"Well, she said a few words."

"Oh? Like what?"

"I don't know exactly. It's all been sort of a blur. She did mention some colors and . . ."

"Biscuit?" Bob interrupted me from the doorway. He must not have heard that we had a conversation going. At four in the morning, though, who hears anything straight? He looked at the manager. "Are you through now?"

"Yes, we are," she said. "I need to go downstairs to wait for Mr. Murphy. Thank you for the use of your phone."

I put out my hand and touched her arm. "Do you happen to know if she mentioned to anyone where her cousin lives?"

"Her cousin? What are you talking about?"

"When we checked in I saw her in the lobby, and she told me she was here to visit her cousin Brenda. I thought it might be a good idea to let Brenda know that Margaret's been taken ill."

Ms. Cappell looked down the hallway. I followed the direction of her gaze. There was a lovely antique escritoire that had some drooping flowers on it. The arrangement clearly needed to be spruced up. Or thrown out. I saw her forehead wrinkle. Somebody in house-keeping was probably going to get a severe talking to in the morning.

"I'll see what I can do about it," she said.

As she turned to walk away, Barry Murphy trudged out of the elevator looking thoroughly disheveled, which didn't seem unusual to me, since I was standing there in a bathrobe with my hair all whompy-jawed.

I felt throughout the furor that I was being catapulted along a roller coaster, with no way to stop the forward momentum. After what seemed like a very long time, we crawled back into bed, and fell asleep curled together like two mealybugs in a compost bin. Only a true gardener would think in such terms, but I've always thought it's so cute the way mealybugs bunch together in little piles.

After a delightful interlude of snuggles and hugs–we were both too pooped for anything more than that–I took a few moments to re-orient myself, then turned back to Bob and continued our conversation where we'd left off. "So, you see, we didn't *start* our honeymoon with an emergency. By then we were old married folks, having been wed at least thirty-nine hours before the drama."

"Your logic astounds me, dear madam."

"I hope I always astound you, dear sir."

After which, we astounded ourselves. Was I going to have enough stamina for this marriage? These stellar performances couldn't last long. I love words, which is probably why I'm a librarian. Take *stellar*, for instance. It comes from the Latin. It means like a star. Or *stamina*, which I wasn't sure I'd have enough of. It's Latin too, from the word *stamen*, which was one of the threads of life that the Three Fates wove. Regardless of the derivation, I was hungry.

Luckily, room service, in which we decided to indulge for lunch, was still operating an hour later, so we ordered Salmon Bisque–a creamy fish soup in my honor–and Brandied Sheffield Pears–whatever that was–in Bob's honor. The food took a long time to get to us, but we weren't in a hurry. Finally, as we lounged over the remains of the meal, my eyes rested on the lamp next to the loveseat.

"Did you know that your wife knows how to freshen up a hat veil on a light bulb if she's forgotten her traveling iron?"

Bob raised his left eyebrow at me as he put on his glasses. Then he looked at me over the rim of them. "What on earth are you talking about, woman?"

"Years ago," I explained, "when I was in sixth grade, all the girls in the class were taken one day to the school gym to see a film called *Growing Up and Liking It.* Our mothers, most of them, were there, which surprised the heck out of us. We hadn't known anything like this was coming. Anyway, it was a film about what would happen when we started our periods."

"Racy stuff for those days?" Bob laughed.

"It *was* racy," I objected. "And we didn't quite know what to do. We wouldn't even look at each other after it was over. And then they gave us each two little booklets. One had the same title as the film. It was a recap of the high points . . ."

"Educational, I'm sure," Bob interjected.

". . . and the other was a book on etiquette straight out of the forties. We were appalled. It was full of such useful information as how to freshen up one's hat veil."

"So how does one do that?" Bob prompted, with a twinkle in his eyes.

"Voila," I said, reaching over to pull the handkerchief out of the pocket of his jacket that he had hung over the bedpost.

The lamp beside the bed had one of those compact fluorescent bulbs, so I scooted across the room to the table near the door. Sliding the heavy lamp closer to the edge of the table, I resumed my instruction. "First, turn on the lamp and remove the lampshade." I matched my actions to my words. "Then, keeping in mind that light bulbs get hot . . ."

"They didn't think you knew that?"

"Shhh. That was 1958. Women had to be *instructed* in everything. You probably never noticed because that's just the way things were then. In women's magazines, ads for floor polishes were always accompanied by an article on how to polish floors." I continued with my demonstration. "Hold the veil tightly stretched between your two hands . . ."

"How else would you stretch it?"

". . . and using the lightest of touches, skim the veil across the light bulb. The heat of the bulb will act like an iron and . . . Whoops!" I removed the silk handkerchief that now sported a big brown scorch mark. "Well, it works with veils."

"Remind me never to ask you to iron my underwear," Bob said as we gathered up the luncheon dishes and he stacked them on the floor outside the door.

"Fat chance, my beloved. If you ever do, I'll starch them first."

Gratitude list for Monday, April 29, 1996 – finally I'm back to writing it on the proper day!

1. This sweet time with Bob
2. A regular schedule – sort of
3. Margaret Casperson, who is hanging on to life
4. The gorgeous flowers all around this place
5. Marmalade, whom I don't always understand,
   but always do love.

Thank you

this wide porch
hedges to hide under
humans who listen
Smellsweet who scratches my ears when I wake her
    in the morning
the catnip treats that Fishgiver gives me

Chapter 4 - 1940's

Tuesday, March 19, 1946

Charlotte McLeod Holvers, second wife of Gustav Holvers, widowed now for well over a decade, tugged down on the front hem of her light-blue cashmere sweater. It *would* keep riding up, and she had to keep pulling it into place, rather like she'd done to Peter all those years ago when he was a child. He was one of those little boys who had always been running to get into things, and she was always tugging at him, trying to get him to settle down, behave, be quiet. He always *would* be riding up against the rules when he was little.

She could hardly remember when she had started disliking him so. He had been only three when his dear mother had died in childbed along with her stillborn baby. In many ways Charlotte knew that she was the only mother Peter had ever known. The first Mrs. Holvers was hardly a loving mother. But back then wives of wealthy men didn't have to raise their own children. That was why Charlotte had been hired in 1901 when she was just twenty or so to care for the first Holvers baby, young Marcus. And then Peter had come along the following year.

Charlotte looked back at that first year with just Marcus to care for. Comparatively speaking, it had been a vacation. Peter, once he arrived, kept her running. He crawled earlier than babies ought to crawl. Once he learned to walk, he ran circles around poor little Marcus, who toddled here and there so sweetly, always behind his younger brother. It wasn't just that Peter ran faster, that he was stronger, that he turned out to be bigger than Marcus. He was mean about it, always rubbing poor dear Marcus' nose in it, always taunting him nearly to tears.

Charlotte pulled again at her sweater, smoothing it over her ample middle, and re-read the note she was holding. The handwriting was deplorable, slanted so far to the right, it looked like the writer was stumbling over her own words. As, perhaps, she was.

Monday

Dear Mother Holvers,

I am writing in the hopes that you will be able to see me for a short time tomorrow morning or Wednesday afternoon. There is something I must discuss with you. As it is of some importance, I hope you can make time for me in your daily schedule.

I have asked the messenger to wait for a written reply, and I will come to you at any time you set. Time is of the essence.

Thank you.
Your loving daughter-in-law,
Mildred

If time is of the essence, Charlotte thought, then she's either dying of some dread disease or, more likely, she's pregnant. And I'd be willing to bet it's not Peter's child. Young people nowadays think they invented sex. When I was a girl, we didn't have automobiles, but we had buggies, and we had back rooms, and we knew what they were for.

Only the grace of God, and a good deal of old-fashioned luck, had kept Charlotte McLeod from conceiving a child. Only a silly quirk of fate had kept her unmarried. The silly quirk was her lover's wife.

And then Mrs. Gustav Holvers had hired her to care for Marcus. And then Peter had come along. And then Mrs. Holvers had died. Gustav had asked her to marry him six months later, to raise his children. It had been a matter of convenience. But she had known what it was to be held by someone. Someone before her husband. Ah well, it was good that all that was in the past now.

Charlotte's hand paused on its way to tug again at her sweater. If I saw *his* handwriting today, on an envelope addressed to me, it would take my breath. After all these years, I know my heart would speed up.

She pursed her lips, and gave a wry chuckle. At my age, that would probably do me in, she thought, and turned her attention back to Peter's wife.

Poor Mildred, as flighty as Peter was serious, no wonder she was always off on those trips of hers. London, Paris. Those cities couldn't be much to see this soon after the war. Surely they're still devastated by the bombing. But Mildred had insisted on traveling. And now she had something to discuss with her mother-in-law. Peter was not going to like learning about this. Peter was the most completely unforgiving man Charlotte had ever known.

She could remember once when the boys were ten and eleven, Marcus had been so excited because he had finally won a game the two of them were playing. The next day Marcus had a broken arm. Although he never blamed his brother, Charlotte had known that it was Peter's revenge. The trouble was, she could never catch him at it. He was very, very sneaky. He was, she had to admit, very, very smart about hiding his tracks. And his older brother was very, very afraid of him.

Charlotte regretted the way things had turned out when the boys were grown, with Marcus being unable to keep the family business afloat through the Depression. What a bad time that had been. What tragedies had played out. Like the Holvers tragedy. Peter, of course, took over and made poor Marcus look the fool. Peter carried success on his shoulders like a toreador's cape. A cape made on the Isle of Always Right. Maybe Charlotte was the only mother he'd really known, but she had never thought of him as her child, the way she did Marcus.

She glanced down at the letter, which she was quietly crushing in her fist. If Mildred was pregnant, it would serve Peter right, but Mildred would be at risk if he found out. She could imagine how he would react. It wouldn't be with loving concern. His property rights were being violated, and he wouldn't like it one bit.

He had been despicable to his half-sister, Charlotte's daughter, when Shirlene was found in 1935 to be expecting a child without benefit, as they used to say, of matrimony. To Charlotte, the child that resulted, her first grandchild, was a treasure. There is so little love in the world, if it has to be expressed in this way, let it be. I love my granddaughter.

Charlotte almost laughed aloud when she thought of all the secret visits they'd had together, so Peter wouldn't find out. It wouldn't have been worth the anger and the retribution. I wish I'd had the nerve to stand up to him, to tell him what an idiot he was for his unforgiving attitudes. But I didn't know how to do that, so I hid the times I welcomed Shirlene and little Sandy back into the house. I never let Peter know about it. I was a good grandmother, though.

And now, I will be a good counselor, Charlotte thought as she heard Mildred ring the front doorbell. I will advise her to keep the baby, and to be very, very sure that Peter thinks it is his.

Saturday, October 19, 1946 – Savannah

Ever since the war ended, people had been flocking to the beach every chance they could get. But today the beach wasn't crowded. That was a pleasant surprise for Joan Fredericks, who had brought her little boy to play in the sand. He toddled around in his yellow and blue striped play clothes, and investigated each stick, each bug, each mound of sand. His pant legs were almost too tight already. He was growing so fast. She sat back on the big blanket she had spread in the dry area above the line of breaking wavelets and watched her baby as he sat down and began to scoop sand over his little legs.

"Hello. Lovely day, isn't it?" The voice surprised Joan, and she raised her arm to shield her eyes from the sun as she looked toward the woman who was walking by in the damp sand at the water's edge.

"Yes, it is."

"My, what a handsome little fellow." The woman meandered up the sand. "A boy, yes?"

"Yes."

"At this age it can be hard to tell for sure."

Both women laughed.

"I remember before he was born," Joan said, "I found it so hard to tell whether little people were boys or girls. I made some dreadful mistakes talking to women who were carrying babies around."

"Yes, I know what you mean. I've done the same thing. Is he about three years old?"

"He's not quite two and a half."

"What's his name?"

Joan reached out quickly to take a good-sized bug out of the boy's grasp just before he could stuff it in his mouth.

"It's Peter," she said. "But I've started calling him Bull."

"I can see why," said the woman again, with what Joan heard as admiration in her voice. "He certainly is a sturdy little fellow."

The sturdy little fellow continued his sand-scooping with a single-minded determination, ignoring his mother and the stranger.

By this time the woman had walked closer to the blanket. She reached down and rubbed her knee. "Would you mind if I sat down for a bit? I tripped on some driftwood up the beach, and my knee feels a little wobbly."

Of course," Joan said as she scooted over to make more room. "Please sit here." She reached into the bright yellow bag that sat on the edge of the blanket and pulled out a clean diaper. "I'll run and wet this in the waves. It's always a good idea to put cold water on a bump so it won't swell as much. Keep an eye on Bull, would you?"

"Of course. I'm pretty good at saving bugs."

They laughed together again as Joan turned toward the water.

When she brought the wet cloth back from the water's edge, she couldn't see any particular swelling or bruising on the woman's knee. "I don't think you're going to have any trouble with it."

"Oh, I'm sure I won't. It was only a little bump. Thank you for your kindness, Mrs. . . .?"

"Call me Joan. My name is Joan Fredericks. I'm a widow."

"In the war? My husband died, too. My name is Star."

"What a beautiful name," Joan said as she reached out to shake Star's hand. She found it hard to believe that such a lovely name had been applied to such a plain-looking woman. Joan tried to study her without seeming to. She was thin and straight-backed. Maybe, Joan thought, she was a pretty little girl and she just grew out of it. The woman's knee, beneath the cool wet diaper had been bony. Her hands looked, for want of a better word, competent.

"Do you come here often?" Star asked a few moments later.

"Oh yes. My little boy loves to play in the sand."

"And eat bugs?"

"Well, he tries to, but I'm usually quick enough to stop him." They settled back and watched Bull for a moment.

"Aren't children wonderful?" Star asked.

"Yes. Thank you. He's such a delight." Joan got up and lifted Bull away from a line of ants. "What about you?" she asked as she sat down again. "I don't think I've seen you here before."

"I grew up in this area, but I have to work to support my children, and I couldn't find a job here." Star picked up a handful of sand and let it slip through her fingers. She reached up to finger a small necklace she was wearing. "I come here for visits when I can. Someday I hope to move home to Savannah. I miss it."

"Do you have family here?" Joan asked. She always assumed that other people had family, even though she didn't. Just her son. Her son.

"No. My parents moved away from here before the war."

Joan thought about her small house and the empty hours stretching ahead of her once her son was in bed for the night. It was always the same. She stayed busy with her knitting and her reading. And, of course, there was the radio. But she felt so lonely for conversation."Why don't you come home with me and have dinner? We'd love the company."

Star's smile almost startled Joan. It was so unexpected on that serious-looking face.

"I'd enjoy that," she said.

For some reason, Joan thought Star looked . . . triumphant. What a strange idea.

* * * * * *

From the *Keagan County Record*
Wednesday November 20, 1946
Myrtle's Musings from Martinsville

It is with great sadness that I have to mention the passing of Obadiah Martin, one of Martinsville's finest sons and a direct descendent of Homer Martin, who founded the town in 1745. I'm sure you've already read all the details in his obituary on page one. I simply want to express my condolences to his family. I have just learned that he will be succeeded as Chairman of the Town Council by his son Leon Martin.

On a happier note, ever since the war ended, there have been so many babies appearing in our little towns along the Metoochie River. They seem to blossoming everywhere, all over the country, but our special little packages here in Martinsville are particularly dear to our hearts. As I mentioned in my column last week, we have already had three babies born since the beginning of the month. And now our own Pamela C. Tarkington informs me that she and Ray now have their first grandchild, a little girl born last week to their older daughter Mildred, who lives in Atlanta with her husband, Peter Holvers. Congratulations, Pamela and Ray. We are very happy for you. And we welcome little "Brenda" to the Martinsville extended family.

Tuesday March 25, 1947

Estelle Placings stood and tucked her steno notepad under her arm. She wanted to reach up to be sure her straight black hair was tidily tucked into its bun, but she would never allow herself to primp in the presence of her boss. She had a firm belief in office etiquette.

"Mr. Holvers?" she said, "I'd like to ask for two days off next month so I can attend the wedding of a close friend of mine."

"Two days?" His left eyebrow lifted a fraction of an inch as he pushed a stack of papers to one side of his desk. "That must be some wedding, Estelle."

"I have to travel a ways to get there, and it's on a Thursday."

"In that case, take three days."

"No, Sir. You couldn't get along without me here."

Peter Holvers' hand paused for three of Estelle's heartbeats on its way to smooth back his already seal-slick hair.

Estelle wondered if she had overdone it, but then he laughed. "You're probably right about that. When is the wedding?"

"It's on the 24th."

He paused another few moments. "I know someone who's getting married on the 24th," he said.

"I'm sure many people are getting married that day, Mr. Holvers."

"You're probably right." He cleared his throat. "Who is she?"

Estelle fingered the single strand of pearls she wore. The necklace felt tight. "Just a long-time friend," she said.

"Well then, that's okay. You go and have a good time."

After Estelle left his office, Peter sank back into his chair. His stomach had been bothering him a lot recently. He wondered if he might be developing an ulcer. Leaning forward to press the intercom button, he said, "Estelle, make an appointment for me to see Dr. Barnett. For a check-up."

He pressed the off button and picked up the letter he had been reading before Estelle came in. There was no return address on the envelope. The postmark was Savannah. The letter was not dated.

Peter,

Thank you for the money order. My son is growing well, and is very sturdy for three years old. I am quite proud of him.

I want you to know that Russell has asked me to marry him, and I've said yes. I'm tired of the charade of being a "war widow" – and it's time my son had a dad to teach him how to play catch. We'll be married at the end of next month, on the 24ᵗʰ. My new friend Star has agreed to be my matron of honor, and Russell's brother will be the best man. Other than that, it will be a quiet ceremony. You, of course, are not invited.

After next month there will be no need for the monthly allowance. I release you from that obligation, for it is time for Peter's new dad to be the one to provide for him. And for me. I do not want any awkwardness between Russell and me. He knows I own the house, but of course, he assumes it was because of "George."

You have "done right by me" Peter, but I never want to hear from you again. I have finally come to forgive your actions almost four years ago, for they gave me a son I love. I have decided no longer to regret your insistence that I give him your name. Also I refuse to hold resentment within me. It is a nasty emotion that eats at one from the inside.

I know the money has not been a burden for you, but I wonder if it has assuaged your guilt in any way.

Good-bye.
Joan

Thursday April 24, 1947

"Joan, you are a beautiful bride," Star told her. "I wish you were having a huge church wedding so the whole town could see you."

"You don't know what you're talking about. I wouldn't want all of Savannah to see me. This blue suit is as simple as they come."

"I know that." Star's heavy face broke into a grin. "But if you were having an enormous wedding, you'd be wearing a long white gown with a train."

"Star! What an absurd idea. I have a child. I can't wear white."

"Well, I wish you could. You would look quite stunning in it."

Joan reached up to adjust the rim of her navy boater. She turned her head a few degrees and quite frankly admired her reflection. "I do look beautiful, don't I? Do you think Russell will think so?"

"I didn't hear that he'd been blinded in the war." Star reached over to tuck in a wayward auburn curl that had escaped Joan's stiff straw hat.

Joan grabbed her friend's hand and held it for a moment. "I don't know what I would have done if you hadn't happened to walk down the beach that day."

"Oh, you would have found someone else to be friends with."

"Quit that! I'm serious. I . . ." Joan groped for words. "You've helped me in so many ways. And you're like a second mother to my dear little Bull. I wish you could move back here."

"I will, Joan. Someday I will. I'd love to stay close to you and Bull."

"Thank you so much for being here."

"Well, of course. I love weddings. Especially yours."

The two friends laughed and linked arms as they walked into the nave of the church.

Thursday April 24, 1947

Estelle Placings got up well before dawn on Thursday morning to catch a bus, glad that her friend's wedding wasn't until 5:00 that afternoon. Estelle hated weddings, but this one she refused to miss. Estelle loved running other people's lives, and she had plans about this friend of hers.

After the wedding was over, Estelle stopped by her mother's house and spent two days with her daughters. Linda was seven now, and Diane was six. It hadn't been hard to leave them to be raised by their grandmother when Estelle was hired by Holvers Enterprises in Atlanta. Estelle was sure she was not cut out to be a mother. And she didn't particularly like children, especially young ones. They were so messy, so noisy. She had more important things to do than herding children around all day. She wanted to provide well for her girls. She wanted them to be a success in life. She wanted them to have all the things she'd missed out on.

On Sunday, she said goodby to her girls, left her mother's house, and took the bus back to Atlanta. She was at work as usual on Monday morning.

Chapter 5 - The 1950's

Wednesday, December 1, 1954 - Martinsville

Pamela C. Tarkington discovered the hard way that all this new-fangled stuff about birth control didn't work when a woman thought she was already past the change and stopped using her protection. She looked across the dining room table at her two grown daughters and figured that this was as good a time as any to break the news.

Monica was hardly complimentary. "At your age, Mother?"

"I always seem to surprise people. Nobody wanted to believe I was marrying your father when I was *only* fifteen. And now you don't want to believe I'm carrying a baby when I'm *only* forty-eight."

"That's nothing to joke about, Mama." Mildred had acted uppity ever since she married a rich man nine years ago. "Can we please work on these seating plans for the reception?"

"I am not joking, Mildred. I am middle-aged and I am pregnant, and I think I will make quite a spectacle sitting in the front of the church at your sister's wedding. I've already ordered my mother-of-the-bride dress, and now it's not going to fit."

Mildred laid down the guest list. She set her gold Mont Blanc pen on top of it. "You are serious? You're really expecting?"

There was no delight. No welcome hug. No offer of help. Not even a question about whether or not she'd been throwing up. "Thank you for your loving concern, girls, but I'm much more worried about what I'm going to wear to this wedding we're planning than about what you think of this."

"I was just . . ." Monica searched for an appropriate phrase. "You must admit, this is rather sudden . . . oh, Mama, how could you? I'll be old enough to be the baby's mother!"

* * * * * *

From the *Keagan County Record*
Wednesday May 18, 1955
Myrtle's Musings from Martinsville

My goodness gracious. We've had a busy few weeks in Martinsville. The Old Church had its First Annual Clean-up Day on Saturday May 7th, and many people showed up with willing hands to help tidy the church grounds and the cemetery. I hope this becomes a real tradition in our little town.

Then, on Tuesday, May 10th, Melissa and James Tarkington made their appearance, earlier than expected, of course, as is so often the way with twins. Their mother, our own Pamela C. Tarkington, is said to be doing well. Their father, Ray Leonard Tarkington, was handing out cigars. He said their "little double bundle" was a blessing that would brighten their later years. Now, isn't that sweet? Just last week, as you know, the twins' older sister, Monica, married George Ingalls. Congratulations Pamela, for making it through the wedding! You were a beautiful mother of the bride.

* * * * * *

Thursday November 10, 1955 – Atlanta

"Yes, Mr. Holvers. I'll get that number for you right away." Estelle Placings pressed the off button on the inter-office line and turned back to look up a phone number. Mr. Holvers was certainly a man of few words, but Estelle liked that in a boss. In a man. He told her to run the office efficiently, and she did it. When he had first hired her in 1942, she was a young Pearl Harbor widow who needed to support two small girls. Linda was almost two, Diane was still a baby. Estelle rented out her house in southeast Georgia and moved in with her parents in Atlanta. Thank goodness her mother was available. The girls were fine with her.

Mr. Holvers, who had been too young for service in the first world war and too old for the second one, had told her right from the first day to start thinking like he did, and to let him know when she felt comfortable doing it. Then, he'd let her make a lot of the day-to-day decisions. As if anybody could really read that twisty mind of his.

In matters of business, though, Estelle soon found that she could anticipate his decisions. After the first six months, she went to him and said, "I think I'm ready to start making more decisions on my own."

"You go and work on it a while longer," he told her. Estelle swallowed her anger and went back to her desk, where she thought a lot about what had just happened.

Two months later, Estelle told him "I'm ready now."

"Ah." Peter Holvers leaned back in his leather chair and clasped his hands behind his sleek head. "Isn't it funny what two little words can do? You went from 'I think' to 'I am'. Now we're getting somewhere."

For several months he asked her, "What would you do with this?" or "How would you answer this letter?" or "If you were in my shoes, which of these men would you hire?"

Finally he stopped asking, and Estelle became the third hand of Peter Angus Holvers. She was the one who came up with the name HolverSilk. She was the one who declined some speaking invitations for him and accepted others. She was the one who put Conrad Robeson's application on the big desk one day and said, "You may want to look at this one, Mr. Holvers." She neglected to mention that Conrad was her younger brother. She also neglected to mention that he was only eighteen. Her brother Conrad had been denied military service because he was born with one leg considerably shorter than the other. But his mind was as clear as Estelle's. She knew he'd do well with Holvers Enterprises, and she wanted him working where she could keep an eye on him.

Estelle was efficient. She was thorough. That was why, when she opened–quite by accident, of course it was just an accident–and read a letter that wasn't meant for her eyes, she calmly retyped a plain white envelope addressed to *Peter A. Holvers (Personal)*. There was no return address on the envelope, but the postmark said Savannah, Georgia, Dec 2 1943. Estelle applied a three-cent stamp to the new envelope, tucked the letter in it, wrapped it up, and mailed it to a cousin of hers in Pooler, Georgia, asking the cousin to send the enclosed letter from Savannah. It was a little joke she wanted to play on her boss, she wrote. When the letter arrived a few days later, Estelle placed the unopened letter from Savannah on the big desk without comment.

The next time a letter came from Savannah, Estelle took it home in her purse. She found that the blue enamel tea kettle worked fine, as long as she was careful to keep her hands out of the steam. The next day, she set another unopened letter from Savannah on the big desk of Peter A. Holvers, President of Holvers Enterprises.

When Peter Holvers married Mildred Tarkington in January of 1945, it was Estelle who ordered the ring. She made sure his tuxedo was cleaned and ready to go. She suggested an acceptable alternative to Marcus as a best man. She mentioned Savannah as a possible honeymoon destination and didn't even smile when Mr. Holvers said he didn't particularly want to go there. She made reservations for them in Miami instead. After the war was over, she booked long cruises and trips to Paris for Mrs. Holvers. Mr. H. didn't like vacations.

Holvers Enterprises had made a fortune supplying sturdy cotton government-issue underwear for the troops, so when, in November of 1946, Mildred gave birth to a baby girl, Estelle thought to order a 14-carat gold baby rattle, which was thoroughly impractical and outrageously expensive. She knew it would be what Mr. Holvers wanted to give his baby. She had the rattle engraved in tiny letters, even though she didn't like the rhythm of the baby's name. It sounded artificial. When it was delivered to the office, Estelle tucked in a card that said, "With love, from your Daddy," and handed it to Mr. Holvers as he left that evening for home.

Soon after this, Estelle began taking the bus to Savannah at least twice a month. It was a lovely city, and she felt she needed time for herself, time to think and to plan. She started simply by strolling through the squares. She began to meet people and make friends. She enjoyed their company. She talked her parents into moving there. Her two little daughters stayed with their grandparents, and Estelle visited them often.

And now, just this afternoon, Estelle had been on the phone ordering a big bouquet of flowers for little Brenda Holvers, who had smashed her leg and her arm that morning. Poor little thing. The hospital had to operate on her right away. And on her birthday, too.

Who would imagine a bicycle could be so dangerous? As she dictated the card, Mr. Holvers walked in. She was surprised to see him at the office while his princess was in the hospital. She was even more surprised that he looked disheveled, somehow. His hair was combed straight back with no part, and looked as severely neat as usual, but his pocket handkerchief was askew. His tie was precise, but Estelle noticed several snagged threads on his jacket, as if he'd run into a climbing rose.

Estelle placed her hand over the mouthpiece of the phone. "I'm ordering some flowers for Brenda, Mr. H. I'll have them write 'Love, Your Daddy' on the card."

"No flowers, Estelle. No flowers."

Estelle canceled the order. A few moments later, the intercom buzzed. She pressed a button. "Yes, Mr. Holvers?"

"I want you to find a detective agency for me. Be sure you get the best one in the city."

"Right away, Mr. Holvers." Estelle turned to the phone book. She never ever questioned his orders, but she couldn't help wondering. Why on earth would he need a detective?

* * * * * *

From the *Keagan County Record*
Wednesday, November 16, 1955
Myrtle's Musings from Martinsville

My, my, my, it is so sad when young ones are injured. Our own Monica Tarkington Ingalls let me know that her nine-year-old niece, Brenda Holvers, was seriously hurt when her brand new bicycle crashed and flipped over a brick wall into a deep gully on November 10th. Little Brenda had to have emergency surgery. She is still in the hospital, but is doing as well as can be expected. It is so good that children heal quickly. Cards and flowers and prayers will be greatly appreciated.

With Thanksgiving around the corner, let us all be grateful for our health and for the well-being of our loved ones, especially the children.

On a happier note, we have a recipe to share that will brighten your holiday table and your spirits. . . .

* * * * * *

Monday August 13, 1956 – Atlanta

Ernst B. Wilhelm III closed his front door, waiting until he heard the latch engage. His evening walks through the small park half a block down the street from his townhouse were one of the high points of his day, even on a stifling summer evening like this. Ever since his wife left him three years ago, Ernst had become a solitary man. He still couldn't understand what had gone wrong. He started to reach for a cigarette, then remembered that he was trying to quit. Nasty habit, but handy for soothing walks.

So much had gone wrong. His wife, Inge. His company, Silk Supplies, Inc. He hadn't been an ideal husband, he supposed. He'd had an occasional fling, but never close to home. It was only when he was traveling on business. And he used to travel a lot. But he'd always remembered Inge's birthday and their anniversary. He was meticulous about sending little gifts for no particular reason at all. He had read once that women liked that, and Inge always seemed to enjoy the attention. True, they'd never had the children she wanted. And she was always after him to talk to her. Why? He talked to her. Every evening, he'd come home and tell her what his day had been like. Busy, hectic, or insane. There weren't any other possibilities in his line of work.

His shoes tattooed the sidewalk as he stepped up into his usual brisk pace. One mile a day. Across the street, turn right half a block, left into the park, around the walking trail, and back up the street. Home, shoes off, slippers on, a quiet drink, a simple dinner that the housekeeper always left for him, some reading, some TV, and bed. It never varied, unless he was on the road.

In a strange way, he missed all the traveling he'd had to do in the beginning when he was the only salesman for his company. His failing company. It did wear thin after a while, though. There'd been too many distractions. Too much drinking, too many boring evenings with women who insisted on dancing with him, too many flirtations. But he'd had a lot of fun, although he had quit telling them he was a Danish Ambassador traveling incognito. Ernst smiled as he turned left to follow the walkway into the park. A few of those women had even believed him. There had been letters from some of them, until he stopped handing out his business card. Now he was home more. Not that there was anyone to come home to. Now his old steamer trunk, the one he had taken on cruises, the one he had inherited from his well-traveled grandfather, the first Ernst Wilhelm, sat in the corner of his bedroom. He hadn't even looked at it in years. Had no idea what was in it anymore. It was just as well. He used to hide those letters in it, but he'd thrown them all out after Inge left.

Ernst looked ahead of him at a short, stocky brown-haired man who was approaching at a steady pace. He'd seen the nondescript fellow almost every evening for the past week. The sort of fellow he wouldn't have hired. There was an indefinable air about the man that spoke of malice. Maybe it was his eyes. They reminded Ernst of a snake. No, a rat. A rat. The man was, as usual, carrying a folded newspaper.

There wasn't anyone else out walking this evening. Just the two of them. Maybe it was the rain from yesterday that had left the air heavy with humidity. He dropped his eyes, unwilling to look the other man in the face, and was surprised when the man's feet stopped right in front of him, blocking the sidewalk. Ernst glanced up as he started to move to his right to pass the man, and saw the gun under the tent of the newspaper, pointed in the general vicinity of his chest. It seemed rather stupidly dramatic.

"If you'll let me reach into my back pocket, I'll pull out my wallet and give it to you. There's not a lot of money in it, but you may, of course, have what's there."

The gun tilted a bit as Rat-face indicated a narrow path that took off into the woods to the left of Ernst. "Just turn slow and walk over that way into those trees."

Ernst stepped off the sidewalk. This was an expressly inconvenient time for nobody to be around. What chance would he have of ducking behind a tree? If he yelled, would anyone hear him in time? If the Rat man had wanted only money, he would have taken the wallet and run. Ernst came slowly to a halt and turned his head to the left. "Can't I give you my wallet right here? There's no one around to see us."

"Why would I want your crummy wallet? I'm making a wad of dough on this job." Ernst did not enjoy the dry humorless laugh he heard from behind him. "Somebody important must not like you much, pretty boy."

"At least tell me who it is."

"Are you dumb or something? They don't tell me, and I don't want to know."

"How do you know he won't betray you?"

"Shut up and keep walking."

The path wound behind a big old oak tree. When the bullet came, Ernst did feel it briefly, but by the time his assailant reached into his pocket and removed the wallet, Ernst was not feeling anything. He did not see his wallet when it landed near his hand. He did not watch as the man trotted farther into the park, around the small lake, and out the other side. And, of course, two hours later his sightless eyes did not see the couple who entered the park and decided to take the small path that looked so inviting.

Tuesday, August 21, 1956

"Mr. Holvers," Estelle Placings said as she swung the heavy mahogany door closed, "we're going to have a slow-down on the new HolverSilk line that you need to know about."

"What's the problem, Estelle?" He set down his pen and looked up at her.

Momentarily disconcerted, since she was used to his looking past her shoulder or above her head or right through her (or so it seemed), but not *at* her, Estelle floundered for words.

"There was a murder. A murder last week."

"Was there?" His words seemed singularly uninterested, but he kept looking directly at her. Estelle couldn't look away. She had known all her life that she wasn't attractive with her angular face and her heavy eyebrows. She had been completely surprised twenty years ago when Thomas Placings had proposed to her. And now she'd been a widow for fifteen years. Was Peter Holvers seeing her, finally?

"Was there?" he repeated. "What does a murder have to do with the HolverSilk production line?"

"The man who was robbed and murdered was Mr. Wilhelm, who is . . . I mean, who *was* one of our biggest silk suppliers. I just received word that his company has shut down production. There's talk of bankruptcy proceedings."

"They can't do that!" Estelle generally admired Mr. Holvers' incisive voice. She had always thought of it as a sonorous pipe organ or booming ocean waves. Now, though, his voice rose in pitch. "They can't close just because their slime-bucket president is dead." He sounded more like a kazoo than a pipe organ. Estelle couldn't believe her ears.

In fourteen years of working for Peter Holvers, she had seen him angry many times. His was anger that burned, that fumed, that exploded, that threatened. But she had never before witnessed a petulant outburst such as this.

"Mr. Holvers? Would you like me to get you a glass of water?"

"No," he snarled, reaching for his pen. "I don't want a glass of water. I want this taken care of. Get Conrad. He can handle it. I want it cleared up today." He was, she noticed, not looking at her any more.

"Yes *sir*," she said, and closed the mahogany door with a decided thump.

* * * * * *

From the *Keagan County Record*
Wednesday, September 5, 1956
Myrtle's Musings from Martinsville

Isn't is wonderful that we live in a county that is so quiet and safe? My brother's wife Elizabeth Hoskins visited the big city two weeks ago, and she brought back a newspaper. My lands, there were so many accidents and awful things that happened. I had my hand over my mouth in disbelief while I was reading. There were houses that got burgled–and here we don't even have to lock our doors. There was a man gunned down and robbed in a park–and here we can stroll around any time of day and night, and feel perfectly safe. There was a car that caught fire right in downtown–and here in Martinsville, the last big fire was in 1814 when the Old Church burned down. I'm proud to live in Martinsville.

On a happier note, our own Monica Ingalls gave birth to a daughter last week on August 26th. She and George have decided to name the sweet baby Margaret, after George's mother, who passed away three years ago. This is the fourth baby born in Martinsville in the past two months, and we're so pleased with all our dear little additions. This town is positively blooming.

* * * * * *

Chapter 6 - The 1960's

Tuesday, May 25, 1965

Even if the four people in the beige waiting-room chairs thought it unusual that Peter Holvers didn't want to see his wife or his daughter while he was waiting to die–and they all knew it wouldn't be long now–nobody said anything. They hung around the hospital wondering how much longer it would be.

Lawyers from Scroop Grey & Cambridge had come and gone several times over the past few days. Conrad Robeson watched the latest parade of senior partners as they glided past the waiting room, with their briefcases and their yellow pads. When the word came out that Peter wanted to see Conrad, a mild riffle of surprise coursed through the small group.

Conrad set down his paper coffee cup and glanced over to where Mildred sat, peering at a book as if completely contented. He'd had two cups of coffee since she last turned a page. Mildred's hair, he noticed, was looking a bit rumpled. She'd been running her fingers through it earlier. He wanted to sit beside her and offer her the simple comfort of companionship. But then, if he were being honest with himself, it was more than simple comfort he wanted to offer her. How long had he been in love with her? Ever since he'd first met her, when she was getting ready to marry his boss. His boss, who now lay dying, eaten up with cancer. Mildred had been so effervescent back then. She had calmed down a lot once she became a mother, but he'd loved her both ways. Giddy and stable.

Conrad stood and took a moment to gain his balance. Most people meeting him for the first time wouldn't notice his limp. He had for years worn a special shoe that helped to equalize the length of his legs, but it had its limits. When he sat for a long time, the heavy shoe made his right leg go to sleep. As soon as he felt the blood flowing to his leg, Conrad stepped around his sister, whose crossed leg was swinging up and down, up and down. A sure sign of boredom, he thought. He smiled at her, and her dark eyebrows raised a fraction.

He smiled at Brenda, too, but without result. She sat there in utter stillness. She could have been a glacier. Of course, glaciers, he reminded himself, aren't still. They melt and re-freeze, they glide, they grind. He hadn't seen her move in hours except to look up each time a nurse walked in.

Following the nurse, who waddled ahead of him at a surprisingly rapid pace, Conrad thought again of Mildred and tried to gauge his own level of contentment. He'd been a faithful employee of Holvers Enterprises his entire working lifetime. When he landed the job all those years ago, it had seemed like a dream come true. Well, there had been some nightmares–how could there not be, working for someone like Peter Holvers?

The man lying in the hospital bed, attached to multiple tubes, black hair sleeked straight back tight against his head, was no longer the big solid presence Conrad had grown to know so well over the years. As he approached the bed, he could hear Peter's shallow, raspy breathing. There was an overlay of jaundice that Conrad could see in the dimly lit room. Flashes of lightning from the storm that whistled and boomed outside the big window beside the bed colored Peter's face and hands with even more of a sickly yellowish sheen.

"I'm dying, Conrad."

"Yes, Peter. You are."

"Don't you even want to argue with me about it?"

"You win all the arguments, Peter."

"Bunch of baloney, that is. You know you've pulled . . . quite a few over on me through the years."

There didn't seem to be a diplomatic answer, so Conrad stayed quiet, waiting as Peter struggled to pull in a breath.

"You might as well know what I'm going to do. . . . My will is all made out, but there are a couple of addendums . . ."

Addenda, thought Conrad.

". . . that nobody but the lawyers know about. One of them will be read right after the will, but the other one won't be opened . . . until the final disposition of the money." Peter shuddered as he tried to take in enough oxygen. His breathing was uneven, like a rabid dog.

"Peter, you need to rest."

"Forget resting." He turned his head toward the window and Conrad saw his eyes go out of focus. He wondered what Peter was thinking. "I need to tell you this," Peter went on, still looking out the big window at the rain. "Stop interrupting me."

Conrad inhaled slowly. "Okay, Peter. I'll listen."

"I've given all my money—most of it—to my children. . . ."

Conrad wondered about the plural. Of course Brenda had always had as much impact as any three young women he'd ever known, so maybe the plural was appropriate.

". . . You'll have control of the company, of course. . . . Wouldn't trust anybody else. But my children get the benefit of . . . all the other investments."

Conrad wondered if anyone other than Peter's investment advisors knew the full extent of his fortune. It wasn't just from Holvers Enterprises. He was reputed to be one of the wealthiest individuals in the world. Hadn't done him much good, though, to look at him here, hooked up to all these tubes. Conrad wondered briefly if he had ever heard Peter laugh. Really laugh. He had sneered and threatened and bellowed. He had oozed charm. Peter persuaded and coerced. He snapped and snarled and stormed. But he never laughed.

Peter was still talking. Conrad brought his attention back to the voice that was gasping. "Going to have to wait for it. . . . Child of my body. . . . Thirty years." Peter's head twisted around in a spasm. It looked pretty painful to Conrad. "By then," he continued, "everybody who's . . . who's known me in business will be gone. Everybody except you."

"Why me?"

"Because you . . . weren't even wet behind the ears when . . . when I . . . hired you. You'll outlast us all."

All the platitudes used around the dying ran through Conrad's mind, but they seemed singularly inappropriate in this case, so he said nothing.

"If my child is dead, though, . . . I've directed that you . . . you get it all. Only if my child is already dead."

"Won't it go to Mildred?" Conrad asked.

"No! Mildred has a trust fund. That is *all* she gets. If my . . . child is dead, you'll get the whole thing. I made sure that's . . . very clear. What good are high-priced lawyers . . . if you can't get them to do . . . exactly what you want."

It wasn't, Conrad noticed, a question.

Peter kept wheezing and talking. Wheezing and talking. "Even with all the stunts you've pulled, . . . getting me to throw away good . . . good capital on your bleeding heart projects, . . . we've still made . . . the biggest bundle ever. I've made you a rich man, Conrad Robeson, and . . . you're going to be . . . even . . . richer because I know you'll run my company . . . my company . . . the right way."

Conrad waited for more, but the dying man seemed to have run down. As Conrad debated whether or not to leave, Peter roused himself and said, "I knew you were her brother all along."

It seemed pointless to argue, so Conrad simply asked, "How?"

"She wrote her . . . maiden name on her application back in 1942. . . . I looked it up. . . . Estelle Robeson Placings. Conrad Robeson. Too much . . . of a coincidence. I . . . don't believe in them."

"Why didn't you say something?"

"I figured if you had . . . half her brains, you'd do okay. And she . . . wanted to feel like she was getting away with something. What . . . what were you, eighteen . . . when you started working for me?" He paused for another even longer labored breath. "I'm giving her a pretty good . . . chunk of change. It ought to keep her happy."

"She'll be grateful that you remembered." Privately, Conrad didn't think any amount of money would keep Estelle happy. All she enjoyed was running other people's lives. Of course, the more money she had, the easier it would be for her to do that.

"You treat my company good. . . . Don't let Brenda take it over."

Conrad almost laughed, but stopped as Peter wheezed out one more demand. "And don't let . . . Marcus in the door."

Conrad didn't answer that one. He knew from the grapevine that Peter's older brother Marcus had been ill, but he hoped it was only temporary. He liked the old guy. Peter might think he could always get his way, but once he was gone, things were going to change.

Wednesday, June 9, 1965 – Atlanta

Mildred Tarkington Holvers sat with her daughter Brenda on one of the elegant love seats in the smaller of her two parlors. The lawyer, a solid-looking man from Scroop Grey & Cambridge, one of the oldest firms in Atlanta, sat across from them, balancing a leather-bound portfolio on his knees. The other people, standing or sitting in varying degrees of discomfort around the room, were concentrating on the words, trying, Mildred imagined, to discern from the legalese whether they would get a pittance or a windfall. Peter Holvers had been the kind who could go either way. He'd be open-handed generous one moment and cut you off the next without even a sniff of his over-sized nose. He had made *"I have to have my Holvers"* a household phrase. The sale of bras and panties and slips and negligees–all tasteful, discreet, quietly elegant, and reasonably priced, except of course for the exclusive and correspondingly expensive HolverSilk line–had soared under his leadership.

Mildred smoothed a wrinkle from the lap of her linen suit. At that moment, she would have enjoyed a comforting touch, but she knew better than to reach for the hand of her daughter. And no other hands, naturally, were available.

Mildred ignored the lawyer, for the most part. She knew, after all, what the will said. She thought it was rather funny, but the smile she held in place looked simply like the brave discipline of a young widow. Not so very young, perhaps, but young enough. Forty-four. She turned to look at her slightly overweight nineteen-year-old daughter. Brenda looked like her Grandfather Tarkington. She also had some of the facial characteristics of the Holvers side of the family. No one would ever mistake that. Mildred was relieved in a way. It made the reading of the will so much easier on everyone concerned.

Marcus, Peter's older brother, the one who had almost destroyed the family's clothing business within two years after The Old Man died in 1932, was standing off to one side, obviously hoping against hope that Peter might have forgiven him at the end. In the wake of the financial disaster that Marcus had been unable to forestall, Peter had turned his back on his brother. He allowed no concession for the Depression. He chose not to excuse any of the experiments his brother had tried to keep the business afloat. Peter had learned from his brother's many mistakes and created a financial empire in the lingerie industry, far surpassing The Old Man's dreams. Of course, the war had helped. The troops needed underwear, and Holvers Enterprises stepped in to fill the orders.

Peter had never talked about it much, but Mildred sensed that if Marcus had been able to hold out a year or two longer, he would have turned things around. As it was, though, Peter had resolved that neither Marcus nor his family would ever benefit from the conglomerate Peter now controlled. Or had controlled until his final illness, a lingering case of cancer that left her once powerful husband gasping for breath. Mildred wondered if Marcus was hoping for a miracle. Maybe that was why he had shown up for the funeral and the reading of the will. He hovered against the étagere, looking slightly jaundiced. Mildred noticed that he looked almost as yellow as the legal pads that sat on the small table beside the attorney.

She glanced over at her sister. Monica sat to the left of the étagere with her only child, ten-year-old Margaret. The attorney's office must have called Monica to be there, because she would have happily gone home after the funeral, never expecting a thing. Mildred wondered what dear Monica would be getting. She couldn't recall Peter ever mentioning her. Skinny little Margaret was as bright as they come. Already she knew she wanted to be a scientist. Even though Brenda hadn't even said boo to her all day, Mildred knew that Margaret was enchanted with her older cousin.

Shirlene, Peter's younger sister, had not come to the funeral. Mildred had to admit that Peter had a way of making enemies. No one would ever tell her precisely what Peter had said to his unmarried and pregnant sister in 1935, but it had sufficed to keep Shirlene away from the entire family for years. When Mildred first met Peter, he had seemed powerful and decisive. Before they'd been married even a year, though, she knew that he delighted in setting one person against another.

When Peter finally got so sick he couldn't function any more, she'd found out he'd had cancer for years. Years. And he never told her. He kept going to work, kept pulling his strings, kept running his underwear empire. How he had ever succeeded in fooling the business community was a mystery. No, she shouldn't be surprised. She hadn't noticed, and she lived with him.

His long-time secretary, the stony-faced Estelle, was sitting on one of the Duncan Phyfe chairs across the room. It occurred to Mildred that Estelle had seen a side of Peter that no one else in the room knew. Mildred wasn't sure she wanted to know all that Peter had been.

Shirlene's twenty-nine-year-old daughter, Sandy Holvers, shunned by Peter as her unmarried mother had been, had shown up at the funeral, and somehow managed to worm her way into the house. Not that there was any point in excluding her. She wore an unfortunate polyester pantsuit in a muddy shade of brown. Sandy was sitting quietly on the yellow wing chair next to Estelle, across the room from her Aunt Mildred. She looked as if she were enjoying herself immensely. Mildred almost envied her.

Conrad Robeson was there, too, as a trusted family advisor. He had been an employee of Peter's for over twenty years and had gradually worked his way up into a position of trust. Despite the difference in their ages, he was the closest thing to a friend that Peter Holvers ever had. Conrad had an incisive mind for business. Mildred knew that without a doubt. He also had something that Peter had never ever suspected. He had a heart. Mildred assumed he had never shown it directly in the corporate offices, but she had heard little rumors from acquaintances who had mentioned a factory that was saved from shutting down by the infusion of more capital and the liquidation of some overpaid upper-level managers. Or they had wondered how the latest product line had avoided using any imports from that country that was using little girls as virtual slave labor in their manufacturing centers. Somehow Conrad had made a difference to Holvers Enterprises. She would have to invite him to dinner soon.

The reading of the Last Will and Testament of Peter Holvers did manage to surprise Mildred after all. It was basically the same will he had discussed with her from time to time, but he had never shown her the actual document. He had always said that he would leave some of his fortune to her and the rest to Brenda, or words to that effect.

She hadn't known that he was restricting the dispersal of the funds, though. He made a few minor bequests to Conrad and to several other businessmen. Mildred heard Brenda, sitting beside her, gasp when Mr. Scroop read that Peter was giving one of his prize cars and a fairly substantial trust fund to little Margaret, who was still in grade school. No wonder she gasped, thought Mildred. Even considering the size of Peter's estate, it was a substantial amount. The bequest, the will instructed, was to be managed through Scroop Grey & Cambridge. Margaret's mother would be the trustee of the fund. Mildred assumed this meant that Monica would be able to drive the Duesenburg until Margaret was old enough. Monica was frowning, Mildred noticed.

Estelle Placings got a reasonable-sized bequest. Mildred supposed she deserved it. Anyone who could put up with Peter every weekday for twenty-five years deserved a medal. She noticed the woman's dry, heavy-browed face lighten a bit when she heard the amount.

Then he left just a few hundred thousand dollars each, a pittance really, to some people from his past. That's what it said in his will – "the following people from my past in appreciation for services rendered." Mildred recognized only one of the names, a man in Albuquerque. The list the lawyer read included a man in Des Moines, a woman in Savannah, a couple in Baton Rouge. He left his watch to his chauffeur.

Peter had set up an elaborate trust fund for Mildred, the interest of which would allow her to live quite comfortably for the rest of her life. After her death, that trust fund was to revert to the main estate.

Brenda was given a small monthly stipend. The biggest chunk of the principal would be held in trust for thirty years and paid out to Brenda in 1996. Actually, the way it read, in all its legal language, was, "the balance of the principal will be paid on May 5, 1996, to the only child or children of my body." May 5th. Peter's birthday. Why 1996? Mildred glanced across the room at her sister, who bent her head and scratched at a dirt speck on her dress. It must have been Peter's idea of a joke. Mildred looked down at her fingers to do a quick calculation, but Brenda leaned slightly her way and said, "I'll be forty-nine, Mother. You'll be seventy-five." As Brenda turned her head back toward the lawyer, Mildred heard her mutter, "Or dead."

Little Margaret Ingalls was being very well-behaved. Her mother had told her that they had to be there. Some lawyer called and said that they were mentioned in the will. Mommy told her she might be getting something pretty from Uncle Peter who was dead now. Maybe a necklace. Margaret wasn't too sure about that. What she really wanted was a horse. But she didn't think Uncle Peter had any of those. She sat beside her mother and swung her legs back and forth, careful not to hit them against the chair legs.

She looked over at her cousin. Brenda was so beautiful. She was in college, but that didn't make her more important than somebody in fifth grade. Margaret would be in college, too, someday. She already had a microscope. It came in her chemistry set that her daddy bought her last year. She liked looking at water and mud and blood and hair. There were little bug things called bacteria in all of those. They wiggled so much. Margaret wondered if you got enough bacteria together and hooked them all up to little engines, could you run the electricity plant with them?

When the lawyer said her name, Margaret perked up and started to listen. He said she was going to get a car. He called it a Model J. She hoped it was the bright yellow one with the pretty seats and the shiny grill on the front. Once a long, long time ago when Margaret was only seven, Mommy and Daddy and Aunt Mildred had taken her out to the big garage–they called it the coach house–to show her all the old cars. Margaret had seen that yellow one and asked Aunt Mildred if she could ever have a car like that someday. Aunt Mildred had laughed at her question, but Uncle Peter must have been in the garage because all of a sudden his loud voice came from behind one of the cars in back. He scared them, 'cause they didn't know he was there. He'd said, "Of course you can have a car exactly like that, if that's what you really want."

Margaret leaned over to ask her mother if the lawyer meant the yellow car, but Mommy was frowning and scratching her fingernail on a place on her dress. Margaret couldn't see a spot or anything. She tried hard not to squirm, but she really wanted to know.

Everyone expected the attorney to put his papers away in his briefcase. Instead, he cleared his massive throat and said, "Peter A. Holvers left specific instructions saying that, after the reading of the will, I was to read the results of a routine physical exam he had almost eighteen years ago on March 31, 1947. There was no reason given. He simply instructed that I read this to the assembled . . ." he cleared his throat again, ". . . mourners." Mr. Scroop extracted two sheets of paper from an envelope that had been tucked inside a file folder. He returned one of them to the folder. The inhabitants of the parlor listened in growing puzzlement as he read. "Peter A. Holvers. Height: six feet, two inches. Weight: one hundred ninety-seven pounds. Cholesterol level: normal. Blood type: AB negative. Blood pressure: 160 over 95. Pulse rate, standing before exercise: 75. Pulse rate after five minutes of exercise: 128. Pulse rate five minutes after exercise: 82. Eyesight: 20/20. Hearing: within normal limits. Deep Tendon Reflex: normal. . . ."

Halfway through the list, Mildred noticed that Brenda's head whipped up and her eyes narrowed in that way she had of staring right through someone. Mr. Scroop didn't see her, which was just as well. That piercing stare of Brenda's could be unnerving. Mr. Scroop tucked the paper back into its envelope, stood, and handed it to Brenda. "We were also instructed," he said, "to give this copy to Brenda Holvers."

After Mr. Scroop was finished, Brenda lifted her head and straightened her back as she stood up. She walked away from her mother without a word.

The attorney glanced up from the small table where he was organizing his papers, and noticed that Brenda's leaving looked rather like the parting of the Red Sea. Or the launching of a battleship. She strode from the room without a backward glance. Even with her variation of the huge Holvers nose, and even with that extra weight that she carried, Mr. Scroop thought Brenda had an elegance about her. No. Elegance was too soft a word. She was self-contained. She had a presence.

The reading of the will had taken forever. Not that Brenda had expected very much. Pop had always been paranoid where money was concerned. Funny that he'd left so much to Margaret, and her only ten years old. She knew what he was doing, holding off her own inheritance for decades. He wanted her to work for it. He expected her to take over Holvers Enterprises as soon as she had her Masters. Brenda knew, though, that Conrad would move into power almost immediately. And he was never one to give way, even to a family member. Mother always said he was a kind person, but Brenda never expected anyone voluntarily to give up a position of command She was too much like Peter Holvers to believe in such a thing.

Why hadn't Pop called her into his hospital room? Why hadn't he let her comfort him? Now she'd never see or hear him again. It wasn't fair. Not that Brenda *believed* in fairness. But it still wasn't fair. Why hadn't he simply appointed her the next head of the company? She could have quit school and kept up the family business. She'd cut her teeth on company business–literally. One of the family jokes was the story of Pop walking into his den one day and finding little Brenda chewing on the binding of the newly printed 1947 Annual Report to the Stockholders. Now, as Brenda stood up to leave the parlor, she wondered for a moment if her father had kept that old soggy report. Probably not. She wished, though, that he had.

He hadn't told the soggy report story in years. And she couldn't remember the last time he'd called her his princess. Brenda's step faltered for a moment. She *could* remember. It had been in 1955 on November 10th. Her ninth birthday.

Before she crashed into that stupid wall, Brenda, the birthday girl, had been very happy. Now, though, with her arm in a cast and her leg pulled up on all these wires and stuff, she didn't feel too hot. They kept coming in to stick her with needles. She hated needles. They scared her. She couldn't help screaming when they started to stick her. Even though Mommy held her hand, it didn't help any. She never wanted to see another needle in all her life, even if she lived all the way to twenty-five.

Her bike was crumpled–she'd heard it crunch when she hit the wall. Now her head felt funny, and the room looked awful swimmy. This was her ninth birthday, but it hadn't turned out the way she wanted it to be. It wasn't fair. That morning she was so excited. It was her birthday and there wasn't any school because the teachers were having some special meeting or something. When she ran downstairs, there was her new bike, just like she'd asked for. It was bright red, and had a loud bell and a basket on the front.

"A bike, a bike! I've got a bike of my very own!" Brenda twirled around the family room and hugged her daddy and her mommy and Aunt Monica, who came to visit so she could be at Brenda's birthday party! She twirled around some more. "Oh, this is just exactly what I wanted!"

She remembered riding down the street to meet her best friend, Ann. Ann had a green bike that she'd gotten last month when she turned nine. Ann had let Brenda practice on her green bike, so now they both were good at bike riding. Ann was going to come to Brenda's birthday party at 3:00, but Brenda couldn't wait to show her the red bike. The two friends took off down the sidewalk, heading for the big church parking lot. They'd planned for weeks that, if they both got bikes for their birthdays, they'd go to the parking lot. It was so big. This was going to be a lot of fun, riding around and around.

They'd told each other that they had to be good and stay away from the lamp post in the middle of the parking lot. Brenda thought that was a dumb place to put a big pole. As she rode for about the millionth time around the lot, she looked back at Ann, who was pedaling furiously behind her. "I missed the pole, I missed the pole," Brenda sang out to her friend. As she turned back, though, to watch where she was going, the red bike hit a small patch of gravel and started to skid. Brenda turned the wheel sharply, too sharply. And there was the low wall that kept the cars from falling off the hill into

the deep gully. Brenda remembered flying over the wall. She remembered the ground coming up fast. She didn't remember anything after that.

Mommy was in the ambulance with her when she came to.
Mommy was crying, and there was a lot of blood and Brenda started
screaming. Everything hurt so much. It was a scary way to spend a
birthday.

Just before they took her out of the ambulance, she looked over
at her mommy. "Will I still have my party?"

"We'll have to see about that, precious."

Here she was now with her leg dangling from the ceiling. Mommy
said she'd had an operation, but Brenda didn't remember any of
that. Daddy was pacing around. Brenda could tell he was bored. He
stopped pacing, smiled at Brenda, and started up again. As he reached
the foot of the bed, he said, "Let's see what they have to say about
my princess." Brenda watched him as he lifted her chart and glanced
through it. There were several pages. He flipped back to the first
page and started reading more carefully, muttering about poor handwriting.

"I have really good handwriting, Daddy," Brenda started to say,
but her daddy looked up at her all of sudden with a really big frown.
He scared her. She thought maybe he was mad about the bad handwriting. "Can't you read what it says, Daddy?" she asked him through
the fog of her fuzzy brain. Her eyes felt heavy, and she couldn't keep
them open. Her daddy didn't answer her. He dropped the chart on
the bed and left the room. He didn't even say goodby to her or
Mommy. Brenda drifted off to sleep, wishing that she could have
had a birthday party.

Yes, thought nineteen-year-old Brenda as she continued on her
way out of the living room, that was the last time he called me princess. And now all I have left of him is an insultingly tiny monthly
allowance and a list of test results. She continued walking through
the crowd, and something in the carriage of her head kept people
from offering condolences, as they were doing to each other, gathering in little clumps.

As she began to climb the wide staircase that *Beautiful Houses*
had called "the most exciting stairway in modern architecture," she
was already planning her life. Now that she knew where she stood
as far as the inheritance was concerned, she could get to work. Thirty

years to go. Unless Conrad died in the next month or so, Brenda would be going somewhere else, far away from here. And in thirty years, he'd be old and washed up, and she'd be rich. It meant turning her back on Holvers Enterprises for now, but she would not *ever* work for Conrad.

Sandy Holvers probably should have laughed out loud instead of holding it in to herself, when she heard that ten-year-old Margaret was getting the best of the deal. Why Margaret? The best of the cars and all that money to boot. Sandy was sure that everyone there had been toting up their degrees of kinship to Peter A. Holvers, trying to figure out who would get what if this one died or that one was shown to be ineligible. Of course, kinship with Peter Holvers never guaranteed anything. Look at her own mother, who was Peter's younger sister. Half-sister. Shirlene was the daughter of Grandma Charlotte, the Old Man's second wife, who had been Marcus and Peter's nanny when the first wife died. And Uncle Peter had tried every way he knew to punish Shirlene when, in 1936, she'd gotten pregnant, with no husband. Sandy admired her mom. It took a lot of guts to be a single mom anytime, but especially back in 1936. And Peter had never helped out. Sandy could remember the secret visits to Grandma Charlotte when none of the men were around. She had liked her grandma.

Well, Peter was as vindictive in death as he'd been in life. It did sound pretty straightforward. He left his money to *the child of my body* – what a strange way to refer to Brenda, the only kid they'd ever had. Imagine making her wait thirty years to get her hands on the money. And what was all that stuff about blood pressure and cholesterol? It made no sense.

Sandy's mom had advised against it, of course, when Sandy mentioned two days ago that she was going to attend Uncle Peter's funeral.

"Why do you want to invite trouble?" was the way Shirlene had put it.

"Mom, I'm not asking for anything from them. I just want to know what Uncle Peter was up to without having to read about it in the paper."

"You can be sure there won't be anything about the estate in the news," Shirlene told her. "Your uncle's high and mighty company will discourage anyone who wants to publish such privileged information."

"Haven't they heard about freedom of the press?"

"They don't believe in it."

"All the more reason to attend the reading of the will."

"What makes you think they'll let you in the house?"

"What makes you think they could keep me out?"

There hadn't even been a fuss. Sandy simply walked in the front door along with everyone else. No one had said a word to her, except Uncle Marcus. She liked Uncle Marcus, even if no one else in the family did. He had certainly tried to make it work. The family clothing empire–former empire–had almost made it. If Peter hadn't barged in and taken over, they all would have been moderately well-off. That is, if Holvers Clothiers had survived the depression.

As it was, though, the Peter branch of the family was ridiculously wealthy, thanks to the war contracts and the lingerie business and the HolverSilk line and Peter's uncanny instincts in the stock market. She'd seen a newspaper article about his death that had said he was the fourth-richest person in the world. And the first most unforgiving, she thought.

The rest of them just muddled along. Poor Uncle Marcus had finally walked out, and then he went and got a job in sales, the only thing he knew how to do well. He'd been a salesman ever since, working for other people, never wanting to handle his own company again. Sandy knew her mom was worried about him. They hadn't seen him for several months, and Sandy was appalled at how yellow and frail he looked. Jaundice wasn't anything to ignore at his age. He would be, what? Maybe sixty-seven or sixty-eight? He ought to be retired by now. Certainly nobody would ever buy anything from a salesman who looked so ill. Maybe he just needed to get out in the sun more.

Sandy turned away from the unhappy sight of her favorite uncle to watch as Brenda sailed from the room. It was a mystery how that girl managed to see where she was going, with her big nose so high in the air. Sandy tried to will Brenda's feet to stumble on the elegant staircase, but it didn't work, and Brenda quickly disappeared from view, still upright and uptight.

"Don't you have a hug for your old uncle?"

Sandy turned to find Marcus at her elbow. He seemed shorter than she remembered. "Can we leave and pick up some lunch somewhere?" she whispered in his ear. "Or did you want to hang around here for awhile?"

"Are you kidding? All I came for was the laughter."

"Too bad there wasn't any," she said.

"The caviar here is way too salty."

"So's the atmosphere. We should have hired a clown."

"Could you stand the blue plate special at Henrietta's Diner?" he asked her.

"Sounds great. Let's split."

Before leaving, they maneuvered over to where Mildred was talking with Conrad. "Good-bye," was all they said. Neither one mentioned condolences, since Mildred was looking rather pleased with herself. Conrad took a moment to pull Marcus aside, and Marcus was smiling as he escorted Sandy through the front door. On the steps outside, he turned to her and said, "What would you think of coming to work for your old Uncle Marcus at Holvers Enterprises?"

"Sounds good to me, but let's eat first. I plan to keep my priorities straight."

Laughing together, they linked arms and walked away from the Holvers mansion.

Later that afternoon, Mildred walked upstairs and approached Brenda's room with a growing sense of doom. She knew how Brenda would react to the suggestion, and she didn't want to face that cold, steely disapproval.

"Brenda, dear?" she called at the door. "May I talk with you for a moment?"

"What is it?" The answer was muffled. The doors throughout the mansion were substantial. Mildred sometimes missed the thin walls of her family home in Martinsville, where everyone always knew where everyone else was. There weren't any secrets there.

"Could I come in?"

There was a long silence. Mildred wasn't sure whether to knock again, say something, turn around and flee, pound on the door, or sit down on the carpet and wait it out. A brief vision of clopping her obnoxious daughter upside the head with a two by four flitted across Mildred's mind, just a hair below conscious thought. As she was turning to leave, she heard a gentle click as the lock turned.

"Sure," Brenda's voice came, finally. "The door's unlocked."

Why on earth didn't the child open the door herself? Mildred didn't like being put in the position of supplicant. How do our children manage to make us feel like insignificant bugs? She reached for the door knob twice before deciding to open it. It would have been a lot easier simply to leave.

She paused in the doorway and looked around at the wide expanse of mottled green carpeting that complemented the faux-finished walls, a subtle blending of shades of mushroom and ivory. Brenda was standing in the middle of the room, in the process of pulling off her tailored jacket. She looked so much like her father in that slant of yellow sunlight that Mildred was unable to speak for a moment.

"Well?" Brenda prompted.

"Dear, Conrad wants to take us all to the zoo as a way of lightening the mood of the afternoon. It'll be for an hour or so, no longer."

"You said, *us all*. Who's included in that invitation?"

Mildred tucked a stray strand of hair back behind her ear. "Well, you and me. And Monica and little Margaret."

"Not that skinny brat. She's been hanging around me ever since she got here."

"She's not a brat, dear. She's a sweet little girl and she's decided she idolizes you. Can't you be patient with her?"

"No."

"Well, if I promise to try to keep her occupied, would you come along just as a favor to me?" For a moment Mildred wondered if Brenda was going to ask her what right she had asking for a favor, but a miracle happened, and Brenda agreed to go along for the ride.

It wasn't a fun outing, but it was memorable. Conrad took one photograph of everyone in front of the elephants. Then Margaret was stung by a wasp, and the event was over. At least they had one photo to show that they were a family. Well, except for Conrad, who wasn't in the picture.

* * * * * *

From the *Keagan County Record*
Wednesday, June 16, 1965
Myrtle's Musings from Martinsville

Next week, two of Martinsville's most promising young men, who have been best friends all their young lives, will be leaving us. Tommy Parkman, son of Cecelia and Charles Parkman, will take off on Monday to begin basic training in the Army. Bobby Sheffield, son of Rebecca Jo and our own Officer of the Peace William Sheffield, will head out on Wednesday for his Air Force training.

They both have said that they will probably end up overseas. We wish them safety throughout their terms of enlistment, and our prayers will follow them through the next three years.

On a happier note, our own Monica Tarkington Ingalls drove home from Atlanta last week in the fanciest bright yellow car you've ever seen. It was the talk of Martinsville. Her husband George told me it was a bequest for their daughter Margaret from Peter Holvers, who married little Margaret's Aunt Mildred in 1945 and made a fortune with his company Holvers Enterprises.

When I asked ten-year-old Margaret what she thought about owning such a fancy car, she said, "I have to get a lot, lot older before I can drive it." Her mother, Monica, had no comment. Then I asked George Ingalls what he was going to do with his daughter's new car, a 1933 Model J Duesenberg Town Car, and he said, "I guess I'm going to have to build a garage."

* * * * * *
From the *Keagan County Record*
Wednesday October 26, 1966
Myrtle's Musings from Martinsville

The Martinsville Cemetery, which perches on the hillside beside the Old Church, has been the focus of some deep concern. In the center of the cemetery stands a stone column that commemorates the lives of Homer Martin, the founder of Martinsville, his wife Mary Frances, and two of his great-grandsons. It has been leaning more and more the past few years. Town records indicate that it was worked on in 1906 and again in 1936, but it needs more work now. The town council has asked for suggestions on how to realign the column. Please submit your ideas to City Hall before the next council meeting. "Maybe we could just prop it up for another thirty years," was the comment made by Leon Martin, chairman of the town council and a direct descendant of Homer Martin.

On a happier note, our own Tommy Parkman came home on Saturday. Tommy, as you know, has been in a physical rehabilitation center in California for the past seven months, following serious injury in Viet Nam when a land mine near him exploded, killing three other young men. Please join me in praying for the families of the young soldiers who were sacrificed in this terrible war, and in prayers of thanks for Tommy's safe return home.

Chapter 7 - The 1970's

September 1974
Illinois Wesleyan University
Bloomington, Illinois

Dr. Dolan D. Bugg glanced once more at the roster for Intro to Biology, wondering if he'd find a kindred spirit among the twenty-four first-year students. Most of them, he knew, would be taking the course because a science class was required, and this was one of those classes that almost anyone could take. It combined some of the basics from the Botany curriculum and some from Zoology. Dr. Bugg preferred botany, but he was fair about presenting both branches of biology. Thank goodness he didn't have to include dissection in the syllabus. He always felt sorry for the frogs. If people chose to go into zoology, Dr. Bugg didn't mind. It had its place, but botany was Dr. Bugg's Holy Grail, his *raison d'etre*, his–if the truth be known–his love.

Occasionally, one or two students would start the semester determined to learn everything Dr. Bugg could teach. And sometimes they kept that fire, that inner glow, that enthusiasm for biology, through all the lists and lessons and field trips and tests. Sometimes, someone would care about the minutiae of life, and, by that caring, would see the larger picture, the grand scheme, the wonder that biology, the study of life, could impart.

They'd begin trooping into the classroom soon, and he was ready. Seven years of teaching this intro class, and he still got a kick out of it. He knew they probably called him Buggsy or Bug Eyes behind his back. That was okay, but he always started each class the same way. "Class," he said, when the big hand was on the twelve, "this class is *Intro to Biology*. If you're supposed to be in a different class, you are excused. My name is Dr. Bugg. Dr. Dolan D. Bugg. And I am, by the way, old enough to have heard every joke there is to make about my name. I suggest we waste no more time over it, particularly class time. You are, of course, welcome to share jokes about my name among yourselves when you are not in this class. And now, before we can get on with the study of life, I need to find out your names."

Margaret Ingalls was sitting in the front row. She listened to his opening speech and sat through the roll call. He looks a bit buggy, she thought, surprisingly like a praying mantis. He had a tendency to wave his front legs–whoops! she meant his arms–around when he was speaking. His pencil-thin moustache under a rounded nose seemed to emphasize his wide-spaced eyes. And his back legs–his legs, Margaret corrected herself–were Ichabod long and skinny to boot.

"Take one and pass the rest back." She took the stack of syllabi he handed her, and followed directions. Hmm, looked like there'd be a lot of experiments. She'd enjoyed that little chemistry set her dad gave her when she was just a kid. One of her earliest memories was when her mother showed her what happened when she mixed baking soda and vinegar. It was so much fun. She'd made a volcano in the bathtub once, and it whooshed all over the tile floor. Mom made her clean it up, but it was worth it.

"Chapter assignments are listed in your syllabus. Questions? None? Then let's begin."

November 25, 1974   Martinsville

It wouldn't have been so bad if Margaret had even thought about the possibility beforehand. It never entered her mind, though.

It was Dr. Bugg's fault.

The second *Intro to Biology* class that September was a field trip. Under Doodlebug's tutelage, the entire class had combed an

Illinois meadow for samples of plants that were edible. "Never," he told them, "never, ever ingest a plant unless you implicitly trust the identification of it." Apparently warming to his subject, he gathered the group more closely about him and said, "Now let's consider plants that are poisonous. Since those plants sometimes grow next to the edible ones I cannot stress enough the importance of knowledge, knowledge, knowledge." Deliberately making eye contact with each student during this little speech, he intoned, "In the quotation about a little learning being a dangerous thing, the operative word is *little*."

He then turned to his left and pointed to a lush patch of greenery. "This, for instance. Would anyone care to identify it?"

The student standing next to Margaret spoke up. "It looks like the garlic my grandma grows along her fence."

"Thank you, Emily. I'm sure it does. You've illustrated my point precisely. This plant that *looks like grandma's garlic* can kill you if you cook it into a tasty stew. This plant is *Convallaria majalis*, better known as Lily of the Valley. All parts of it are toxic. If you cut the flowers to bring inside in a pretty vase, the water in that vase becomes toxic, too."

Margaret sighed. They looked like any other short green plant to her. She hoped he wouldn't have little plant pictures on the test. Lists she could memorize, but this felt beyond her.

In October they tested the eye colors of the fruit fly *Drosophila melanogaster.* And then Doodlebug started lecturing about other bugs. Crickets and grasshoppers and spiders and beetles. "Always remember," he told them, "that bugs communicate non-verbally. Without voices."

What about grasshoppers singing and crickets chirping, Margaret thought as she sat there in the front row.

"You may think that crickets chirp or that grasshoppers sing," he said, "but they make those sounds by rubbing various body parts together . . ."

Margaret could sense a stirring in the room as the males in the class experienced a burst of testosterone. Talk about non-verbal communication . . .

". . . They are not using voices to produce these sounds, because they have no voices. I repeat, they have no voices."

Margaret wondered why he was making such a big deal about it.

"Non-verbal communication gives us many clues. Reading body language is a valuable skill."

He went on like this for quite a while, but Margaret's mind was wandering.

And then, in early November, they learned how to take a sample of their own blood, and type it. They were supposed to list all the possible combinations of parental blood type. The mother could be this or that, and the father could be that or this. Then they had to go further and list what parental blood types could not possibly lead to their own blood type. Dr. Bugg let them take home a couple of typing kits over the Thanksgiving break, so they could practice their lab skills and earn some extra credit by submitting a report on their findings.

Her dad agreed right away. "Anything to help my scientist," he said. But it took Margaret a while to talk her mom into cooperating. "It's only a little bitty prick, Mom. It won't hurt at all. All I need is a couple of drops of blood from each of you."

Dad set his paper aside, stuck his hand out and made a big show of being the brave one in the family. Margaret took her task seriously, making sure that she swabbed her father's index finger carefully before sticking the sterilized lancet into the tip. She placed one big drop of blood on each end of the slide that she had already labeled in a meticulous print.

Then she repeated the procedure, using a new lancet for her mom, who disappeared into the kitchen as soon as her blood was shed.

There were two little toothpick-sized plastic sticks in each blood-typing kit. Margaret used a different one on each drop of blood as she stirred a carefully-placed drop of Anti-A serum into the blood on the left end of each slide and Anti-B serum on the right end. Mom's blood didn't change at all. Dad's slide showed no change on the right end of the slide. On the left, the drop of blood clumped together like sour milk.

Margaret checked the labels, and looked again at the tiny vials of anti-A and anti-B serum. Left end. Right end. Mom was type O. Dad was type A. That couldn't be right.

"Dad, what's your blood type?"

"That's what you're supposed to be finding out."

"I know. This says you're type A. Did I make a mistake?"

"No, honey. You did it just right. I can tell you're going to be a scientist some day. I have A-positive blood."

"What's Mom?"

"Come to think of it, I don't rightly know."

"I'll, uh, I'll ask her later. I need to . . . to clean these up. Thanks for your help, . . . thanks." Margaret bent over the table, and George Ingalls turned back to reading the *Keagan County Record.*

That afternoon, Margaret lit a cigarette to give her hands something to do. Then she cornered her mother in the kitchen as soon as her dad went outside to mow the lawn. She delivered what amounted to a lecture on blood types, and concluded, "so, since you're type O and I'm type B, my father had to have either B or AB blood. And Dad just told me my test was right. He has type A. Was I adopted?"

"No . . . no, you weren't adopted," Monica told her. She poured herself a cup of coffee and walked over to the breakfast table. "I suppose you had to find out eventually. You see, dear, I've never really known for sure. I didn't know the details about this blood type business. And there was a very good chance that your dad was truly your father."

"Mom, how can you be so calm about this? My world has turned upside down, and you're not even embarrassed?"

"Oh, sweetheart, I got over the embarrassment a long time ago. Please don't smoke in the house, dear. You know we have a rule about that."

Margaret threw the cigarette in the sink. "So, as long as I don't smoke, are you going to explain?"

Monica looked as if she had thought about what she would say if this ever happened. She did straighten herself up in her chair, but Margaret couldn't tell if she were steeling herself or simply getting more comfortable. "It was about six months after your dad and I were married. He was on a business trip for two weeks, so I went to visit your Aunt Mildred to be with Brenda on her birthday." She toyed with her coffee cup, twisting it this way and that.

"And . . .?" Margaret prompted, not knowing if she truly wanted to hear what was coming.

"Her birthday," Margaret's mother repeated quietly. "That was the day she toppled over a wall into a ravine and smashed her shin, her ankle, and her arm. The gully was fifteen or twenty feet deep. It took them an hour to haul her up to the ambulance. It's a wonder she didn't break her neck. She eventually had four operations because there were complications."

Margaret watched as her mother's eyes traveled outside to where Dad . . . George . . . Margaret didn't know what to call him . . . was standing in the driveway, glaring at the mower. "The funny thing, really, is that it was your dad who suggested that I go there. He said it would give me something to do while he was out of town."

Margaret walked to the end of the kitchen, turned and retraced her steps. "But he's not my dad."

"Yes, he is, dear. He's the one who loved you and held you and hollered at you and worried about you and supported you. He's your dad."

"Okay, but he's not my father. He's not even the one who's putting me through college. It's Uncle Peter's trust fund that's paying for school."

"Your Uncle Peter . . . he liked you a lot."

"Yeah, but would he have liked me if he'd known I was a bastard?"

"Margaret, you will curtail your language when you're in this house. And please sit down. You're making me DIZZY with all that pacing."

"Oh sure, Mom," Margaret spit out. "You can sit there and talk about how my dad may or may not be my father, but I can't tell it like it is."

"Margaret, what I didn't particularly want to tell you–ever–is that there was always the possibility that Peter Holvers may have been your father."

"Uncle *Peter*? What were you doing sleeping with Uncle Peter?"

Monica stirred her coffee for quite a long time. "It wasn't quite like that."

"Oh, no, of course not. I'm sure it was all perfectly innocent. Excuse me, Peter, I just got married to George Ingalls, but if you'd like to screw around, please help yourself."

"He raped me, Margaret."

"He . . . he what?"

"You heard me. It was Brenda's birthday. The day she had the accident and the first operation. Mildred was going to spend the night with her at the hospital. Peter came home in the afternoon and didn't say a word. He simply grabbed me and pushed me onto the floor. I fought and fought, but he was a big, strong man. You were born nine months and two weeks later." Her words were staccato, like drums beats. Like lightning flashes. Like Margaret's heart.

Margaret stood transfixed as her mother continued. "I spent almost five years in therapy as a result of that attack, so you can get off your high horse and understand that you don't have a clue what you're talking about. And please sit down. Now."

Margaret sat down. She couldn't look at her mother. "Did you ever tell Daddy?"

"No, dear. I suppose I should have, but at first I was afraid he'd kill Peter, and I didn't want him to go to jail. By the time he got home from his trip, most of the bruises had healed. He asked me about the ones that were left, and I said I'd tripped on something. Later on I simply could not tell him."

Margaret looked up when her mom paused. She had taken off her glasses and was rubbing her eyes. This, Margaret thought, is non-verbal communication.

"You see, dear, we didn't talk about this sort of thing in those days. It was like such things were invisible. We didn't want to see them or hear about them. So, no, I didn't tell him. And of course, by then I knew I was expecting and I had you to think about. So I never said anything. When you were about six I went to a therapist, and of course, I told him about it. I never told my sister, either. I doubt she would have understood."

"She probably would have killed him."

"No, dear. He was Mildred's gravy train."

The afternoon sun was shining in Margaret's eyes. That was why they were watering, of course. "You must have hated me," she said.

"No," Monica said as she reached out to lay her hand over her daughter's. "No, my dear girl. I always saw you as a gift. Well, except for when you were colicky. And your dad loved you so much."

Margaret pulled her hand away. "Which one?"

"Please try not to be bitter, dear. Your Uncle Peter never knew. He may have wondered about the possibility, but even if I'd been sure, I wouldn't have let him know. And George really has been your dad. He's the one who loved you right from the start."

The sound of the mower criss-crossed the afternoon. Back and forth. Back and forth.

"Mom? Why didn't you tell me before this?"

Monica tilted her head to one side and raised her right eyebrow. "Would you have wanted to know? Anyway, I always thought that nothing had come of that one time. I never had a bit of morning sickness, so there was no way of knowing at first."

"Did Uncle . . . did Peter ever say anything to you?"

"Not a word. In fact, the only thing he said that day was something strange, after it was all over. He stood up and said that this would serve her right."

"What was that supposed to mean?"

"I have no idea. I got up and threw my things in the car and left as fast as I could. After that I never visited Mildred unless your dad was with me. When she called to let me know that Brenda was out of the hospital, I asked her if she and Peter were getting along okay, and she said they were. Another time I asked her if they were happy together, and she said that she couldn't be happier, having Brenda and all."

"So . . . so this is why Uncle . . . why Peter gave me the car and all the money?"

"I never told him, dear. But he might have suspected. Especially when no other children came along after you."

"Mom, this makes me feel so awful–like all this money I have is . . ." Margaret reached up to rub the tears from her face. "It's blood money."

"Well, even if it is, dear, nobody else knew the reason. They all thought he was looking after his wife's relatives."

"So he got points for being a nice guy, is that it?"

"Yes, dear. That's it."

"No, Dr. Bugg," Margaret said the following week, in response to his question. "I didn't write up my report for extra credit."

"That's okay, Margaret. I'll accept it tomorrow. Bring it by my office."

"Dr. Bugg, something went wrong. I . . . messed everything up, so I don't have anything to report." She couldn't meet his eyes. She knew he thought she was lying about it. She wanted to forget the whole thing.

The next day Margaret stopped by her faculty advisor's office and changed her declared major from Botany to English.

* * * * * *

From the *Keagan County Record*
Wednesday June 14, 1978
Myrtle's Musings from Martinsville

I love those weeks when all my news is happy news. Our own Bobby Sheffield has been officially named the Martinsville Officer of the Peace. Officer Bob is not new to the position, simply to the title. He's been filling in ever since his father died four months ago. Drop by the Martinsville City Hall and say hello to Officer Bob. We wish him well in his new civic position.

On another happy note, we'll have a wedding to celebrate next year when the bells will be chiming for our own Margaret Ingalls, daughter of Monica and George Ingalls. She's going to be marrying Sammy Casperson, son of Constance and Patrick Casperson. Sammy graduated from Illinois Wesleyan University two years ago, and Margaret graduated from the same school last week. They're planning their wedding for May of next year. The spring flowers should be lovely then.

* * * * * *

Chapter 8 -The 1990's

Saturday, September 24,1994   Martinsville

Margaret Ingalls Casperson would never have known, if she hadn't decided over a breakfast of soggy scrambled eggs to drive the one hundred and twenty-five miles to poke around her favorite antiques malls in Atlanta. She wasn't much of a cook, although she loved to eat good food. Sometimes she wondered why Sam put up with her the way he did. And heaven knows she wasn't anything to look at. Years ago, she had been astonished when gruff-sounding Sam, as sweet as a marshmallow on the inside, had asked her out during her sophomore year at IWU. He was a senior at the time.

She and Sam had grown up together. He'd never seemed to notice her, though, until they were away at the same college in Illinois. Her cousin Brenda, so elegant and refined, had told her once, that day at the zoo when Margaret was crying over the wasp sting, that she was as homely as a bucket of mud. Thank her lucky stars that Sam didn't seem to mind.

What a relief not to have to worry about that, Margaret thought as she finished her coffee. When she stood up to clear the breakfast dishes, she told Sam she was going to drive down to the city.

"Are you planning to stay overnight?"

"I'll let you know. It'll depend on what I find."

"What are you looking for?"

"Oh, a late fortieth birthday present for me."

"You already got a present."

Margaret smiled at the heavy gold chain on her wrist. "And I love it, too. But I thought I'd look for a solid gold four-poster bed to go with it."

Sam shook his head and rolled his eyes under their shaggy brows. He adjusted his glasses on his wide nose and went back to reading his paper.

Margaret happily walked up and down the aisles in her favorite antique place on Five Forks Trickum Road in Lilburn, a few miles northeast of Atlanta. Her feet weren't hurting her too much. That was a miracle. She peered into each little booth. Some she ignored. She wasn't interested in the knick-knacks or the children's furniture. She could easily live without a dozen cast iron kettles. And she already had perfectly lovely dining room furniture, although that early Duncan Phyfe hutch was spectacular. At the next booth she paused to inspect a mahogany sleigh bed and an impressive oak armoire that had intricate bird's-eye maple insets on the doors.

Margaret couldn't understand where the usual Saturday afternoon crowd was. Oh well, she thought, I might as well enjoy the elbow room while I have it. Her gaze passed over an old trunk sitting next to the armoire, and lingered in disbelief on one of the ugliest chairs she'd ever seen. No lines to it at all. Country Victorian had never impressed her. No grace. It was a bunch of junk people had made trying to make it look expensive. "Even that old trunk is more attractive than this chair," Margaret remarked to the air in general.

More to verify her last comment than for any other reason, she looked back at the trunk. It was a nondescript dark brown, with wooden reinforcements arching over the domed lid. A heavy leather band circled it halfway between the bottom and the lid. There were brass corner-protectors that looked somewhat the worse for wear. Good quality, she decided. Margaret leaned closer to look at the brass plate centered on the lid. It was engraved with what Margaret assumed was a name, surrounded by a bold design of leaves or flowers. Or maybe it was a fish motif? The owner may have been at sea. In fact, one end of the trunk was a bit scuffed and stained. That, thought Margaret, is probably where the trunk was dropped as it was being loaded aboard the . . . Her mind cast about for a suitably impressive-sounding ship. . . . the *Lusitania*. No, that one was torpedoed. Well, maybe this was on the voyage just before the one when it sank. She continued to gaze idly at the sturdy old trunk as her mind concocted a romance between Margaretha de Casperosa, the lovely young heiress or, better yet, the astonishingly beautiful young princess who owned the trunk, and the dashing ship's captain, whose name would have been . .

"Ernst Wilhelm?" she gasped, as she finally noticed the name engraved on the brass plate. Whoo-eee! she thought. Imagine seeing my cousin Ernie's name on such a romantic old trunk. There couldn't possibly be two Ernst Wilhelms in the world. Of course, her crazy cousin Ernie–that was how she always thought of him–wasn't Ernst Wilhelm. He was Ernst Wilhelm Robeson. And he wasn't crazy crazy. Just zany. You never knew what Ernie would do next. Sometimes he'd call in the middle of the night, and he'd be in Louisiana for the weekend because he had a chance to grab a flight. He'd stick the phone out the hotel window so she and Sam could hear the sounds of the New Orleans night life. Sometimes he'd rent a guy in a baboon suit to deliver a get-well message when Margaret wasn't even sick. Once he had hired an orchestra–well, a string quartet–to show up on her doorstep playing Happy Birthday. He was crazy, all right. But he was crazy with heart. Margaret wished there were something she could do for him. He was such a good kid.

Well, hardly a kid anymore. Ernie was a dozen or so years younger than Margaret. He used to come from Atlanta to stay summers with his grandparents, the Tarkingtons, and he'd ended up spending a lot of time with Sam and Margaret.

Ernie's mother, Margaret's old Aunt Mildred, said she had named him Ernst Wilhelm for some great-great-grandfather or uncle or such. But Margaret's mother always swore she couldn't remember any such person anywhere in the Tarkington family tree. In fact, Mom had often said privately that Mildred wanted her son to sound like Scandinavian royalty. Imagine anyone mistaking cousin Ernie for royalty. That would be the day.

Margaret bought the trunk on a whim. She'd never thought of herself as an impulsive person. Her other cousin, Brenda Holvers, complained once that Margaret never thought about anything first; she went ahead and did it. That was the day they'd gone to the zoo. Margaret had wanted to see the elephants better, so she climbed up on the fence railing right next to a big bush, and that was when the wasp stung her. Brenda had said, "Don't you ever stop to think about anything?"

Margaret thought that wasn't a fair comment. She did think about things a lot before she acted. The trunk had been different though. She *had* bought it impulsively.

When she brought it home, Sam shook his head. "You buy a lot of worthless things, Margie, but this one's about the ugliest so far. And it's not very practical. You can't even stack anything on top of it with that domed lid."

"They did that on purpose," Margaret explained. "These trunks were called Saratogas, and the domed lids meant that they were always stacked on *top* of everybody else's luggage."

"Makes sense, I suppose," Sam admitted. "But it's still ugly as homemade sin."

"Wait till you hear the story behind it."

"There's always a story, isn't there?"

"Yes. And you usually enjoy them, even if you pretend not to."

"Next time I'm going with you to keep you on the straight and narrow."

"You'd be totally bored, and you know it," she said, clicking the garage door opener. Nobody else in Martinsville had a garage, except her mom and dad next door. The houses just weren't built that way. Sam had insisted, though, on building one beside the house right after they were married. It was a big double-doored structure, with lots of room for the car and all of Sam's tools on the right-hand side. "Now, before you haul it in here, take a look at the name on the lid."

Sam pulled his glasses out of his shirt pocket and peered at the brass plate. "What's Ernie's name doing here? Did you steal this thing?"

"No, I did not steal it. Would you pay attention? It's a funny coincidence, but once I get this cleaned up, I'm going to show it to him."

"Maybe it was his and he gave it away."

"Silly, it wasn't Ernie's trunk. This nameplate is original. And the trunk has to be almost a hundred years old. It was probably handed down in some family for three or four generations."

Sam scratched his head with the allen wrench he was holding. "And now the last one in the Wilhelm family died?"

"Or decided they didn't want a musty old trunk around anymore."

"Are you going to give it to Ernie for his birthday?"

"No, I'm going to turn it into a cute little linen chest. I think it'll fit in the powder room, right beside the statue of the swan."

Sam lugged the trunk into the left side of the garage, where Margaret kept all her junk. He found a place near the side door and plopped it down in front of a table she was refinishing. And there the trunk sat for a long time.

Saturday April 6, 1996

"I'll be over in about an hour to help, dear." Monica said as her daughter Margaret walked out the kitchen door. They'd had a good long talk. Grown up children are such a joy once you don't have to worry about them all the time. Monica was delighted that Margaret had asked for advice about refinishing an old trunk. That was an interest the two of them had always shared. Now that Margaret was grown, Monica sometimes felt they were more like sisters.

Nothing like Mildred, her real sister, of course. Mildred was only ten months older than she. They'd been great friends growing up, but it all went to pot once she married that awful Peter Holvers. Monica's teeth started to grind together until she remembered how much she'd paid for her crowns. She took a deep breath to calm herself. Of course, since Peter's death in the mid-1960's, they'd seen more of each other, but it still wasn't the same as when they were young girls together.

Monica had never been much of a party girl. Unlike Mildred. Even after Mildred snagged old Peter Holvers, she still kept up a carefree life, taking off on cruises and flying to London and Paris to shop.

Well, at least she'd settled down after Brenda was born. That was something in her favor. Brenda had been a big baby, one who seemed to require a lot of attention. Lands! That child could holler when she wanted something. She had a way of getting what she wanted like a train rolling through the town after midnight. It wouldn't stop for anything. And neither would Brenda. How did flighty Mildred ever end up with a kid like that? Brenda had certainly been her father's daughter right from the start. What a relief when Brenda stopped coming along on the odd times when Mildred drove to Martinsville for a visit. Monica hadn't seen Brenda since she was eight or ten, except for the funeral.

"I'm glad Brenda wasn't a boy," Monica said to the icing she was spreading in swirls. That Peter Holvers might have been as rich as this double-chocolate cake, but he sure would have been a lousy role model for a boy. Thank God Mildred married Conrad second time around, although that was too late for Brenda. I am so blessed to have George for a husband, she breathed quietly. And Margaret for our daughter.

Margaret stood in her garage, tilting her head from side to side, trying to imagine the trunk next to her dresser. It was time to do something about it. Mom would be coming over to help her once she finished frosting her cake.

The trunk had been taking up space in the garage for more than a year now. It was too big to fit in the powder room, so she was going to install it either next to her dresser or in the little nook beneath the window at the end of the hall. She had measured. Maybe she could get a bit of a head start, before Mom got here.

She dragged the trunk out into the sunlight on the driveway, admiring again the bold designs around the edges of the nameplate. She ran her fingers over the rounded brass studs that ringed the lid before she removed the long brass key tied securely to the old leather handle. Those leather handles usually decayed, but this one was still intact. And the lock must have been kept well-oiled, because the key turned easily. A faint, musty odor escaped as Margaret opened it.

Instead of the usual paper lining, this one had a dark blue fabric, stained and torn in places. It needed a good airing out. Why hadn't she thought to prop it open while it was in the garage? She turned the trunk around so the sunlight shone directly into it. All along the bottom, there were little snags in the fabric, as if something sharp had been stowed in there without having been wrapped properly. Margaret quickly decided she would have to rip it all out and fumigate the whole thing before she replaced the lining with some lovely taffeta. Maybe a bright yellow would lighten up the inside.

"What are you going to do with that disreputable-looking thing?" Sam called out from under the Duesenberg. He was changing the oil. Again.

"I already told you. I'm turning it into a linen chest," Margaret said over her shoulder.

"You'll never do it before your mother gets here." Sam was always so practical.

"No, she's going to help me, but I can at least get it aired out a bit." She backed up close to the bright yellow car, where she could look at the chest from an angle. "Most of the problem is cosmetic. If I replace the lining and shine up the brass and use some wood putty to fill in the holes . . ."

"Won't that destroy its value as an antique?"

"Sam Casperson, you *are* interested in antiques, you old stinker."

"No I'm not. I just don't want you to lose your money throwing it away on junk."

Margaret stood still for three heartbeats. "Is that what you married me for? My money?"

"Of course not, you silly female." Sam stuck an oily hand out from under the car and stroked her shin, leaving a shiny streak on her bare leg. "I married you for this car."

Margaret couldn't get angry with him. She laughed and turned back toward her trunk. He was such a tease.

"This rotten glue is going to be the death of me," Margaret groaned later as she ripped out yet another piece of stained lining. The heavy blue material, of fairly good quality when it was new, was glued onto the inside of the trunk. Every time she pulled, a square of lining came off in her hands, leaving behind a large rectangle where the glue, laid down in a wide checkerboard pattern, held a strip of lining firmly to the inside of the old trunk. Her mother had finally left, saying "I have to put my chicken salad together. And it's a good chance to get out of the messy work."

"That's about the only reason I can think of to want to cook," Margaret muttered to herself as her mother walked next door.

Margaret's knees were complaining, too. The concrete driveway was a lousy workplace. Even with this old pillow to kneel on, she knew she'd be limping when she tried to stand up. She shifted off her knees and sat down on the sun-warmed concrete, which reminded her of Uncle Peter's funeral back in 1965. It was a relief to be able to think about him now without feeling all that old anger. Of course, in 1965, she'd still thought he was just her uncle.

She was in fifth grade when he died, and she got out of school for the funeral. That was the last time she'd seen Brenda, her cousin.

After that, Brenda had totally disappeared. Margaret missed her, even after all this time. She could remember that day, waiting for the limousine from the funeral home to pick them up, sitting on the warm concrete steps in front of her Aunt Mildred's house, watching some ants carrying tiny pieces of something green in a line across the cement. Her mother had told her to keep her dress clean. Otherwise she probably would have followed the little trail off through the grass. That would have been a lot more fun than riding what had seemed like a million miles to sit through a stuffy old ceremony. Then she had to be quiet and listen to the reading of the will that same afternoon. Of course, she'd gotten her first car, the Model J, out of it. Hadn't been able to drive it until she was old enough. When she was still a kid, she used to go outside and sit in it and look at the needlepoint flower designs on the back seats. Somebody had gone to a lot of trouble to make that car.

Her mother wouldn't let her take it to college. That was probably a good thing. Otherwise she might have suspected that Sam asked her out just so he could drive the car. Margaret turned slightly to look back over her shoulder into the open garage door. There it sat, the car of her husband's dreams, with its distinctive grill, topped by a flying arrow. It was on Sam's side of the garage, of course. Her side was full of projects. He babied the car. She refinished furniture. They had two other cars that sat at the curb for everyday use.

Margaret called herself back to present time. The trunk sat there, looking as if it might at one time have been fancy enough to ride in the Duesenberg. Not now, though. Its insides were hanging out, a bunch of little blue frog tongues lopping over the edge.

Margaret reached for one of the little tongues and tore it out impatiently. As she did so, she noticed something shift underneath the lining near the far-left bottom corner of the trunk. When she brushed her fingers over that area, she could feel the outline of something about the size of a greeting card. The lining, stained and worn, had several long slits in it.

Margaret stepped into the garage and lifted a small pair of long-nosed tweezers from her crowded work table, intending to lift the card, or whatever it was, carefully from its hiding place. In the middle of fishing gently around, trying to grasp the paper, she paused, rolled her eyes, and laughed out loud at herself. Taking hold of the edge of the slit, she ripped the material away, and out fell several sheets of paper, folded in the middle.

Setting the tweezers aside and ignoring her sore knees, Margaret unfolded the ivory-toned paper. The date in the top right-hand corner was April 8, 1946.

"My Dearest Ernst," she read, "I have the most astonishing news for you, my darling. . . ."

The writing was slanted so far to one side, it was hard to decipher. Margaret had known only two other people who had such heavily-slanted handwriting. One was Doodlebug, her freshman biology professor at Illinois Wesleyan. The other was her old Aunt Mildred, who still lived in Atlanta. Now here was someone else with that funny slant. Thinking that her mother would probably enjoy seeing this, Margaret sat down again on the warm concrete of the driveway and continued to read.

My dearest Ernst,

I have the most astonishing news for you, my darling. We, that is to say you and I, are going to have a child. I have wondered for the past few weeks if that might be a possibility. And now I know for certain.

Yes, my darling. I can hear your question. Yes, it is your child. It has been almost four months since I have had relations with my husband. He has been, of course, so involved in all his business ventures. Well, my dearest, you know all about that. You listened so sweetly to all my ramblings when we met at the Eiffel Tower.

I am writing simply to give you the wonderful news. I want you to know that I am carrying your child, and that I will always treasure him–I'm sure it will be a boy. I will name him after you, my dearest.

How I wish that week in Paris could have gone on and on. But that could never be. Even though I have known we will never again see each other, I want you to know that your name will live through your son. I don't want to burden you with this next piece of information, my dearest, but I need for you to know this–I must arrange to lie with Peter tonight or tomorrow. He must never suspect that this child is not his. Luckily our family doctor is a rather stodgy old man. I'm sure I can lead him to believe that this child is the son of my very wealthy husband. Maybe he will even be born early. That would help matters immensely.

I dreamed last night that my husband died and that your wife left you to return to Denmark. It was a lovely dream of our being together, of sharing our lives, of loving wildly and magnificently. But I know, my dear Ernst, that it was only a dream. I know that we two will have no life together, other than what we had that one lovely week.

I will bear your son. I will name him for you. If all goes well, he will be born in November. Look for the announcement in the society column.

Oh, my dearest, I just thought how awful it would be if someone from your embassy noticed your name in the birth announcement. No. I will not risk your reputation. I will not bring even a hint of scandal on you. I will not give our son your first name, only your middle name. Brendan. It has a certain ring, don't you think?

I suppose this is good-bye. I cannot risk discovery. Peter is an unforgiving man. I will be a good wife to him, as best I can. Good-bye my dearest, my love. Even such a brief love (as ours was) can last a lifetime.

Mildred

Margaret dropped the letter into her lap. This was the strangest turn of events she'd ever heard of. Brenda? It had to be. Mildred. Peter. Brenda, who should have been a boy named Brendan. Who the heck was this Ernst guy?

And the funniest–no, the saddest–thing of all was crazy cousin Ernie. His mother, Margaret's Aunt Mildred, had been forty-five when she married Conrad Robeson, the year after Peter died. Forty-six when she gave birth to Ernie. It was a family joke about how Aunt Mildred was so surprised when she got pregnant after all those years. And she'd named the boy Ernst Wilhelm Robeson. From the look of this letter, they'd had a one-week fling. Pathetic. That crazy woman! Had she carried a torch all these years for some long-ago guy? Enough to name Conrad's son after him? At least, Margaret was sure that Ernie *was* Conrad's son. He was the spitting image of his dad, except that Conrad had that one short leg, and Ernie's legs were fine.

Ernie was a sweetheart. Margaret had been in her teenswhen he was born. After she married Sam, Ernie used to come to Martinsville to spend his summer vacations with them. After college, he moved to Russell Creek, a small town that was a hop skip and a jump up the road, where he worked for a catalog company. Margaret brought her wandering mind back to the letter and the questions it posed.

How did Brenda manage to get the Holvers nose, though? When she walked into a room with that big nose in the air, it fairly screamed *the heiress apparent*. Wait. Maybe what Brenda had was a Tarkington nose. Of course. Old Aunt Mildred didn't have a big nose, but Brenda might have gotten it from Granddaddy Tarkington. That would certainly explain things. If Brenda wasn't Uncle Peter's daughter, that might explain a lot. Uncle Peter, ha! If anybody deserved to be cheated on it was Uncle Peter. There was a gleeful part of Margaret that cheered Aunt Mildred for doing something that . . . No, she thought. That's revenge thinking. I won't sink to that. No matter who it happens to, things like this are sad.

She couldn't wait to tell her mother. In the meantime, she'd have to tell Sam. No, on second thought, she wouldn't say a thing to him about this. She'd never even told him that her dad wasn't her father. For her, that piece of information had almost ceased to exist.

Poor Brenda, though. She wouldn't like the idea of being a bastard. Maybe that was too strong a word. But she certainly wasn't a Holvers. No, she certainly wasn't.

Margaret stood up with some effort and dusted off the back of her pants. She should not have sat on the ground for so long. She refolded the letter, smiled, and walked on feet and knees that ached, next door to her mother's house.

Monica waved the letter in front of her as she faced her daughter across the crumb-scattered plates. "You realize what this means, don't you, dear? It means that you're the one who's going to inherit *all* that Holvers money. If Brenda's not his daughter, you'll get it." She reached for the glass carafe. "Do you want some coffee?"

"Not a chance, Mom. I don't want it. The coffee or the money."

"What do you mean, you don't want it? It's a fortune." She poured a big spoonful of sugar into her cup and added a dollop of cream from the small blue pitcher. "A fortune," she repeated.

"First of all, I wouldn't do that to Brenda. I may not have seen her for years, but she's still my cousin and I looked up to her a lot when I was a kid. Secondly, even if the blood typing said Peter Holvers was my father, he was not my dad, and I don't want anybody to know what he did to you. Don't you think the papers would snap that right up? *Holvers Fortune Goes To Small-Town Girl in the Boondocks. . . . Love Child. . . . How to Make Millions Overnight.* I can see the headlines now. We'd have reporters from the city swarming all over this town."

"But, it's a fortune."

"So what, Mom? I've got plenty from the trust fund. Sam and I are happy. I don't need anything else. Brenda needs the money a lot more than I do, because her da . . . I mean Peter hardly left her anything. And if we never tell about this letter, it won't make a bit of difference to anyone."

"I still don't see how you can give up a fortune without a second thought."

"What would I do with it? I've already got the Duesenberg, and Sam couldn't possibly love another car as much as he loves that one. We've got good friends, a lovely house, our lives are pretty settled. The trust fund keeps churning out the interest and I get a huge check every month until I die. How could hurting Brenda and hurting you and stirring up gossip all over town possibly help anything?"

Monica kept stirring her coffee. "But it's a fortune," Monica said again. "Couldn't you do a lot of good with that much money?"

"Mom, I hate to be trite, but you sound like a scratched record. It is not worth the hassle. It is not worth the heartache that would come from telling this to lawyers. Let Brenda have it. I truly do not care."

"But . . ."

"And think what everybody would be saying about Dad if this was in the papers."

Monica stopped her coffee cup halfway to her lips. "Oh. I hadn't thought of that." She took a long breath. "I guess you're right."

"You're darn tootin' I'm right."

"You really mean that, don't you?" Monica asked.

"Yes, Mom. I will not hurt the people I love to get something I don't honestly need. I will not hurt Dad. I will not hurt you. And I will not hurt Brenda. I don't care if she isn't his kid. She still deserves that money, and I'm never going to show this letter to anyone."

"But, dear . . ."

"No. And promise me you won't say anything about it, either. I think this is so sad. Maybe Brenda knows. Maybe that's why she disappeared."

"She didn't *disappear*, dear." Monica took a long sip of well-stirred coffee. "A couple of months after her father . . . Peter, that is . . . after he died, she changed her last name and transferred to a different college."

"Why?"

"Because she was tired of being automatically associated with the Holvers underwear kingdom."

"Where is she now?"

"Down south of here somewhere. I have her phone number in my address book."

"What's her new last name?"

"Heavens to Betsy, I don't know. The only reason I have her phone number is just in case something happens to Mildred."

"Why didn't you tell me all this?"

"You never asked."

Margaret was almost ready to laugh, when she saw the color drain from her mother's face. "Mom, what's wrong?" She stepped around the table and knelt beside her mother's chair.

Monica's voice, when it finally came out, was shaking. "That's what he meant, when he said *This will serve her right*. This is what he was talking about. He must have found out. Somehow. My own sister. He did it to get back at her."

"Did what? What are you talking . . ." Margaret stopped. She stood up and returned to her side of the table. "Oh, Mom," she said as dropped into her chair and stared at her mother's trembling hands. Monica was trying to pick up her coffee cup. And failing miserably.

＊ ＊ ＊ ＊ ＊ ＊

"Try it, just once, and see if you like it," Ernie Robeson coaxed, to no avail. She slid out from under his outstretched hand and careened around the corner, down the hall, and into the bedroom. "How can you already have such definite opinions when you're only two months old?" he asked in the general direction of the dust ruffle, which was quivering from the kitten's passage. "Come on, Puddin Head." After a while he began to feel faintly silly talking to the floor. "All right. Be that way." He set down the bowl of cat food and retreated to his recliner, where he slipped off his shoes and socks, and picked up the remote.

Ernie simply did not understand women, and that apparently applied to the feline variety as well. Out of the corner of his eye, he noticed her sneaking around the corner. He stretched his foot out in her direction and wiggled his toes to entice her to come closer. He had a lot to learn about kittens.

The bandage was entirely too fat, and his toe still hurt. It looked like he wouldn't be able to get his shoe back on. He wondered what he'd do tomorrow when he had to go to work. Maybe he could tell them he'd had a skiing accident in Aspen. Maybe they'd believe a car wreck. Maybe he could just not say anything and seem mysterious. He certainly wasn't going to admit to having his big toe mauled by a kitten.

If he hadn't been in the bathroom trying to fix the bandage, he probably wouldn't have heard the car when it coasted into his driveway. "Who on earth would that be?" he asked Puddin Head, as he gave one final wrap of tape around his toe. Gently prying the kitten's needle-like claws out of the bandage again, he pulled the curtain aside. Moonlight created a sinister shadow around the car, as if some fiend had finally settled on Ernie's house for a showdown.

"I have entirely too much imagination," Ernie told the kitten, as he watched someone, a woman, hoist herself out of the car and head toward the back door. So much for the fiend idea. "It's only Margaret."

He waited until she knocked. Had she really driven the fifteen miles to Russell Creek hoping to find him home at nine o'clock at night? Why hadn't she called first? What if he'd been gone? What if he'd been in the hospital? What if he'd had a hot date? The kitten must have agreed because she purred loudly.

"Fat chance of that," Margaret told him over a cup of the world's worst coffee when he asked her those same questions. She had come inside, taken one look at his lollipop-sized toe, stripped off all the gauze, and replaced it with a neat, thin, and relatively comfortable bandage. His shoe slipped on just fine now.

"Fat chance," she repeated as she stroked the little yellow kitten sleeping in her lap. "You're always here." The kitten stood up, kneaded Margaret's lap briefly, turned around, and settled back in to continue her snooze. Margaret looked up and shifted conversational gears. "You'll never in a million years guess what I found out."

"You're pregnant? You struck oil? Your mother used to be a stevedore?"

"Would you shut that mouth of yours? I'm not at all happy about this. I found out that Brenda is not entitled to that fortune she got from Uncle Peter."

"She hasn't gotten it yet. Not until next month. And why not?"

"Because she's not his daughter, that's why."

"But the will says it's for her."

"No it doesn't. I thought it did, but this afternoon when I showed Mom this letter, she told me that the exact words were *child of my body.*"

"Of course she's the child of his body. All you have to do is look at her profile. It's as big as his. I've seen pictures."

Margaret settled back into the kitchen chair and frowned at her cousin. "I tell you, she didn't get her nose from Uncle Peter. She got it from Grandpa Tarkington. That means the fortune will go to Aunt Mildred . . ."

"Mom?"

". . . and then you'll get half, since you're her son."

"But Brenda is her daughter."

"Exactly. She'll get the other half."

"That's three halves," Ernie pointed out.

"Oh phooey, don't be so exact. Anyway, it's still a lot of money for both of you. Or all three of you. Doesn't that make you happy?"

Ernie grimaced as he set down his coffee cup. Margaret thought at first he was recognizing what terrible coffee it was, but he veered off to another topic that had nothing to do with coffee. "I wish," he mumbled, "I wish I could have known her. I would have liked having a sister. A real sister."

"Well, I bet the payout date will lure her out of hiding," Margaret said. "Then you'll get to know her really well."

Ernie peered into his coffee cup. "What makes you think Brenda wasn't Peter's daughter?"

"I found this in that trunk I told you about, the one that says Ernst Wilhelm on the lid." Margaret pulled the evidence from her purse, took another sip of his execrable coffee, grimaced, and handed him the letter.

"It's Mom's handwriting for sure," Ernie said after a few moments.

Margaret settled in as he read the letter over a couple of times. After he finished it, he looked up toward the ceiling and said, "I wonder why Mom named me for her old boyfriend." Margaret could have kicked herself for having shown him the letter.

"Oh," she said after a moment, "my mom has that all figured out. She said your mom really liked the name and thought it made you sound like royalty." Margaret wasn't sure he was convinced, but at least he stopped frowning.

"I wasn't going to show it to anybody," she told him, "but then it occurred to me that you wouldn't mind sharing a fortune with your half-sister, right?"

Ernie scratched his head and stared at the kitten in Margaret's lap. "Somehow I don't think it's going to be as easy as all that."

Sunday, April 21, 1996 – Savannah

With a snap of her sturdy wrist, Officer Columbine Sloan turned down the volume on the scanner. She was in no mood to take another domestic call. This was the fourth in thirty-six hours. She began making a U-turn.

"Brando," she asked, "is it a rule that when we're headed this way, we get a call that sends us that way?"

"You're right," he said. "And if we're headed that way, we have to turn around and go back this way. It's written in the regulations, chapter 482, subsection Q, paragraph 3."

Keeping up an easy banter with the new partner she'd been assigned to three months ago, a piece of Colly's mind stayed on her earlier concerns.

What on God's lovin' earth were married people doin' when they got married or stayed married to people they hated? Didn't make a blamed bit of sense to her. Colly was tired of trying to coax guns and knives away from men intent on carvin' holes in the women they'd promised to love, honor, and cherish. *Till death do us part* seemed appropriate, in a twisted kind of way.

She glanced over at Brando Williston, whose freckled face sported a bright sunburn from the field trip with his grandson's first-grade class. Even in the light from the oncoming headlights, she could see the bright red. Looked like it might be sore. Thank goodness he was a big man. Made the domestics a lot easier. Her last partner had been a scrawny little squirt who just wanted to get promoted. He was never any help at all. Served him right when he caught the mumps with complications–she could guess what *those* were–and had to quit the force. She pushed her shoulders back against the dark blue seat of the cruiser, to try to ease the tension down her spine. She and Brando took turns with the driving. Tonight it was her turn.

"You don't know how glad I am that we have next Friday and Saturday off. I hate workin' weekends. Especially the night shift. Makes me feel like I'm fifty-five like you instead of almost thirty-five like me." She sensed Brando shifting in his seat, but he didn't say a word. That was his style. For an old white guy, he wasn't too bad. He always let her vent for a while and then took the conversation back to police matters. What Colly really hated was her own whiny attitude about working Sunday nights. Way down underneath, Colly believed that folks should take what life handed them and make it serve. She should have been a plumber, though, like her daddy.

In fact, the only reason she hadn't gone into plumbing was that she was scared to death of snakes. And wouldn't you know, her first day on the force, she was called to rescue a kid stuck in a crawl space under a house. There were two little garter snakes under there that had skittered off when Colly crawled through the opening, but they might as well have been twenty-foot pythons as scared as they got her. If the kid hadn't been crying, Colly would have backed out and resigned right then.

Colly's daddy was born during the Depression and raised by his widowed mother. Never saw his own father who was killed in a train wreck. Went to work when he was a kid to help out his mama. He always managed to be so cheerful, and he believed in that saying about making the lemons in your life into lemonade.

He had been pretty much paralyzed by a stroke when he was in his late fifties. He made it serve. He worked like the dickens to learn to walk again, and to talk. Kept on laughing and joking. Made friends of every person on the rehab team, even that snooty head doctor. She never heard him complain about the pain or the frustration, until three months before he died, when he told her he was feeling too tired to keep on fighting. That was when he gave up, and started to shrivel inside. A week before his 64th birthday, he passed.

So, why couldn't she stop grousin' about something little like having to work weekends? Her partner didn't seem to mind it; but Brando's wife was a nurse who worked the weekends, too. Evening shift, three to eleven. Colly knew that Patch, her sweet husband, certainly understood, since he used to be in uniform himself. Trouble was, weekend work hours took away time she could have spent with him. That was what she really resented. Here she was, heading out to try to keep Horse Munson from beating the heck out of Bunny again, and all she wanted to be doing was sitting down beside sweet Patch, with something cool to drink in her hand and some ever-loving jazz in her ears.

Patch Sloan had been Colly's best friend in childhood. They lived next door to each other and were always in and out of each other's kitchens, idolizing each other's mamas, and generally getting underfoot together. Or getting lost together. It was almost like a storybook. They'd helped each other through all sorts of broken hearts—his because of his girlfriends and hers because of boyfriends. One day when they were both twenty-eight—*old enough to sneeze, and dry behind the ears*, as her grandmama used to say—they looked at each other and saw the light. Now they'd been married for a sweet, sweet seven years.

Last week, her sister-in-law had told her that lots of marriages failed in the seventh year because that was when all the wedding gifts broke—the toaster and the TV and the microwave. "If you have to throw that many things out," she said, "sometimes it seems to make sense to get rid of your spouse at the same time. Don't you believe it, though." Of course, Beatrice had been married going on twenty-eight years, so she ought to know. She was ten years older than Patch—a whole decade.

Colly chuckled to herself as she remembered what Beatrice had told her once a long time ago. Theodore, her husband, had raised his hand to her only one time, about a year after they got hitched. She picked up her cast iron frying pan that was sittin' there handy, and said, "Theodore Black, you can choose right now between the best home-cookin' you've ever known and watchin' my backside walkin' out the door. Which'll it be?" He lowered his hand and never even thought about doing any physical harm to her. Ever again. The fact that the frying pan was full of her drool-over-it-delicious fried chicken and a heck of a lot of hot grease might have had something to do with his decision. "Funny thing was," Beatrice admitted, "to this day, I can't recall what we were fightin' about."

Colly sure wished Horse and Bunny Munson would come to that same sort of accord. They'd been giving each other hell from day one. Trouble was, all the shouting bothered the neighbors who called to complain, and Colly and Brando always seemed to be the ones on duty. She didn't really think they'd actively kill each other, but you never could tell.

"One day," Brando remarked, "that Bunny is bound to get tired enough of all this to do something about it. Think she'll kill him or just shoot his balls off?"

"What are you doin', partner, readin' my mind? We could lay bets on it, I suppose." Even as she joked with Brando, Colly's mind was on another track. "You know, when I took that class on domestic violence at police trainin', I had a hard time believin' that any woman would put up with such nonsense."

"I know what you mean."

"Do you? My parents loved each other. Really loved each other. That was the best sex education I could have had, watchin' them hug and dance in the living room, watchin' dad pat my mama's fanny when he kissed her goodbye in the mornin', even watchin' them argue without bein' mean about it, and watchin' mama's eyes go all soft and honey sweet while she told me about what it meant to love a man and be loved back. That domestic violence class made no sense to me at all. At all."

"You're in a rare mood. Better reel yourself back in or you're liable to do in Horse before Bunny gets a chance."

"Don't you go makin' fun of me, Brando. I'm not understandin' this job right now."

"You want to be home with your honey, don't you?"

"You got it, partner." For a man, and especially for a police officer, Colly had to admit that Brando was an okay guy.

By the time they dealt with Horse and Bunny, taking him to cool off overnight in his usual jail cell, and sending Bunny to stay with her sister, Colly needed a break. She was starting to mosey toward Barnacle's, the best all-night diner in the area, when the radio went off. Colly turned the cruiser around and sped in the opposite direction.

From the personal notebook of Colly Sloan:
glad this notebook isn't official. got horse and bunny separated just in time to turn around and head the other way to see about a noisy dog. miss witherspoon was complainin again. every time we get there, though, the dog's quiet. hard to track down a silent dog. almost like it's invisible. miss w said her carpenter heard the dog all day yesterday while he was repairing her front porch. why didn't she call then? finney, his name is. i'll check with him tomorrow at a reasonable hour.

Chapter 9

Wednesday April 24, 1996 - Savannah

Linda Finney, working the front desk at the River Landing Hotel, ducked her head slightly as the general manager, Millicent B. Cappell, strode past. It could have been interpreted as a nod of respect, but it was designed to hide the fact that Linda was chewing a bite of chocolate chip cookie, forbidden but luscious. Employees were never allowed to eat on the premises. Ever. Linda supposed it made sense, but she needed to sneak an odd bite here and there when no one was looking. Not that she was even hungry, but the chocolate helped her stave off her craving for a cigarette.

Linda did not like Ms. Schnozz, as all the employees called her behind her unyieldingly straight back. Linda's husband kept telling her that she shouldn't make Ms. Cappell angry. Even Linda's mother told her the same thing. "You have to get along with your employer, Linda," she'd say. "I always got along just fine when I was working as an executive secretary." *Yeah, yeah, yeah.* Linda had her mother's whole speech memorized. Why should she care, though? Estelle Placings, Linda's mother, was always pushing her around.

For that matter, her husband was always pushing her around, too. No wonder her mother liked him so much. The two of them must have come out of the same mold. You'd think they owned the world. Linda was tired of being told what to do. Oh, she supposed her mother was okay. So was her husband. But Linda felt lost, somehow, between them. They were tall. She was short. They were bossy.

She was, well, meek. They were sure of themselves. She could always see two sides to every argument.

And now, here she was at the Landing, a gracious old building she truly loved, caught between Barry Murphy, the pompous owner, and Millie Cappell, the bull-headed manager. She had tried talking about her ideas for streamlining the reservation system so regular patrons wouldn't be shuffled around to rooms they didn't want, but Barry Murphy told her to talk to Millie Cappell, and Millie Cappell said it would cost too much. This place should be packed year-round, the way it used to be. Barry Murphy had definitely let the standards drop after he bought the place four years ago.

It had taken a long time, though, for the ripples of his dissolution to be seen. It wasn't so much what he did. It was all the little things he didn't do. It's sheer laziness, Linda thought. On the surface, the Landing was still a wonderful place to stay. But Linda could see that important things had begun to slip. Housekeeping wasn't what it should have been. They had switched to a linen service that did shoddy work. It wasn't effective to cut costs at the expense of quality.

Don't get me started on this, Linda thought, although she was already well started on her list of what she would do if she were in charge. Sally, that insolent youngster who worked the front desk on the late shift, hadn't been trained worth beans, but with good supervision and specific training, she could have been an asset to the Landing. The restaurant was cutting corners on the menu. They needed a decent budget, and John, the chef, needed a good assistant. The patrons were beginning to complain about how long it took to get anything delivered by room service. And what could Linda do but apologize? Barry wouldn't hear her complaints, and Millie Cappell ignored them.

She watched until that gray-suited back disappeared out the door to the courtyard. Then Linda glanced around at the quiet lobby and popped the last bite of cookie into her mouth.

* * * * * *

"Why did I ever buy this place?" Barry Murphy thought as he padded toward the lobby. He hated his hotel, but he hid that thought behind a magnificently polished smile. He had always wanted to travel, and he resented the people who had the time and money to do it. At least they left a lot of their money with him. The River Landing Hotel was not cheap. Not at all. Over the years, as the reputation of the place spread by word of mouth from satisfied guests to prospective guests, people began to come regularly to be pampered and appreciated. The previous owner had built up a reputation for the Landing that was impeccable. Everything about the River Landing was low-key and high-class, except the current owner. He knew that, but he tried hard.

Barry didn't have a cultured background, but he knew how to fake a terrific smile. And he had learned everything else fast. Barry was never one to be inconspicuous, to stay behind the scenes. That would have been hard to do anyway. Barry was a big, big man. He was tall. He was wide. His feet splayed out like a couple of phone books. The only reason his big ears didn't overwhelm his face was that his face was as big as the rest of him, with round eyes and full cheeks and a nose that was . . . Barry turned his head to one side to look at himself in the big mirror that graced the Landing's front hallway. Now, his nose wasn't that big. Linda in reception had a big nose. And Millie Cappell, the manager, had a big nose. Even Bull Finney, the carpenter who replaced that broken window in Barry's house, had a big nose. This city was swarming with big noses, so what did his matter? He wiggled his heavy eyebrows at his reflection and ran through a mental list of the guests, searching for more big noses.

Barry always remembered every name and every face of every guest. It was a trait he had developed growing up, the second son in a family of eight children. Nobody in his home town of Martinsville had ever thought of those eight as individuals. They were always lumped together. Larry, Barry, Gary, Mary, Sherry, Perry, Harry, and little Derry, who wasn't so little anymore.

All of the Murphy children had left home as soon as possible, although Larry, a retired barber, had returned to Martinsville and inherited the huge old family house. Barry owned the River Landing Hotel, Gary and Perry had dead-end jobs, Mary had six loud-mouthed kids, Sherry went into real estate, Harry quit talking to the family twenty years ago, and Derry was a lawyer at some hot-shot firm in

Atlanta. Barry's wide-lipped mouth crinkled up into what for him passed as a real smile as he recalled that when Derry was a little girl, she liked to draw on those yellow legal pads, and now she had a briefcase full of them.

He noticed, as he passed the reception desk, that the painting he detested across the hallway was slightly askew. He detoured around and stood in front of it, scowling. He'd never liked that painting, but it seemed to be expected that a hotel called The River Landing would have paintings of ships on every wall. He had drawn the line at that, but couldn't dump this one, since it had been a gift from a satisfied guest—one who came back often and always ran a white-gloved hand along the edge of the frame. Hadn't white gloves gone out of style decades ago? The *Savannah* was the first steamship to cross the Atlantic, from here to Liverpool in 1819, and the forebears of the wealthy guest had something to do with the building of it. Come to think of it, she hadn't been here lately. Maybe just as well. Last time she was here she'd been complaining about her room. Fussy old biddy. Still, it wouldn't do to have people not coming back. He'd ask Linda to do something about that.

Barry shifted his considerable weight from one leg to the other. He wondered if the jogging he was doing was a mistake. He'd lost a few pounds, but his legs were sore. And looking at these depressing paintings all day long didn't help his spirits any. He grimaced once more and continued on his way to the back office. He had expected Millie Cappell to be waiting for him. She was usually punctual. He buzzed the front desk. Nothing happened. He pressed the button again.

When Linda answered, he cut her off between "front" and "desk". "Why did you take so long to answer my buzz? And where is Ms. Cappell?"

"I walked across the lobby to straighten the *Savannah* after you looked at it . . . sir. And Ms. Cappell is outside checking the gazebo."

"Tell her to see me when she comes in."

"Yes, sir."

* * * * * *

Millie lit up a cigarette as soon as she walked in her front door. It was a pain in the patootie not being able to smoke on the job, even though she was the one who had made the rule herself. She pulled her jacket off with a sigh, wishing, not for the first time, that she'd gotten her masters degree. She could have amounted to something instead of running one stupid hotel after another. This one was better than the last one she'd worked at. A good job in a lot of ways. She had this house rent-free, with perks like yard maintenance and free utilities and free meals at the Landing Restaurant. She got to make all the decisions, but that was only because the owner was lazy. It wasn't the power-packed life she'd always imagined for herself. And she was sick and tired of fencing with that asshole Barry Murphy every day.

She took one more drag on her cigarette. It brought her no joy. She had tried to quit several times, but when she did, she gained weight she'd worked so hard to whittle off herself. She had no photos of herself as a kid, but she seemed to remember that she had been skinny then. By the time she was in high school, though, she was chunky. And ugly.

Rummaging in the cabinet, Millie couldn't believe that for someone who considered herself ultra-well organized, she had such a chaotic kitchen. Of course, organization was easier when it was business-related. She pushed a box of microwave popcorn aside, wondering if she'd stuck the spaghetti behind it. No. She found a can of spiced peaches and pulled it toward the front so she would remember to eat it for breakfast the next day. Ridiculous. Here she was, almost half a century old, and eating canned peaches for breakfast because she couldn't think of anything better. Her cigarette didn't taste so good, not that anything did anymore, so she heaved it out the back door into the butt-bucket. One good thing about smoking, she thought. Food didn't taste good. Easy to keep that weight off.

Shuffling things around, she piled a couple of pairs of rubber gloves on top of the popcorn box, shifted the canola oil over to the side of the cabinet, wondering as she did so what the hell a canola was. She stuffed a bag of solidified brown sugar into a box with some packages of green peas and black-eyed peas and dried lentils. Why she ever bought that healthy junk, she'd never know. She'd get to thinking she could enjoy cooking if she'd just do some simple things. What could be simpler than pea soup? But there the little plastic bag still sat, filled to the bursting point with those self-satisfied-looking little flat half-peas. Millie's hand hovered over the bag, snatched it up, and heaved it into the garbage can. That felt better.

Finally she pulled out a box of instant rice, then wandered over to the fridge to see what she could find to put together quickly. She'd already eaten the quiche she bought last week. There was some dip and a cheesecake, and two small containers of potato salad, one with mustard and one without. Big deal. Where was the egg carton? Thank goodness there was a deli in the grocery store. Millie hated cooking. Scrambled eggs were her limit. Anything else had to be eaten cold, heated up or ordered.

She'd seen a poster once that said *You Are What You Eat*. Ridiculous. If she was what she ate, she'd be two-thirds stuffed in a plastic container and sitting on a deli shelf.

The other third was what she ate at the Landing's restaurant. Not bad food, but it didn't seem to taste as good as it used to. Maybe she was just used to it.

Today, though, she was unwilling to sit there at her table for one. Her fancy table for one. What did she have to show for her life?

This wasn't like her. Not at all.

She'd let Linda Finney get away with snacking on the job this afternoon. Why did she let it pass? Oh, nothing made any sense any more.

She had figured on working for a year or two after college and then going back for an advanced degree, but the year or two kept on stretching out longer and longer. She knew her ship would come in one day, but in the meantime, she was tired of going nowhere.

She found the egg carton, adhered to the back of the top shelf. No telling how old these eggs are, she thought. After cramming the rice back into the cabinet, Millie broke three eggs into a pan and whipped the dickens out of them. Tomorrow she'd move Sally to the day shift and put that trouble-maker Linda Finney on the evening shift, starting Monday. No, she'd start her the following week. Give her seven extra days to stew about it.

* * * * * *

From the *Keagan County Record*
Wednesday April 24, 1996
Myrtle's Musings from Martinsville

All of my news is good this week. It's nice when digging in a cemetery is a happy event. Martinsville has been refurbishing the stone column that was erected in honor of the town's founder, Homer Martin, and two of his great-grandsons, both of whom were killed in the tragic fire of 1814 that destroyed the first church building in town. Fortunately, the stone wall that surrounds the small plot where Homer, his wife, and the two boys are buried, did not have to be disturbed. Now the stone column is standing straight and tall again on a solid concrete footing, thanks to the efforts of the men of the town, headed by Hubbard Martin, the Chairman of our Town Council and a direct descendent of Homer Martin.

Hubbard said the concrete should keep the column in its place. "We almost lost it thirty years ago, when my father Leon Martin was chairman," he told the assembled workers. "This time," he added, "it should stand for a century or more."

* * * * * *

Chapter 10

Thursday April 25, 1996 - Savannah

What a lousy week this had been. The light was blinking on the thin woman's answering machine when she finally got home. Nobody ever called her, unless it was somebody from work. It wasn't like she had any friends. She took a moment to peel off her black linen jacket. Before she stepped into her bedroom, she pushed the button with the blinking light.

"Brenda? You'll never guess who this is," came the voice through the metallic filter of the machine's innards.

"You're right. I'll never guess," she growled at the machine as it parroted the woman taking a deep audible breath.

"This is your little cousin Margaret, remember? From Martinsville?"

Oh my lord, how did she ever find me? she thought.

"Well, I'm going to be in your area on Sunday, and I wanted to see you. It doesn't have to be a long visit if you don't have the time, but there's a lot to catch up on. . . ."

Nothing I'm interested in finding out about.

"You know. All the news from Martinsville . . ."

As if I cared.

"And I want to hear all about your exciting life in Savannah."

Exciting. Right.

"I have to go to a wedding here on Saturday, so I can't be out of here any earlier than Sunday. If it's okay with you I'll leave real early Sunday, around five o'clock in the morning, and I should reach Savannah by early after. . ." BEEP.

The second message said, "It's me again. Your machine cut me off. I'll call you back this evening so we can arrange a time. My schedule is pretty clear. Well, truly I don't have a schedule, so you just let me know when you want me to come, and I'll be there. I have something, . . ." The voice changed to a deeper tone. ". . . really important to tell you about. I don't think you're going to like it, but it's important for you to know."

Brenda looked at the machine as it clicked off. This was not a welcome turn. What could that skinny little kid have to tell her that she wasn't going to like? The last time she'd seen her was at the funeral, when Margaret got the Model J and the trust fund that amounted to a minor fortune.

The last person she wanted to see was cousin Margaret. Rich cousin Margaret.

But curiosity got the better of her, and when Margaret called around 8:30, she arranged for a visit on Sunday afternoon. "Come after lunch. I'll be here." She gave directions to her young cousin and listened to some rhapsodic exclamations of excitement.

It did occur to her a couple of hours later, as she was drifting off to sleep, that her skinny little cousin wasn't so young anymore. It had been thirty years or so since the funeral, so little Margaret would be almost middle-aged. Hard to fathom.

The day after that funeral, Brenda had left home to go back to the summer session at college, and the last time she'd seen her mother was the next Thanksgiving, when her mother told her she was marrying that awful Conrad Robeson, who limped around all the time and had wormed his way into her father's confidence. Marry him? Mother? What a disgusting idea. She could remember the fatuous, misty-eyed look her mother had. It was revolting, how anybody that old could get all goo-goo over someone who'd taken over the company that should have been hers. Hers.

The only good thing Conrad Robeson had done as far as she was concerned was he'd gotten that gorgon Estelle Placings to retire. Estelle had never paid any attention to her. She was always too busy doing for Daddy. Estelle was Daddy's right hand. Estelle could do no wrong. He depended on Estelle. Estelle ran the office. Estelle knew what he was thinking. Estelle could always anticipate what he needed.

She remembered seeing Estelle looking at Daddy with *that look* on her hatchet face. The same look Mother had over Conrad. She hated Estelle. She was glad Conrad had gotten rid of her.

But then he hired back Uncle Marcus after all those years. That was exactly what Daddy didn't want him to do. And he'd dropped some of the most lucrative overseas sweatshops. Who cared who made the underwear, as long as it brought in the most profit? But no, not the almighty Conrad.

Brenda had felt so angry she could hardly spit out the words. "Choose between us, Mother," she had said. "It's him or me."

It was him. She hadn't gone to the wedding, and she hadn't been home since.

* * * * * *

"You, my red-faced wife," said Bull Finney, "are simply going to have to settle down. I know you're madder than a wet hen about being moved to the evening shift, but at least you won't be working weekends any more. Maybe you could talk to Barry Murphy."

"Ha! Don't even think about it. If Ms. Schnozz caught me going over her head, she'd fire me in a heartbeat, and then where would we be? You think anybody would hire a fifty-six year old woman who's been working as a desk clerk all these years?"

"Quit saying that. I can support us fine without your help."

"Then why do you always get upset when I talk about quitting?"

"Because you need something to keep you busy."

"You think I didn't keep busy enough raising three kids and working too?"

"They're out of high school, for Pete's sake."

Linda's hands were on her hips, and her lower lip trembled as she said, "Here we go again. You sound like my mother. She's so proud of working for twenty-five stupid years, but she was never there when we came home from school. Instead she handed us off to be raised by Grandma without even thinking twice about it."

"You two turned out okay. You married the best guy in Savannah. And Diane married the second best."

"Bull, quit joking. I love that hotel. I want it to bloom the way it used to be years ago. But Schnozz and Barry between them have a strangle-hold on it. And there's nothing I can do about it. I feel so frustrated about the whole thing. They've got me working the front desk when I used to be in line for manager until Schnozz came along. I don't want to work evenings, and I hate Millie Cappell."

"Why didn't you quit when Millie was hired? You already hated her."

He was right. Linda had disliked that woman from the moment they first met at the church bazaar, when Millie had refused to donate even one red copper cent to the Ladies Auxiliary. She'd turned that nose of hers up in the air and said, "I've always thought women should make their own way in life rather than being mere auxiliaries to their husbands." Linda felt her blood pressure go up just thinking about it.

"So," Bull's usually loud voice lowered a fraction, and he went back to his question. "Why don't you just go on to work and quit beefing about it? Tell you what. I'll pick you up after work on Monday and we'll go out to dinner."

Just when Linda was really fed up with this man, he'd go and do something nice like this. She blew her own over-sized nose and settled down a peg. But she still hated Millie Cappell.

Chapter 11

Friday April 26, 1996 - Savannah

As I am approaching the steps of the River Landing Hotel, I see someone drive up who looks so much like my father it almost stops my heart. The pain flows over me. I stand still. I cannot move. He stops the car and a woman gets out. She works at the Landing. I see her often. I want to see more of him. I wonder if he would sound like *Him* if he spoke to me.

* * * * * *

Linda closed the car door with a gentle thud. "Thanks for the ride, Bull," She leaned down and looked at him through the open window. "My car should be ready by the time I'm off work. Will you remember to come get me this time?"

"Yeah, yeah. I'll remember. Don't rub it in." His indignation boomed out for all to hear. "I forget once, and it's a capital case."

"Bull, it's not a capital case. I simply want you to pick me up so I can get my car."

Since she didn't receive any answer as the car pulled away from the curb, Linda shrugged and clutched her purse closer to her chest. Life wasn't much fun lately. There were so many little prickles between the two of them. What happened to the easy camaraderie they used to have together when they were young? Before they were married. He should have been my brother, she thought. That way we might have stayed friends.

Linda wasn't paying much attention to which way she was headed, and she bumped into a woman who wasn't watching where *she* was going either. Linda dropped her purse and had to scramble to grab her lipstick before it rolled into the grass. The woman, dressed all in black, didn't offer to help. She just stood there staring off into the distance, and tapping her finger idly on her tape recorder. Funny thing to cart around, Linda thought. Don't people on vacation always carry cameras?

There was a really skinny-looking woman just standing there, too, blocking the walkway, and Linda had to step onto the grass to get around her. She'd seen that woman hanging around a lot recently. She wasn't staying at the Landing. Oh well, it's no crime to stand around on a sidewalk.

Thank goodness I'm not late. She breathed a big sigh. That monster Millie Cappell was standing at the front door looking at her watch.

* * * * * *

Atlanta

Derry Murphy had been looking forward to this. She pushed a stray lock of her shoulder-length blond hair back behind her left ear as she pulled the white envelope from the file folder. The instructions on the sealed envelope were quite precise. Derry wondered what all the hooplah was about, but she knew that this client, long-since dead, was still responsible for a large amount of income for the firm. The legal firm of Scroop Grey & Cambridge had been managing various trust funds for Peter Holvers' estate for over three decades. His will had specified that this sealed envelope was to be held until *April 26, 1996* it said. And *Open at 3:00 p.m.* it said.

As she reviewed the file, she was surprised that a senior partner wasn't handling it, simply because of the amounts of money involved,

This directive seemed fairly straightforward. Derry made notes on a yellow legal pad. She had always enjoyed pads of yellow paper, and had not been particularly surprised, but rather had been gratified, to read a study that proved people were more likely to remember words written on yellow paper, rather than on white.

Well, this would be easy to remember, she thought. The papers in the envelope named Peter Holvers' heir, *the only child of my body,* and directed that Scroop Grey & Cambridge set up a meeting with said heir. The heir was to be contacted first by phone. No specific amounts were to be mentioned at that time. Next the heir was to be notified by letter on April 29th of the terms of the inheritance (text included in the directive). Finally, Scroop Grey & Cambridge was to meet in person with the heir on April 30, 1996, to disclose the amounts involved. The large amounts, thought Derry. The payout was to begin on May 5, 1996, which would have been the 94th birthday of the deceased. If he had lived. It seemed to Derry to be an elaborate way of yanking the heir's chain. Who would make a loved one wait more than three decades for an inheritance? But a directive was a directive.

She buzzed her secretary. "Betsy, I need to reach the Holvers heir." Giving the name and last known address, details that were in the directive, Derry settled back with another file, expecting a long wait. She was right. It was half an hour before her phone rang.

"I have the party you requested, Ms. Murphy."

"Thank you, Betsy. You're a wonderful help." The gentle click let her know that the heir was on the line.

After a bit of explanation, Derry arranged to meet the heir on the following Tuesday, April 30th at 3:30 p.m. "I'll send you a letter explaining the terms." She held the receiver away from her ear a bit. Heirs tended to become excited. "You will receive my letter before I arrive on April 30th. Please read it carefully and jot down any questions you may have."

Derry said a cordial good-bye and hung up the phone. Lifting the directive and looking at it again before she started composing the required letter, she wondered what on earth Peter Holvers had in mind when he wrote "if anyone else claims to be a child of my body and therefore my heir, run a blood test."

Chapter 12

Saturday April 27, 1996 - Martinsville

Glaze McKee," she said to herself in the front hall mirror, "you did a great job today, and now you deserve a bowl of ice cream." As if she needed it, after that big piece of wedding cake she'd eaten. It was a delightful day. And she was so glad it was over.

Biscuit and Bob had been the first to drive away of course, in a flurry of good wishes and bubbles and bird seed. The party kept going, though, as people flowed from group to group talking happily about the fun of this extraordinary wedding. Marmalade's part in it had generated quite a few laughs.

What was so funny?

Finally, though, everyone had left and Mrs. Sheffield, mother of the middle-aged groom, had quietly set to work tidying up the living room and the porch, and everything else in sight. Biscuit's kids and grandkids left in a noisy bustle. And of course, Tom Parkman and his catering crew dealt with all the food leavings. He offered to stick around and keep Glaze company, but all she wanted was some quiet time to herself. Well, herself and Marmalade.

Thank you.

She glanced down at the sweetest cat she'd ever known. Marmy was the only cat she'd ever known, but Glaze was sure she was the sweetest anyway. Marmalade purred back at her and twisted her head to rub it against Glaze's shin.

It was only a few steps to the big old kitchen, but Glaze's ankle, the one she had sprained, was aching by the time she completed the short journey. Grabbing up a small carton of French vanilla ice cream and a spoon, Glaze hobbled out onto the side porch where the swing creaked gently in a warm breeze. "A bite for me, a nibble for Marmalade; a bite for me, a nibble for . . . Don't you want any more, Marmalade?"

That is enough for me. Thank you. I cannot brush my teeth.

". . . Suit yourself. It's probably not good for you, and there's not much left anyway. We finished most of it up the day I got here." Was that really only a week and a half ago? Seemed like forever. Seemed like no time at all.

Marmalade settled into Glaze's lap while Glaze ate the last few bites. She stuck the lid back on the carton and set it off to one side, twisted herself sideways and raised her legs onto the swing, then settled more carefully against the comfy cushions.

"It was a good wedding, wasn't it?"

Yes.

"I hope they enjoy their honeymoon."

I am sure they will.

"Oh, Marmalade, what am I going to do?"

I do not understand why you are not happy, but I will do my best to comfort you.

Glaze raised Marmalade's purring little body up to her shoulder and burrowed her face in the soft fur. And cried.

* * * * * *

Savannah

Colly and Patch Sloan were all set to head back toward their favorite table, the one back in the corner of the Yellow Moon Restaurant. As they walked in the door, however, a rousing burst of singing, more enthusiastic than musical, stopped them on the threshold. Patch wound his arm firmly around her back.

"You were in on this, you stinker," she hissed at him.

"Your indignation is not convincing, my lady. There's a suspicious upturning at the corners of your mouth."

"I give up," she grinned, and plowed through the happy throng who were singing an upbeat, double-time version of *Happy Birthday to You*, complete with sound effects from what looked to Colly to be some leftover New Year's Eve noisemakers.

"Don't blame the song on me," Patch said as the song ended and they wove between the tables. "It was probably Brando's idea. Looks like he talked everybody else in the restaurant into singing along."

Colly looked ahead of her and saw Brando Williston sitting with his wife, Diane, at the corner table. Colly liked Diane's solid good sense. Colly never wanted to be in a hospital, but if she had to be, she wanted Diane taking care of her. "What's Diane doin' here? She works the evenin' shift."

Patch, who must have been planning this surprise party for some time, said, "She traded with another nurse. She gets off tonight and she has to work the night shift on Monday."

As they continued making their way between the yellow-and-white-checkered tablecloths of the Yellow Moon, Colly recognized some of the people she passed. They lived on her beat. She gave a high five to old Mr. Higgins, who was sitting near the door, and lifted her hand to wave at Mary and Eugenia Crabb, the two sisters who happened to be Mr. Higgins' next door neighbors. She nodded at Ms. Cappell, the manager of the River Landing Hotel, who was sitting alone, and frowned a bit when she saw a solitary woman, dressed all in black, perched at one of the small round single-seater tables. There was a tape recorder on the table beside her. Colly remembered having seen her in the park two days ago, just sitting on a bench. She'd been holding the tape recorder then, too. Funny thing to carry along on vacation. She wished she had talked to her in the park, but she was in a hurry at the time. And this, Colly thought, is probably not the time to approach her either–at my birthday party. If I see her there again tomorrow, I'll ask her what she's up to.

Colly paused as she passed the table where Peter Finney, the carpenter, was sitting with two women. One was probably his wife. The other woman, who had improbably black hair, was old enough to be his mother. She had the kind of face that didn't invite confidences. Built-in frown lines. Finney was the carpenter who was fixing up Miss Witherspoon's front porch. He'd told her he'd be happy to testify that he'd heard that dog yowling all that morning. There was something about that man that she didn't like, though. Nothing she could put her finger on. Just felt like something was off. Maybe it was his black hair slicked straight back with no part. Her mama had always told her you can't trust a man who doesn't part his hair.

Patch nudged her gently, so she moved on, passing by an emaciated-looking woman at the next table, who sat by herself. Quite a night for singles, Colly thought.

When she got to her own table, Colly turned and bowed to the room before reaching to accept the glass of beer Brando handed her.

"What happened to you, partner?" she asked, as she noticed the big bandage on his left index finger. "Looks like you got put through a wringer."

"I was playing tug-of-war with Knucklehead, and he chomped a little too far up the rope."

"When are you goin' to train that mutt to catch criminals instead of harming Southeast Georgia's finest? I'll have to swear out a warrant if he gets too rambunctious."

"Can she really arrest a dog?" Diane asked her husband.

Brando patted her hand. "No, don't worry, hon."

Colly winked at Diane. "It sure would be temptin' to try."

"Leave my dog out of this," Brando objected.

"You're the one who accused him of assault and battery, partner. But, just to show you what a good sport I am, I promise to let your dog maul you any way it chooses." Turning to Patch, she said, "I think you ought to show him your wound. The two of you look like twins."

Patch held up his right hand. The index finger was sporting an impressive-sized gauze creation. "You've got me beat on that one," Brando admitted. "What happened? Did our Officer Colly clop you with her nightstick?"

"No, I was repairing a computer at work and had to crawl under the desk to get at the wiring. Somebody had broken a glass and hadn't swept up all the pieces."

"You're kidding," Diane chimed in. "Almost the same thing happened to me yesterday, only I was the one who broke something. I dropped a bowl. Stupid me. I knelt down to clean it up, and a sharp piece of it sliced my knee." As she was speaking, she stood up, lifted her skirt a few inches and revealed a large white lump that showed where a bandage lurked underneath her stockings.

"This is bizarre," Colly said. "We're all injured. I was trimmin' my nails this mornin', and I clipped a little too close. I have some gauze around my big toe."

Brando threw up his hands in alarm. "Please, please, don't show it to us," he wailed.

"Behave yourself, partner, or I'm gonna fire you."

"We could call ourselves the Society of Sores," said Patch.

Diane spoke up. "Or the Bandage Band."

"How about the Bloody Brigade?" Colly offered.

"Yes!" the others chorused.

One of the women sitting at the neighboring table with the carpenter laughed and held up her left pinky finger. It looked like a bulky white lollipop. "Can I join your group?" she asked. "I fell off the stool in my kitchen this morning and jammed my fingernail against the counter."

Diane laughed and motioned to the woman. "Come on over here and meet my friends. Linda, this is Colly and Patch Sloan. Colly and Brando are teamed up now. This is my sister, Linda Finney. I call her Shorty, but nobody else better do that or she'll get mad."

Once Linda stopped sticking her tongue out at her sister, and laughing as she did it, Patch reached out to shake Linda's hand. "Consider yourself a full-fledged member. We collect no dues, there are no mandatory meetings or membership lists, and the only requirement is a bloodied badge of courage."

"In that case," the woman said, "my husband can join too." Turning to the man and woman still sitting at the nearby table, she said, "you two come on over here and meet Diane's friends. And show them your arm, Bull."

Shaking his head, the man stood up, rolling his sleeve up over a muscular forearm. "Come on Ma," he said in a booming voice to the elderly woman who was still seated. "We've been summoned." As they walked the few steps to Colly's table, he revealed a small patch covering the inside of his elbow.

"Drug user?" Patch said, with a laugh that took the insult out of the question.

The man shook his head. "Blood donor. I give twice a month."

"I thought it was every eight weeks," Colly said quietly as an aside to Patch.

"You're right," he told her, just as quietly. "It's every fifty-six days."

The woman Finney had called Ma nodded her head at Colly and the rest. "I'm Estelle," she said. She went on to explain, rather proudly Colly thought, that Bull could donate that often because he gave platelets. "He has the rarest blood type." For such an old lady, Estelle had a surprisingly strong voice.

The man looked around at the people from nearby tables, who were listening to Estelle's broadcast of his medical details. Colly noticed that he flexed the muscles of his shoulder before he said, "It's nothing at all. Just a few needles and a big machine. They take the blood out of one arm and spin out the platelets. . ."

That was the last thing Colly wanted to hear. To the left of his elbow she could see the Crabb sisters turning a little green. The woman in black, the one with the tape recorder, seemed to be trans-fixed by his loud voice. Colly raised her own voice and interrupted. "It's my birthday party, and I suggest we change the subject." Colly felt Patch's hand on her shoulder, and she softened her tone a shade. "Well, you're all three welcome to some of the birthday cake that I'm assumin' these jokers are goin' to give me after we eat dinner. And I thought your name was Peter. Why does she call you Bull?"

"It's an inside joke. My middle name is Angus."

"Hey," Patch said, "that's almost as good as my middle name. It's Seuliman."

"Soolyman? Patch Soolyman Sloan?"

"Go ahead and laugh, Diane. Patrick Seuliman Sloan. It was my grandma's idea. She thought it sounded like a doctor, which I didn't become. It was hard getting through high school once kids found out."

"Why'd you ever tell them?" Diane asked.

"I didn't. I had one teacher in tenth grade who called out everybody's full name the first day of class. It was all over after that."

Colly noticed the scrawny-looking single woman again. She was still watching them from her nearby table. They were putting on quite a show for the whole room. She turned back to Bull. "Are you a Scot?"

"Don't think so, why?"

"Angus sounds pretty Scottish."

"My mom told me she named me for an old friend of hers."

"What kind of friend?" Patch was leering as he asked, so Colly poked him with her elbow.

"Not that kind," Bull objected. "Put your eyebrows down. She's my mother for heaven's sake."

Colly wondered why Estelle didn't object to the joke, but when she asked Patch later that evening, he told her that Estelle was Linda and Diane's mother, not Bull's.

"How'd you know that?"

"I was talking with Brando the other day, and he said something about he was glad Diane's mother lived with Linda and Bull instead of him and Diane."

When the dinner was over and the plates were cleared, everyone shifted so Linda and Bull and Estelle could squeeze their chairs in. There was, indeed, a big birthday cake, topped with a little blue plastic car. "Happy 75th Birthday to our Friendly Pop," said the meticulous icing script across the face of the sheet cake.

"And what in the ever-lovin' heck is that supposed to mean?" asked Colly with a pointed glare at her husband and friends.

"Oh phooey, phooey, phooey!" Diane spluttered. "I wrote out what I wanted. Happy 35th Birthday to our Favorite Cop."

Brando leaned forward and spoke in a stage-whisper. "You know your handwriting is nothing but a bunch of chicken-scratching. It's a good thing I didn't ask her to marry me in a letter, because the reply would have looked like gup, gup, gup, instead of yes, yes, yes."

Patch glanced over at Colly, who was rolling her eyes at him and shaking her head. "Let's cut it up real fast so nobody will see it."

"At least they wrote Birthday instead of Anniversary," Colly said as she began the cutting job. They ended up asking for a stack of small plates and offering cake to everybody in the restaurant, delivering little icing-topped squares to each table. Later, as people were leaving, most of them came by once more to wish Colly a happy birthday. The Crabb sisters insisted that she come by some time next week for a cup of tea. Colly thanked them sweetly and said she just might find time to do that. Then Old Mr. Higgins told her how much he appreciated all the fine service the men in blue . . . "Well," he said, "that is to say, the men and, uh, the women . . . in blue . . . do."

Once Mr. Higgins was out of earshot, Patch turned to Colly and crooned, "When the blue do / what the blue do / well then you do / the dooby-doo doo."

As they began to tone down the volume a bit, Millie Cappell stood and came over to add her good wishes to the others. "I couldn't help overhearing your conversation about the bandage club," she said. "I wish I could join, but I haven't been in to give my monthly blood donation yet, so I don't have any wounds. " Turning around to face Linda's husband, she said, "So you're a platelet donor?"

Bull straightened up again and sucked in his stomach. Colly saw Linda clench her teeth as Estelle spoke up. "Yes. He's AB negative. Very rare."

Millie ignored both the women. Turning back to Colly, she wished her many happy returns, and left.

"What does that mean, anyway? Many happy returns?" asked Colly. "I've always wondered."

"It means," Patch half-sang, "that whatever the blue do, it keeps on coming back."

"Let's get this guy home before we have to fire him from the Bloody Brigade," said his wife.

* * * * * *

I followed him to this restaurant. He did not look behind him. He does not know I am here. I take a chance and sit at a small table close to him, so I can watch him and hear his voice. He has so many of the gestures I remember. He has the same sweep of black hair that he brushes straight back from his forehead.

He is with his wife. I know her. I do not like her. And there is another woman with him. I recognize her face. I see her look over at me as I sit down, and I am sure she does not know who I am. Have I changed that much? Why should she recognize me now, though, when she never paid me any attention before? Even at his funeral, she was all wrapped up in her own concerns. And He left her a lot of money. Now she is old and even uglier than before.

His voice has the same quality as my father's voice. He calls the other woman "Ma." Ah, so that is who she is to him. Is that possible? I cannot tell how old he is, but it could be. She was so close to *Him*. She took it as her job to keep *Him* happy. There are many ways to do that.

Now I am sure. His name is the same as *His*. She named him after *Him*. I hear them laughing. I hear that his blood type is rare. He looks like my father. He is named for my father. His blood type is the same as my father's. So is his voice. She is responsible. I will kill her son. He is a danger to me. He is a child of my father's body. I hate her for doing that to me. After I kill him, I will kill her.

Chapter 13

Sunday April 28, 1996 - Martinsville

The phone was louder than Glaze expected. Not that she had expected it to ring at all. Who'd be calling on Sunday morning?

She cleared her voice and said a few tentative words before picking up the phone. "Hello?"

Tom's voice sounded amused. "Good morning, sleepyhead. Did I call too early?"

Yes. Smellsweet was still asleep. I was merely resting my eyes so I would not disturb her.

"No, I always yawn like this when I answer a phone."

"Would you like some breakfast? I'd be happy to whip up a little omelette for the best man and the maid of honor."

I enjoy eggs, too.

Glaze stifled another yawn. "I'm not awake yet, and you want me to think about food?"

"What else would a professional chef and restaurateur expect?"

"Quit laughing at me. Give me half an hour to get myself decent."

"See you at 8:30, then. We can eat and I'll drive you to church. . . ."

Church? He expected her to go to church?

". . . Hello? Are you still there?"

"Oh, sure, Tom. I'm not thinking too clearly yet. Okay. I'll have some coffee ready when you get here."

The coffee wasn't ready yet. In fact, Glaze was picking her way downstairs on an ankle that hurt more than she expected, when Tom knocked on the front door. Of course, he installed Glaze in one of the yellow chintz-covered chairs at the big old table in the kitchen, made the coffee himself, and produced a vegetable omelette that was worth drooling over.

Yes, but I do not drool.

* * * * * *

ANNOUNCEMENTS FOR THE WEEK OF
APRIL 28, 1996

The church trustees have decided to hire someone to be in charge of the sign board outside the font of the church! Supplicants should talk to Ralph or Hubbard, and they'll tell you what to do!

Our Church was the scene of a restive ceremony of marriage yesterday! We extend our congratulations and our prayers for a long and happy marriage to our dear parishioners, Bob and Biscuit Sheffield!

Our 42nd Annual Clean-Up Day is coming soon. Saturday, May 18th. Plan to come early! Bring rakes and good garden gloves! Some lawn bags would be a help, too, because we have a lot of broken branches from that last big thunderstorm! Margot and Hans are supplying their hasty doughnuts for the workers, and we'll have plenty of coffee on hand! Come be a part of the fun!

Glaze couldn't help herself. She slipped a pen out of her purse and started making corrections. "That's the front of the church, not the font," she muttered to herself.

"What was that?" Tom asked as Sadie Masters settled in beside him on the narrow pew, smoothed the lap of her yellow dress, and looked at her own bulletin.

Glaze held up the announcement page so Tom could see the circled words. "It should be festive, not restive. And Biscuit kept her maiden name. And what on earth are hasty doughnuts?"

Tom was used to the creative spellings of the weekly announcements. "When they got a computer with a spell checker on it, they forgot how to edit. Those are tasty doughnuts. Tasty."

Glaze kept marking. "What's with all these exclamation points?"

Sadie leaned across Tom and pointed to another word. "It should be applicants, dear. We always have fun seeing what Sophia has come up with."

"Is it always this bad?"

Sadie leaned across Tom again and patted Glaze on the knee. "No dear. Sometimes it's much worse."

The piano increased its volume as Reverend Pursey walked in from the side and stepped up behind the podium. "Let us raise our voices in praise with hymn #42 "A Mighty Fortress is Our God." Glaze had already noticed that the bulletin said "A Mighty Buttress . . ."

They left the church after the final hymn, listed in the bulletin as "Oh God, Our Hep in Ages Passed." Tom helped Glaze into the car. "I like this seat cover," she told him. "It's soft and cushiony and comfortable."

"Glad you like it because you're going to be sitting there quite a while."

"Oh?"

"We're going for a little ride to look at springtime." Spring had always been Glaze's favorite time of year. Although she never paid much attention to what bushes were planted around the towns up and down the Metoochie River valley, she thoroughly enjoyed their springtime display.

Tom took a circuitous route around the upper streets of the little town, giving Glaze a chance to see all the azaleas and dogwoods. "They blossomed later than usual this year," he told her. "It must have been the drought." After the Martinsville tour, he headed up to Braetonburg and Hastings, on through Garner Creek and into Russell Gap. At the crossroads, he headed away from the river. The road wound through wooded hills where redbuds and wild cherry trees were floating in the landscape, pink and white clouds that had settled between the taller pine trees. By the time they reached the next set of towns, Glaze had pretty much forgotten about her sore ankle. And when they stopped for a Sunday afternoon milkshake at a roadside diner, she hadn't a care in the world.

But when Tom looked at her before proposing a toast to the best best man he'd ever seen, Glaze crashed right back into her slump. What on earth was she thinking? This would never work.

* * * * * *

Larry Murphy hated the old house. It had been his inheritance as the oldest son and the only one of the eight Murphy kids who wanted the old hulk. Oh sure, he'd taken care of his dad through that last illness. Well, he hadn't exactly done all the caring. He'd left that to some of the neighbor women who were real suckers when it came to sick people. But he'd paid the bills. Well, he'd paid for groceries when he had to. Which wasn't often. Most of those women walked in the door with food in hand. Wasn't that what women were good for? And, he thought, he had paid Marvin Axelrod an arm and a leg–yes, an arm and a leg–to come haul off the body after it was all over.

Larry gave an extra swipe with the old broom he used for cleaning up his barber shop floor. Nothing worse than a dirty barber shop. Floor was spotless. Chair was always in good repair. Counters were clean and tidy. Scissors were just so. It paid to take care of your investment. Larry always said so to anybody who would listen. You got 'em in the chair and you could talk all you wanted to and they couldn't do a darn thing about it.

As he straightened up, Larry glanced out through the wavy glass of the barber shop window. Drat it! Those pesky Irish Shepherds were at it again, frisking around his azaleas. Yesterday they bounded across one of the bushes and broke some of the stems. Larry hated dogs. There was one of those Labrador Receivers from up the street who peed on his hydrangea every time it walked by. He really hated that one. But these two Irish Shepherds were the worst. They ran right into his yard any time they felt like it. He was going to have to do something about them.

"Here, Big Red! Here, Little Red!" came a call from half a block away.

"Get outa here, you mangy curs! Out of my yard!" The broom made a good enough weapon as he rushed the two long-haired dogs, who simply bounded away from him and raced back up Maple Street, responding more to the voice of their human than to Larry's imprecations. Larry turned in disgust and noticed that more branches of his pink azalea had been broken off. He was reaching for one of them when it was snatched up by an orange and white cat who grabbed the little branch in its mouth and ducked under the hedge. "Come back, you thief! Get back here with my azalea!"

This was not Larry's day.

* * * * * *

Glaze enjoyed the afternoon anyway, and both her spirits and her smile revived soon after the milkshake. When Tom drove up in front of 213 Beechnut Lane, Glaze was looking forward to a hot cup of tea and a nice relaxing hour in the swing with Marmalade.

Marmalade, though, was perched, yowling, on a high branch of the Leyland Cypress tree, while a short, skinny man stood at the base of the tree and hollered up at her. Tom bounded from the car without even bothering to help Glaze out.

"What the tarnation are you doing to that cat, Larry? You leave her alone!"

Larry folded his arms across his concave chest and pulled himself up to his full five and a half feet. "Don't you go yelling at me, Tom Parkman. This cat is a nuisance and a thief, and I intend to stop it from happening again."

"Thief? What do you mean, a thief? That cat couldn't steal anything. . . ."

Yes I could.

Tom paused as an indignant meow came from the cypress tree. ". . . she's only the size of a postage stamp."

"He's big enough to pilfer my bushes."

Glaze, who had managed to extricate herself and her ankle from the soft front seat of Tom's Volvo, walked up beside Tom. "What on earth are you talking about?"

"He broke my azalea bush . . ."

No I did not. The Irish Setters broke it.

". . . and stole one of the branches. The proof is right here." Larry held up a six-inch long stem with a few bright spring-green leaves and a splayed-out bunch of funnel-shaped flowers at the end. "See this? He stole it right out of my yard. I saw him, and I don't want it to happen again."

"Larry," Tom said as he stepped forward and peered down his nose at the barber, "you are the biggest crock of bull I ever saw. Get out of this yard and don't come back. And leave that cat alone from now on."

"You just see that he leaves me alone, you, you . . ." He paused as if searching for the worst insult he could think of on the spur of the moment. ". . . You chef!"

Glaze looked up at Tom. Tom looked at Glaze. And they both burst out laughing.

Once Larry was well out of the yard, Marmalade calmly jumped into Tom's outstretched arms. He carried her into the house in triumph.

Savannah

I watched Margaret Casperson as she padded out of the hotel lobby. Small world. Travel all the way from Martinsville to Savannah and run into a neighbor. Dear old Margaret. She had the most comfortable face, and such a peaceful way about her. There always seemed to be a bubble of laughter under the surface, too. Part of me knew that I was older than she was, but she seemed so happily placid, it was hard to think of her as anything but old, rather like a cow that was ready to be milked or an elephant about to have a baby. This was ridiculous–how would I know what a pregnant elephant was like?

She is a kind lady. She gives me saucers of milk when I visit her.

Her feet must hurt her. I bet that's why she walks the way she does. I hope she enjoys her visit with Brenda. I could hear Bob behind me at the River Landing's front desk, explaining that we had a reservation. For the bridal suite. At my age!

I was watching the beveled glass door close behind Margaret's ample rear end. I wondered for a moment what I looked like from the back. But then Bob was there, gently taking my arm and saying, "This way, woman." We shared the elevator with two other couples. After we all turned to face the front, I told Bob what Margaret had said and asked him if he knew much about Brenda.

"Not much," he said as the elevator door creaked and groaned and stuttered its way closed. I sincerely hoped we weren't going to get stuck. They should have oiled that door.

"I know Brenda turned her back on her family years ago. Her Aunt Monica was pretty mad at her from what I've heard for not going to the wedding when her mother married Conrad."

The woman standing in front of me cocked an ear our way. I could imagine her trying to figure out what the heck we were talking about. People who eavesdrop have to take their chances.

"So you didn't know her well?" I asked him, trying to ignore how slowly the elevator was rising.

"Not at all. She stopped coming to see her grandmother when she was a little kid, maybe seven or eight. If Monica wanted to see her sister, she had to go to Atlanta to do it. That Brenda usually got her way. She always did have a mind of her own. Or so I remember. When she decided something, you couldn't talk her out of it. None of us missed her at all. But Margaret liked her for some reason."

"I think Margaret likes everybody," I ventured. Although I hadn't known Margaret long, just the year I'd been the Martinsville librarian, I was always struck by how kind she was. And how quietly happy she always seemed. The gift she'd given me at the surprise wedding shower the ladies of the town threw for me was a pair of big stone lions for the library. I was going to have them installed beside the front stairs. They must have come from one of her antiquing trips. I'd have to ask her the history of them the next time I saw her.

And then the elevator door opened, and the other people got off ahead of us and turned to the right. We went to the left, toward the bridal suite. I could feel a blush coming on.

* * * * * *

A rather chunky woman trundled up the walkway.

"Brenda?" The woman's voice was tentative. "Brenda, is that you?"

Brenda opened the door wider. "Of course it is."

"You've changed so much I wouldn't have recognized you."

Brenda thought she could just as easily have said the same thing to Margaret. Instead she said, "I've lost a lot of weight in the last thirty years, if that's what you mean. I believe in taking good care of myself." There was only the slightest emphasis on the word *I*.

After the usual dance of settling in, after the *what a cute house* and the *how have you been* and the *it's so good to see you again* routine, Margaret set her purse down beside the couch and walked over to the window that overlooked the small back lawn beside the oleander hedge. Underneath the hedge, there were banks of little purple flowers blooming.

"Those oleanders out there are about the only thing I see that I can identify," she said. "I learned that years ago in a biology class. I don't have a green thumb the way you must have, and I certainly don't garden." Glancing back over her shoulder, she asked, "Did you know they're poisonous? I mean those oleanders."

"Are they?"

"Yes. My old professor told us that you don't have to go to a botanical garden to find toxic plants. Look in your own back yard, he said. Almost every garden has rhododendrons, lily of the valley, azaleas, hydrangea, yew hedges. And oleanders down South. It's funny how I remember the names. I memorized them for a test. But I don't remember what they look like. Except the oleanders."

"Margaret," Brenda said, trying to keep the edge out of her voice. "Did you drive all the way from Martinsville to tell me that?"

"Of course not. I drove here to tell you something important."

Brenda clenched her teeth again and glared up at her cousin's back. "That's what you said on the phone. Why don't you just tell me and get it over with?"

"You're not going to like it much, but I had to say something. I had to let you know. And," she turned and walked back across the room. "I had to do it in person."

"Margaret, sit down and quit dithering."

Margaret sat and took a deep breath as she perched on the edge of the couch, facing Brenda across the little coffee table. "I found out something, Brenda. At first I thought you might be pretty inter-ested in it, but as I was driving here I realized you might not want to know." A deep wall of red washed upward over Margaret's wide and homely face. "But you had to know eventually, so I figured it would be better if I was the one who told you instead of someone else. I hope nobody ever finds out about this whole . . ."

There was a long silence. Brenda could hear a faucet dripping in the kitchen. She waited for Margaret to finish her sentence. When that didn't happen, Brenda stood up and walked over to the sink. She grasped the faucet handle and wrenched it to the right until there was no more drip. As she turned back to Margaret, she said, "Go ahead, cousin. I'm ready."

Margaret reached down and picked up her capacious purse. "You see, I found this letter in an old trunk that I bought in Atlanta a couple of years ago." She rummaged around as she spoke. "I couldn't believe it at first, but—well, here—I brought it for you to see." Marga-ret extracted several sheets of paper. She handed them across the coffee table to her cousin and sat back to wait while Brenda sat down and read it, every word. Twice.

"How long have you known about this?" Brenda forced her voice to sound almost conversational.

"I found the letter three weeks ago, but I was never going to say anything. I didn't think it would make any difference. And then, Mom mentioned that the payout of Uncle Peter's will is going to be next month. And she said that . . ."

Was the woman having hot flashes, Brenda thought. She was turning bright red again.

"Oh, Brenda, I don't want you to think I'm interested in the money. Uncle Peter left me so much with that huge trust fund, it's not like I need any extra. I always thought you'd get everything."

"What are you talking about?"

"Please don't go all tight-lipped like that. I'm talking about what Mom said. The wording of the will. Everybody always said he gave it all to you. But Mom told me he left everything to *the child or children of my body*. And, Brenda, . . ." She stopped for a moment, looking as if she were trying to gauge her cousin's mood. "I'm so sorry. I truly don't want the money. It seems right for you to get it, since you always thought he was your dad. And since I didn't know for a very long time that he was mine."

Brenda's eyes narrowed only a bit as she asked, "What are you saying?"

"Oh, I didn't want you to have to find out like this, but Uncle Peter was my father."

"He what?"

Margaret seemed to shrink somewhat as she hunched her shoulders forward. "He was my father."

Brenda sat up straighter. "Would you like to explain that outrageous statement? What was your mother doing playing around with my . . . my father?" Brenda couldn't think of what else to call him. Except bastard, but she wouldn't give Margaret the satisfaction.

"She wasn't! She wouldn't do that. He . . ." Her voice dropped to a raspy whisper. "He . . . raped . . . my . . . mother."

She wants my money, Brenda thought. That's what this is all about. "You don't know what you're talking about."

"Yes I do. It happened that time you had your big bike accident, and she never told him, so he didn't know. I was born nine and a half months later, so Mom thought I could have been my dad's daughter, but when I was in college we did a blood-type experiment, and there's no way I could have come from my dad. I thought maybe I was adopted. I cornered my mom and made her tell me the truth." Margaret was leaning so far forward she was in danger of falling off the chair.

"Does your mother know you came here to tell me this?"

"No. She thinks I'm off on another antique-buying binge. So does Sam."

"Does she know about the letter?"

Margaret studied her cousin's face, the cousin she had adored from childhood. Even though she hadn't seen her since the funeral in 1965 . . . My goodness, thirty years. How did that happen? . . . Even so, Margaret continued to hold a special child-like warmth in her heart for her elegant cousin.

Now the spare, almost bony woman looking at her from across the table, seemed strained. Well, of course she did. This was a terrible blow, to find out all this—it must be earth-shaking. Poor Brenda looked so miserable, Margaret didn't have the heart to embarrass her more. "No," she said. "I didn't tell anyone about it."

"You're sure?"

It was only a little lie. And it would make Brenda feel better. "Of course I'm sure. It's your private information."

Margaret watched Brenda glance out the front window, where the early afternoon sun was reflecting off Margaret's car parked at the end of the walkway. She felt relieved when Brenda spoke up. "Why don't we have some dessert?"

"Oh, I couldn't. I'm too hungry. I skipped lunch. If I don't have a real meal, I'll probably faint. I need to be on my way, anyway."

Brenda held up her hand. "Well then, stay for dinner. It's too late for you to head to Atlanta anyway. We can call around and find you a good place to stay."

"I've already checked in at the River Landing. It's not far from here. Do you know it?"

"Yes, isn't it the one just down the street? I've heard it's a nice place."

"Yes. I've got a lovely room on the top floor."

"So it's settled." Brenda looked down at her hands. Margaret noticed how steady they looked. Her own were shaking. She was so glad this was over. And so glad Brenda was okay about it.

Brenda stood up. "You sit here. I'll bring out some snacks, and then we'll eat dinner about 7:30. I would cook a big meal, but I never got around to grocery shopping this week. There's a great little place ten or fifteen miles up the river. We can eat there and then come back here for some cheesecake. That way we can both get to bed early tonight."

"Wouldn't it be easier to eat at the River Landing? They have a restaurant."

"It's no trouble. This other place is nice and quiet. In the meantime, how about a quick tour of the house and the yard? There's not a lot to see, so it won't take long."

"Oh, I'm so glad you're not angry about this."

"Angry? Why should I be angry? But I do expect you to give me half the money."

"Brenda, nobody knows about the letter, so you can have it all. I really mean that. The trust fund is enough for me. And anyway, you're like a big sister."

"Right," Brenda said.

As the two women walked around the tiny house, Margaret made a point of commenting with great enthusiasm about the furniture, the framed prints, the fresh flowers in containers of all sizes. The enthusiasm wasn't hard to produce. Margaret loved this little house.

Brenda identified the tiny sprigs of violets in shapely little bud vases. In the corners of each room, she had positioned white plant stands. Tall vases held huge sprays of red, white, and pink blossoms. Margaret ran her fingertips over the little funnel-shaped flowers.

"What are these, Brenda? They're beautiful."

Brenda looked at her cousin. "You really don't know what they are?"

"No. That's why I majored in English, not Botany. I can't tell one plant from another, except those oleanders out there."

Brenda nodded. She dropped her eyes to the pink-flowered spray. "These are the bush form of violets."

"Oh. That's nice."

When they stepped outside, Margaret took a quick moment to light up a cigarette. Some day she was going to quit. She walked around the tiny yard, delighting in the landscaping. She had never been a gardener, herself. Sam teased her sometimes that she couldn't tell a daffodil from a crabapple. All she really knew were the lists of poisonous plants that Dr. Bugg had made them learn. Oleanders and castor beans and those things they make rosaries with in some countries. Paternoster peas. Funny how she could remember strange bits of information after all these years.

Still, even if she didn't know what was planted here, she could tell when she liked the way a yard looked. And she liked this one. It was so small, it could have been only a hedged-in swath of grass, but there were flower beds tucked here and there, and mounds of those flowering bushes with the funnel-shaped blossoms. Already she'd forgotten the name. Bush something or other.

The overall effect was colorful and restful at the same time. Margaret reached out to touch some bright green leaves, but thought better of it when she noticed the long thorns on each branch. Could they be roses? Since they weren't blooming, she couldn't be sure. "Do you do all this yourself?" she asked.

"Yes, of course," Brenda said. Nodding in the direction of the thorny bushes, she added, "I planted all of these roses. They're beautiful when they're in bloom. All I do is prune and fertilize them, and spray them to kill the bugs. And then I get to cut fresh flowers to bring in and arrange."

"How do you ever find time, even for that?" asked Margaret, looking around for a discreet way to get rid of her cigarette butt. She always kept a bucket of sand next to the kitchen door at home.

"I keep to myself on my days off. I need a way to get away from my work. It would take over my life if I let it."

"Brenda, I didn't even ask you what kind of work you do. I'm so sorry. I guess I've just been thinking about myself."

"Oh that's okay. I work in management. Big company. High stress level. It's fascinating work." Brenda pointed toward a stubby white pot, with yellow and purple irises painted on it, tucked behind a bushy shrub. "Dump it in there."

"Even your butt-bucket is pretty," Margaret said. "Did you paint it yourself?"

"Yes, of course." Brenda walked over to the nearest flower bed and bent to pluck a few blossoms from the purple flowers that were growing at the edge. "Did you know these are edible?"

Margaret tossed her dying cigarette in the painted pot and listened to it sizzle, then took the little flower that Brenda was holding out. "Edible?"

"Violets are good to eat; didn't you know that? Try a little nibble. After dinner we'll have some flowers on our cheesecake."

Margaret raised one eyebrow, but then straightened her face with an effort and said, "Okay. I'm willing to try it. Only a little, though?"

"It doesn't take a lot."

"The dip? Of course," Brenda called out later from the compact kitchen. "Of course I made it myself."

"You always were so talented. Seems like everything you do comes out just right."

"I'm glad you like it." Before she sidled from behind the kitchen counter, Brenda checked her watch. 6:42. She tucked the clear plastic carton far down into the trash and threw a paper towel on top of it. Picking up the refilled glasses of sweet tea, she carried them out into the minuscule living room.

Margaret had made herself comfortable, now that the difficult part of the trip was finished. Her shoes were tucked neatly to one side, and she was using one nylon-encased foot to massage the other. "Oooh, that feels so good. I swear shoes were invented by a sadist." She reached up to take the tea, and smiled sweetly at Brenda. "Thanks. And thanks, too, for taking this so well. I was afraid you might be angry at me. You know, sort of like Rome where they shot the messenger who brought bad news."

"There weren't any guns in ancient Italy."

"Well, you know what I mean."

"Yes, I do. I certainly do. Help yourself to more crackers and dip. We'll head out for dinner in about fifteen minutes." Brenda sipped her tea slowly. "How long were you planning on staying?"

Margaret raised her hand as she chewed her way through a bite of cracker mounded with the delicious homemade spinach dip. Once the food was safely down her throat, she said, "I thought I'd drive straight from here to Atlanta for some antiquing, but by the time I got here I knew it would be too late, so I checked in at the River Landing. I'll leave first thing in the morning. Then I can be home by Tuesday or Wednesday night." She reached for another cracker, and piled it high with the creamy dip.

"Why don't you stay here longer and look up some of the antique dealers on Dupont Circle? As long as you're here, you might as well sight see and shop."

"What a lovely idea, Brenda." Margaret thought about it. "Thank you. I'll take you up on it. I think the River Landing is gorgeous. It might be nice to stay some extra time. They don't seem to be too busy."

"Is your husband expecting you back any particular time?"

"Heavens, no. He knows I get caught up in antique fever and may not show up for days."

Margaret watched Brenda lean forward to pick up a single cracker. What was wrong with her? She must be starving herself.

"But surely," Brenda said, "you talk to him a couple of times a day?" She stopped to pick a single crumb off her sleeveless black knit shirt. "Don't married people do that?"

"Usually I don't call but every other day. Sam's pretty good at entertaining himself. I swear he must spend the whole time polishing the Duesenberg. Or fishing. And he's a fair cook, too. I don't worry about him." She switched feet and sighed in contentment. "I'll call him tonight to let him know I'm staying an extra day or two."

Brenda picked up the phone and handed it to her cousin. "Call him now, why don't you? That way you won't have to remember to do it later tonight."

Margaret didn't want to embarrass Brenda by mentioning their earlier conversation about Peter. Anyway, Sam still didn't know about the letter. She'd tell him when she got home. Why she'd told Ernie and not Sam, she had no idea. Maybe because the trunk had Ernie's name on it.

So she told Sam that she was in antique mode and would be home in a couple of days. "I looked up my cousin Brenda while I was in the area. . . . Yes, I've had a nice visit with her. . . . Oh, fun stuff. . . . She talked me into eating a violet. . . . Yes, violet petals. They're an interesting taste. . . . We're going to dinner in a few minutes. . . . Yes, dear. I promise not to eat the centerpiece. . . . I love you too. Bye." She was smiling as she hung up the phone. "That Sam," she said. "He's always good for a laugh."

"Hungry Harry's?" Margaret couldn't imagine herself ever choosing to eat at a place called Hungry Harry's. On the other hand, Brenda was such a good cook—that spinach dip had been divine. Surely she wouldn't eat at a place that had bad food.

The menu, though, was mediocre. Spaghetti and meatballs, macaroni casserole, house salad, hamburgers.

"Did they just have a change in management?" she asked her cousin as they looked over the choices. Such as they were.

"Not that I know of. Why?"

"Just wondering. The menu seems a little . . ." How to find the right word? ". . . ordinary."

"The food's good though," Brenda said, and ordered a salad from the freckle-faced waiter.

As Margaret was waiting for her spaghetti, she fingered the little vase of flowers sitting between them. "Could I munch on these until dinner comes?"

"Excuse me, Ma'am," said the waiter who had materialized at her elbow. "Did you want ranch or thousand island?"

"Are those my only choices?"

"Yes Ma'am."

At least he was being polite, Margaret thought. "I'll take ranch." Then, in an effort not to sound too abrupt, she added, "My cousin Brenda here has been feeding me violets."

"That's nice, Ma'am." And he walked away.

"I wonder if he even heard what I said," Margaret asked.

"I doubt he'd care," Brenda said, as she picked up her water glass.

"So, my question still stands. Can I munch on the flowers?"

Brenda laughed at her. "What would we do for centerpieces if you ate them all?"

"Excuse me Ma'am." It was the waiter again. This time he was speaking to Brenda. "What did *you* want? Ranch or thousand island?"

Martinsville

Late Sunday evening, Glaze walked out onto the front porch and took a big sniff of the most delicious air. It seemed to be coming from that big bush with the snowball-sized white flowers. She carried her mug of hot tea to the side of the porch and set it down on the railing. House-sitting was fun, particularly since she hadn't had to do any cooking. It was rather like being at home. As she turned and glanced toward the climbing rose that was beginning to leaf out at the back corner of the porch—the verandah, she corrected her thought–she noticed three little azalea branches in a pile right in front of the swing.

Savannah

Sally Whitehead stopped filing the long nail on her left index finger and watched the old fat woman plodding across the lobby toward the front desk. The last thing she wanted to do was listen to somebody telling what a simply lovely time they'd had shopping. This looked like somebody who'd expect Sally to listen to the story of her whole day. The way she was walking it looked like her feet bothered her. No wonder, wearing those ugly shoes.

"Good evening, dear," the old lady said to her. Sally hated it when people called her dear and she didn't even know them and didn't care either.

"Can I help you." It wasn't a question the way Sally phrased it. She'd found that a certain tone of voice kept people from confiding in her. It wasn't impolite enough to make them complain to that monster Millie Cappell. But it saved Sally's ears from having to listen to a bunch of boring stories.

"Have you had a nice evening?" The question startled Sally. Nobody ever asked her how she was doing. Except for the usual 'Hey, how you doing,' which wasn't a question at all. It was just a way to start a sentence before you got to the important part of what you really wanted to say. When she started working at the Landing, she met a lot of people coming in from up North. They always answered it like she even cared how they were. The right answer was 'fine, how are you' and then the first person would say 'fine' and then both people could get on with whatever they were thinking about in the first place. Which wasn't how you were doing. And now somebody was asking her like she meant it. Somebody who sounded like a real person. Not somebody from up North.

She took a closer look at the dumpy-looking lady standing there. Sally was never going to let herself get that broad. It made clothes hang the wrong way. It looked messy.

"Yes, Ma'am." Sally may not have liked any of the guests, but she didn't want to lose her job, especially now that she'd soon be on the day shift. Maybe that wouldn't be as boring as the evening shift. Sally wanted something to do. "Yes, I've had a real nice evening."

"Well, so have I. . . ."

Oh dear, here it came, the story Sally didn't want to hear.

"I spent the most delightful time with my cousin. I haven't seen her since I was a little bitty girl. . . ."

Which was about a million years ago, thought Sally with less than a charitable bent of mind.

"She showed me all around her little house and yard, and we had dinner at Hungry Harry's Restaurant up the river." She paused to take a breath.

"That's nice," Sally said.

"Well, it wasn't the best restaurant I've ever eaten at, but it didn't last too long. My cousin Brenda brought me back to her little house afterwards and we had some delicious cheesecake with pretty pink violets on it."

That startled Sally out of her determination not to get involved in a conversation. "Violets?"

"That's right. Pink violets. Well, she had the ordinary purple kind, but she gave me the pink ones since pink is my favorite color. They're edible, you know."

"No, Ma'am. I didn't know that."

"Well, neither did I." The woman gave a little shudder. "I didn't particularly like the taste, but I didn't want to hurt Brenda's feelings."

"I didn't know violets came in pink."

"It's the bush variety, dear. I've been learning a little bit about plants from my cousin."

"Oh." Sounded crazy to Sally. Who'd want to eat flowers? And Sally knew darn well violets didn't grow on bushes. That cousin must be stupid.

The woman said good night and headed for the elevator. She was as dumpy looking from the back as she was from the front. But she'd been nicer than anybody else that evening. Sally was grateful, for one brief moment. And then she went back to filing her nails, holding them low behind the desk so that Millie Cappell wouldn't see her if she came in unexpectedly.

Chapter 14

Monday April 29, 1996 - Savannah

Well, after scorching Bob's handkerchief on the lamp, there didn't seem to be a lot for me to do, so I suggested that we stop by the hospital to check on Margaret. It didn't occur to either one of us that the hospital wouldn't give us any information about her condition. We were politely but firmly rebuffed at the nurses' station.

So we headed toward the lobby, and happened to see Millie Cappell walk in. She noticed us and came over to ask if we'd heard anything about Margaret. When we told her that they weren't allowing any visitors, she shook her head, said a quick good-by, and turned to leave. Bob stopped her with a quiet question. "Ms. Cappell?" he asked in his soft, rumbly voice. "I can't help thinking that you look familiar. Have we met before?"

I'd have to figure out a way to let him know that what was simple curiosity on his part sounded like he was trying to pick her up.

"No," I heard her say with finality. "Not unless you've been a guest at the River Landing before this."

"No. I've never been to this area."

"Well, I probably remind you of someone you met once." At that she turned and left the building through the big double doors.

We wandered into the gift shop to see if we could buy some flowers to send up to Margaret, but were told that flowers were not accepted in the ICU. I was beginning to feel like a ping-pong ball, bouncing from here to there without accomplishing anything. The good thing, though, was that once we walked back outside the gift shop, and stood there wondering what to do next, the front door opened and we saw Ernie and Sam step in and look around. We waved, and they headed in our direction.

As much as we would have liked to talk, it seemed to be far more important to get them in to see Margaret, so we led them upstairs to the ICU, then stepped aside while Sam talked to a nurse. We watched as she led him around the circular desk and into one of the rooms. Bob asked Ernie, "Do you want us to wait with you?"

"Of course he does," I said, leading the way to the waiting room, where I sank onto the dark blue couch and patted the seat next to me.

Ernie perched on the edge and kept an eye on the doorway.

"Don't you worry, Ernie," Bob said. "She'll be okay."

Ernie looked as if he wanted to believe it, but didn't quite. "Have you seen her? Is she any better?"

"No," I told him. "We haven't been able to see her because we're not next of kin, and they're real careful about access to patients in the ICU. But that means they're keeping a close watch on her. She's going to be okay, Ernie."

He looked up at me with his fine, dark eyes. I could see red veins in them–a sure sign of not much sleep. "You're the librarian lady, aren't you?" he asked. "We met once, last year."

"Yes."

"I'm Ernie."

"Yes."

He glanced over at Bob. "Thanks for calling me. It took me quite a while to track down Sam." Ernie stifled a yawn, then went on, "I checked out every fishing hole I could think of. Then I thought to look and see if his car was at home. It was. He'd gone across the river on the footbridge. I found him at dawn right across on the other side of the pool. He was going to camp out in one of the caves for a couple of days."

The Metoochie River, which is really not much more than a creek, runs through our little valley. The whole eastern bank of the river is a steep hillside covered in old forest and riddled with caves of all sizes. I knew Bob and his friend Tom had been lost in one of them for a while when they were kids.

I was born in one of those caves. I walked across the small bridge to the houses when I was young.

The pool is right in front of the main shops on First Street. It's a wide place in the river, just down from some boulders that make the water upstream tumble noisily. The pool is deep enough to swim in, wide enough to fish in, and toward the middle it's quiet enough to skip rocks across—a skill that Bob has mastered.

We're proud of the Metoochie, even though it's so small that most of the rest of the state doesn't know it's there. Eventually it runs into the Chattooga River, which forms part of the border between Georgia and South Carolina. Metoochie seems to be a messed-up version of an old Indian name. We've tried to trace the beginnings of the name, but haven't found anything definite yet. In some old diaries that were given to the town library, we found references to *the river*, but never a name.

The squirrels call it "chatter water".

Ernie was telling Bob that they had "run up the hill for the car and took off for Savannah without Sam hardly even changing his clothes." I hoped he wasn't going to be too redolent; I know what a fisherman can smell like after a few days of camping. Bob likes to fish.

Thank goodness.

Ernie paused to take a breath, which turned into a big yawn. He turned to me saying, "I have a kitten, you know. I named her Puddin Head."

Is she yellow pudding or chocolate pudding?

I was about to object to such a frivolous name, when it occurred to me that I called a perfectly dignified cat—Marmalade.

My name suits me well. It is the right color.

On the other hand, it might not be a dignified name, but it truly does describe what she looks like.

"You own the library cat, don't you?" Ernie was asking.

Own?

"Well, I wouldn't exactly say I own her, but she does live with me."

I have chosen a person of discrimination, who understands fine shades of meaning.

Bob spoke up. "You and Sam just missed meeting Ms. Cappell. She's the general manager of the River Landing. She dropped by to try to see Margaret a little while ago."

"That was nice of her. That's a good old Martinsville name."

"What is?" I asked.

"Cappell," Ernie said. "My grandma was Pamela Cappell before she married Grandpa and turned into a Tarkington."

"I should have thought of that, Ernie. I'll mention it next time I see her. Who knows? You two might be fourth cousins or something."

"Well," Bob said, returning to the original thread of thought, "Margaret *is* a guest there, so Millie was probably here just on business."

I looked over the choices of waiting room reading material. The low table that sat in the middle of the square of two couches and four chairs was covered with all the usual news magazines and movie star magazines and home decorating magazines. What about *Horticulture, Fine Gardening,* and *Mother Earth News*? Then I'd have something to read.

No wonder Ernie was yawning so much. He'd been looking for Sam half the night and then had driven almost nonstop from northeast Georgia to Savannah. I stood up and moved over to one of the chairs. "Why don't you stretch out on the couch, Ernie? There's no telling how long Sam will be in there."

Ernie was snoozing softly by the time Sam dragged into the waiting room and slumped down on a chair across the table from us.

"The nurse said the doctor's going to be out to talk to me in a while. They think it may be some form of food poisoning, but she wouldn't say much else."

We said all the usual stuff about her being okay, it'll take some time, keep up hope. And Sam didn't believe any of it.

When the doctor came in, we offered to leave, but Sam asked us to stay. Ernie was still asleep on the couch, so we talked around him.

"Your wife is extremely lucky, Mr. Casperson," the doctor said after he had explained all the symptoms. "We just received the laboratory results. Poisoning by *carbohydrate andromedotoxin* is very rare and usually fatal."

"Was it the violets she ate?" Sam asked.

"Violets? No. Violets aren't poisonous. She ate azalea blossoms."

"She said she was eating violets."

I couldn't help interrupting. "Sam, when did she say that?"

"She called me yesterday afternoon from Brenda's house, just before I left to go fishing. Said they'd been eating violets."

"Brenda?" came a muffled voice from the couch, where Ernie was apparently waking up from his little snooze. "She saw Brenda? I thought she was on one of her antiquing trips."

"She was," said Sam, "but she looked up Brenda while she was here and they ate violets."

"Brenda's here?" Ernie asked. "Did she show Brenda the letter?"

"What letter?" Sam said, at the same time Bob and I echoed him. "What letter?"

Before Ernie could answer, the doctor reached for the phone and handed it to Sam. "Please call her cousin immediately, Mr. Casperson, and be sure she's all right."

"I don't know her number, doc."

The doctor motioned to the volunteer on duty and asked for a phone book, but I interrupted him. Again. "That won't help any. She changed her last name years ago after she left home. Nobody seems to know what her name is now." I turned to Ernie. "You ought to know. What's her last name?"

"Mom never talked about it. I don't think she ever told me."

The doctor excused himself, saying that he was going to check with other hospitals and clinics in and around Savannah. "They may have a case of poisoning on their hands and not know what it is."

"Doctor, please wait." I was getting good at this. "Margaret didn't get sick until late last night or early this morning. So it couldn't have been what she was eating yesterday afternoon."

"That's good thinking, but the reaction time is at least six hours."

"Is it possible that Brenda is immune to the poison?"

"Not a chance," the doctor said. "We need to find this Brenda as soon as possible. Now, if you'll excuse me, I'm going to start calling around." He walked away before I could think of anything else to ask, and I turned to look at Bob.

"Are you thinking what I'm thinking?"

"Woman, I seldom have a clue what you're thinking. But I'm thinking we'd be smart to call the police and tell them what the doctor said."

I had forgotten about Sam sitting there with his head bent over and his elbows resting on his knees. "Sam, don't you think we should call the police about this? They can help us find Brenda."

He nodded. The poor man probably didn't know which end was up. One minute he's fishing. The next minute he hears his wife is sick. Then he travels for hours to get to her side and finds out she's been accidentally poisoned. And it could be fatal. This is not a good way to spend a day.

From the personal notebook of Colly Sloan:

so our little friend ernie knows about a letter that shows this cousin won't be entitled to the inheritance. wonder if the letter was real or if margaret casperson forged it to make it look like–no, that doesn't make any sense. but if ernie said–let me see– "it'd be just like margaret to show brenda the letter" then we've got a real motive on our hands. now if we can just find her. it's like lookin for one particular oyster in a whole fish store.

Martinsville

Right after an early supper of canned bean soup, Larry finally decided he needed to relax. It had been a hard two days. A hard week. His life was hard. Working all day when he was supposed to be retired. Of course, it was boring sitting around watching TV all the time, so he might as well work, but he'd been cutting hair for so many years he must have barbered a couple of thousand heads. Maybe a million. Well, maybe ten thousand. What he needed was a chance to sit down and relax.

He wandered out into his front yard and looked around to be sure those pesky dogs weren't anywhere near. He'd bring him a chair outside under the tree and sit and smoke a good cigar and maybe have some iced tea. That'll be relaxing, he thought. That'll feel good. I ought to get my blood pressure checked. Been having some symptoms. But it means driving all the way up to Russell Gap. I'll be doggoned if I'm going to go see that young squirt at the other end of Second Street. I want a real doctor. I forgot my cigar. Stupid stairs. Oughta leave this chair up on the porch. That way I can see the street better. No sense sitting in the grass. Where's that cigar? It's around here somewhere. I set it down while I was moving the chair.

Here it is. This oughta be relaxing. Rats and damnation, I forgot my iced tea. Stupid idea, sitting out here. I need my lighter anyway. I'll get that while I'm getting the iced tea. What's relaxing about all this anyway?

Once Larry had his tea and his lighter in hand, he headed back across his porch just in time to see that orange and white cat running around the corner. "Stupid cat! What're you doing here? Get outa my yard!" How's a guy supposed to relax with all this rat's-ass stuff going on? Where's my cigar? Where's my stupid cigar? Stupid cat! I'm gonna get you for this!

* * * * * *

Tom dropped by the Beechnut Lane house with a doggie bag in hand. Marmalade appeared from around the corner of the porch and padded up to meet him at the front door, which was standing open. He stuck his head in and called out, "Hello? Anybody home?" at which point Glaze hobbled out of the kitchen with a big bowl of popcorn.

"I was going to sit down and rock for a while. Want to join me?"

"Sure."

"I hope you like popcorn."

"It's okay for movies, I guess. Could we have it as an appetizer? I was hoping you'd let me cook dinner for you. And I brought a treat for FurBall here."

You are the only one I will allow to call me that.

Glaze settled herself into one of the big rockers and looked at Tom for several seconds. Marmalade hopped into his lap as he sank into the other rocker. "Aren't you supposed to be running your restaurant instead of tending to me?"

"Oh, we're closed on Mondays."

"Mmph." Sounded like a pretty thin excuse. How was she going to tell him that she really liked popcorn for dinner once in a while? It was a full meal as far as she was concerned. "Tom, thanks for your concern and all that, but I'm fine just the way I am. I'm going to munch popcorn for a bit and then turn in early." No she wasn't. She wanted to stay up late reading a good book. "It's been a long day." No it hadn't. She had done little else than clean the litter box and feed Marmy. And she'd washed up the few dishes from breakfast and lunch. That was it.

"It's all right. I don't mind cooking for you."

"Tom, it's not that. I know you don't mind. It's just that I don't want a full meal tonight. I want to sit here and munch and then go get a good book off Biscuit's bookshelf. I want to read and scratch Marmy's head and think and turn in early."

She didn't like looking at the way Tom pulled back his head as if he'd been slapped. She watched in silence as he stood up, setting Marmalade gently back onto the chair.

"I'll set this goody bag in the fridge on my way out. It's salmon for the cat."

The cat? You are calling me the cat? What happened to FurBall?

"Thank you." How lame did that sound? She lowered her eyes as he walked around the corner of the porch and out of sight.

Glaze was still sitting there, with her bowl of uneaten popcorn in her lap, when Marmalade jumped up and hopped off the rocker, sliding around behind it in a fluid movement that reminded Glaze of a seal in water. A moment later she heard footsteps stomping up onto the porch, followed by a loud knocking on the front door. "I'm around here," she called out.

Larry Murphy's unwelcome form materialized around the corner, scowling at her. "Your cat went and did it again."

"Branches?" Glaze asked.

"Nope, worse than that. He stole my cigar."

Was the man serious? Glaze stifled her impulse to laugh at the ridiculous image of Marmalade puffing on a stogie. Perhaps with a little pool hall music in the background.

"I'm serious. Don't you think I'm not. He stole my cigar, and I saw him do it."

"She. Marmalade is a girl."

"I don't give a rat's ass about that. It's a thief. That's what it is."

Glaze felt somewhat at a disadvantage sitting down, but she was halfway afraid to stand up. A huge bandage on her leg might have helped. Or glasses. Would he hit someone who had glasses on? Without either of those props, though, she decided to try a good imitation of the Czarina. "Mr. Murphy, I don't know what you're talking about, but I suggest if you have a complaint, you take it up with Officer Sheffield when he returns from his honeymoon. It is, after all, his cat to whom you are referring."

It must have worked, because Larry stomped off the porch and across the lawn, at which point Marmalade slipped back up onto the lap she had just abandoned. "Chicken," Glaze muttered at her, but without much conviction.

The better part of valor is what Widelap would say.
"Of course, you were probably smart not to provoke him any further, . . ."
My thought exactly.
". . .but did you really steal his cigar?" Glaze asked the purring kitty.
By way of answer, or so it looked to Glaze, Marmalade hopped down once again, and walked over to where the Lady Banks Rose clambered up the corner of the porch. She fussed around a bit and pulled out a somewhat battered . . .
"A cigar? You DID steal it? Whatever for, Marmalade? I'm so glad he didn't see it. Otherwise we both would have been in deep trouble. And I hope you understand I'm going to have to tell your mom about this."
Yes, please do. She will think it is funny. She needs to laugh.

* * * * * *

From the personal notebook of Colly Sloan:

heaven save me from new-comers. why do I have to get a waiter who remembers both their names and their entire conversation but has been there only a week and never saw margaret's cousin before. he said she's really skinny. that's about a third of the female population around here. piece of cake. I just walk up to every skinny woman I see and haul her in for questioning. that woman has to be somewhere. i'm goin to find her. somebody has to have seen her. somebody that is who knows her.

* * * * * *

Savannah

Once Bob and I got back to our room, I gave a quick call home to find out how Marmalade was doing.
I am doing quite well, thank you.
Glaze sounded somewhat worse for wear when she answered the phone. "Oh, I'm so glad it's you, sis," she said.
"Why? What's wrong? You don't sound like you. . . ."
She is unhappy.

"Is everything okay there?" I had sudden visions of disasters, and was thoroughly unprepared for Glaze to say, "Marmalade stole a cigar."

"I can't understand why she did it," Glaze said after explaining what had been happening there. It sounded funnier than heck to me. I couldn't figure out why she sounded so depressed.

"I hardly think it's a problem," I assured her. I wondered what was really bothering her. A cigar and a couple of flower stems seemed hardly worth her notice.

"You don't understand, sis. He was really, really angry. And I didn't appreciate having to sit there and listen to him ranting."

I tried to soothe her, but without seeing her face to face, it was hard to read exactly what the problem was. "Bob will handle it when he gets home. Meanwhile, try to keep Marmalade a little closer to home, and maybe he'll forget about her." I remembered Larry's style. Or lack thereof. "Just to be on the safe side, though, why don't you make sure you keep the doors locked?" The last thing I wanted to do was to have to worry about my sister while she was babysitting Marmalade. . . .

I am not a baby.

And what was getting into that cat anyway? . . .

That cat?

I'd never even considered that she might be destructive.

Destructive? Three broken branches and one smelly cigar are not destructive. You would not want to see me if I chose to be truly destructive.

"Maybe," I suggested, "you could ask Tom Parkman if he'd spend some time with you in the evenings, to be on the safe side . . ."

Oh dear. You just said . . .

"Glaze? Are you still there?"

Before she hung up on me, she spit out, "You are no help whatsoever."

What did I say?

. . . the wrong thing.

I was trying to explain to Bob what Glaze had said, but she called me back a few minutes later with an apology. I could tell she'd been crying.

". . . So, what I basically told him was to go away and leave me alone, and I didn't mean that. Not really. I can't believe I said such a mean thing. It tumbled out, and I don't know how to take it back, but I truly did want him to leave me alone right then, and I'm so mixed-up about this I don't know . . ." She paused and I heard a loud honk as she blew her nose. ". . . don't know what to do, and I shouldn't be bothering you about this because you're on your honeymoon and you don't need to be worrying about a sister who can't get her act together when it comes to men, and there's nothing you can do anyway."

I waited for her to wind down, made a few encouraging noises into the phone, and wished that Savannah weren't so far from Martinsville. Why hadn't we stayed home? No, that's not what I wanted. I simply wanted my sister to stop hurting. And I wanted to understand the problem–whatever it was. She was not making a heck of a lot of sense. "Glaze, hon, we'll be home in a few days. Do you think you can stick it out a while longer and then we can sit down over a nice cup of tea and work this out?" Even as I said it, I knew that was no help whatsoever, so I tried again.

"On second thought, I want you to take a big breath and then tell me something good that's been happening. Surely you can think of at least one thing."

"Okay." She sniffled a bit, and then seemed to settle in. She blew her nose again rather loudly and too near the phone. But she's my sister, so it was okay. "Well," she continued, "I was looking through your Wayside Gardens catalog."

"Why? You're not a gardener."

"No, but it was sitting here and I picked it up and started looking at it. And you'll never guess what I found."

"You're right, I can't guess. What did you find?" I asked, playing right along.

"I found a Joe Pye Weed!"

It was nice to hear some animation in her voice, but she stumped me as to the subject matter. "Glaze, whatever are you talking about?"

"A Joe Pye Weed. You know, that big thing you had in the middle of your bouquet? You said if we didn't know it was a weed, we'd be willing to buy it, or something like that."

I vaguely remembered being teased by Glaze–and Melissa too–when I chose some weeds for my bridal bouquet.

"Well," she crowed, "they sell it in the catalog. And the picture's beautiful."

"Of course they sell it. The plant *is* beautiful," I told her. "And it's not considered a weed everywhere. I guess we're just lucky that it'll spring up like a gift in our yards." I was hoping she'd get the message.

"Are you preaching at me, big sister?"

I guess she got it. I could hear her smiling as she said it.

* * * * * *

What an ordinary conversation that had been, I thought as I sat in the waiting room. The waiting room. What an appropriate name. I was waiting for my husband to recover. We'd never suspected when we went to bed on Monday night, that our lives would change so drastically within an hour.

* * * * * *

On Monday evening Bull picked up Linda after work. This was the beginning of her last week before she started on the late shift, and she didn't like the idea at all. They went to the Yellow Moon for a long, quiet dinner. Linda loved going out to eat. She always took a long time over her food, even though Bull finished his meal in minutes and then sat there like a lump. She didn't care. She wanted to enjoy her food. Food she hadn't had to cook. On plates she wouldn't have to wash.

Bull once told her that if she wouldn't spend so much on cigarettes, they could afford to eat out more often. He'd always complained about her smoking, from the time she started in high school. But there was no way she was going to be able to quit now. The money angle was merely an excuse. He'd never even tried smoking, so what did he know?

By the time they finished dinner and got back to the Landing, the night was quiet, and the wide pathway along the river looked pretty well deserted. Bull surprised Linda by getting out of the car and walking her over to where hers was parked. The hotel was still, except for someone Linda could see sitting on the rose arbor bench down near the end of the parking lot. And here came Millie Cappell walking down the stairs. As she approached the two of them, she asked, "What are you two doing here at this time of night?"

Linda didn't even try to keep the resentment out of her voice. "We went out to dinner." She shouldn't have to explain. She was on her own time now. "We came back to pick up my car."

Bull stretched, for no reason that Linda could think of. "Yeah, we left it here." Why did he always have to preen his feathers around any unattached female?

Millie looked at Bull, nodded without comment and stepped past them toward her own car. On what sounded to Linda like a sudden impulse, Bull turned to Linda and said, "Let's go for a quick stroll along the river, sweetheart. It'll help us digest that chocolate cream pie."

She knew what he was doing. Millie could still hear them. He was playing the good attentive husband. A walk was what Linda wanted, though, so she figured she might as well play along and be the happily satisfied wife.

"You're right. But let's make it a long walk. I'm stuffed."

They crossed behind Millie's car as she was sliding into the driver's seat. As Millie drove away, they rounded the side of the hotel. Linda smiled at the woman who was sitting under the climbing roses. She smiled back and reached down to pick up what looked to Linda at first like a book. On second thought, she'd seen that woman before, and she'd been carrying a tape recorder. Linda wondered about it briefly as the woman walked quickly past them toward the parking lot, and Linda heard her footsteps receding. She and Bull started down the wide pathway that led alongside the river.

"I wonder what the tape recorder was for?" she asked.

"What tape recorder?"

Didn't this husband of hers ever pay attention to anything? "She had a tape recorder."

"Who?"

"That tall woman we just passed."

"Hell, Shorty, everybody looks tall to you."

"Forget it." They walked on in silence.

Another woman, this one equally tall and quite thin, approached them. Linda said a pleasant hello. The woman simply ducked her head and kept walking.

The Savannah River swooshed along quietly, with just enough noise to cover gaps in conversation. Bull Finney had to rein in his footsteps to match his wife's shorter stride. They walked slowly, accompanied by the sounds of the night birds and the somber river tune. There didn't seem to be anything much to say. Bull didn't talk a lot when they took walks like this. He had his own thoughts. He didn't know what she thought about. He enjoyed her cooking, but he didn't understand her. She'd been a little distant lately. He briefly wondered if maybe she was going to start talking about a divorce again. They'd had that conversation three or four times, but they'd always managed to avoid splitting up. Usually dinner and some flowers would quiet her down. He didn't know what else to do. And his ship would be coming in soon. She'd see. Her mother liked him a lot. Wasn't that something in his favor?

Weather hasn't been too bad, Bull thought. We could use some rain, though. Wonder if those Crabb sisters are going to hire me to put up that big bookcase they're thinking about? I need to remember that big meeting tomorrow. Dinner was pretty good tonight. It's time to replace the blade on my band saw.

Linda had known when she was walking down the aisle that this marriage was a mistake. She and Bull had been friends growing up, but that didn't necessarily make for a long-term marriage. Her mother was best friends with his mother. It was good, naturally, to be friends with the man you were going to spend the rest of your life with, but she'd always thought of Bull Finney more as a brother than anything else. The little boy almost next door. After all, she was four years his senior. She still felt like she was the adult, and he was still the kid. Why couldn't he grow up? Why did he always have to joke about everything she said? Mean jokes, too, most of the time. Why couldn't he take her seriously at least once in a while? Why didn't he talk to her? Why couldn't he quit seeing himself as the center of the universe?

She wondered sometimes why her mother had pushed her so hard to accept his proposal. Her mother had seemed almost desperate to have Linda marry Bull. Why did I give in? Linda asked herself in time to their footsteps. She supposed she had tried to keep on loving Bull. Well, she *did* love him. Sort of. But he bad-mouthed her a lot in front of the kids. She could remember once when they'd been planning a canoeing trip. He wanted to take along ten times more equipment than she thought they needed. He even wanted to take lawn chairs. In a canoe! What was wrong with sitting on a stump? They'd ended up loading *two* cars with his stuff. Then, he'd gotten the kids together and had them draw straws. "Whoever loses," he said, "has to go with mom."

If the kids hadn't been little, she would have walked out right then. In fact, she had talked to her mother about it, but of course her mom had told her to stick with him. He took her mother's side all the time. Called her *Ma*. He'd done that all his life. I don't call his mother *Ma*, Linda thought. I call her Joan. I don't even call my own mother *Ma*. Sounds juvenile. And she wasn't here for us anyway. Grandma raised us, really. Grandma would have understood, if she hadn't died ten years ago.

Linda brought her thoughts back to her husband, walking along beside her. She could hear his breathing. It was loud.

And he wouldn't cook, even if he didn't have a job going. She was so tired of running home after work to get another one of his favorite meals on the table.

Now, on the other hand, he was a platelet donor. That was a good thing, but she figured he did it just because it made him a hero. He took her for walks, but he never brought her flowers unless he thought she was mad at him for something. If only he knew how often she was really mad at him. The man didn't have a clue. She had asked him to go to counseling, but he didn't want to spend the money.

"Let's just talk about it," he'd say. And he'd start talking, telling her all the reasons why counseling wouldn't work, and all the reasons why they ought to stay together. The only one that was important to him, though, was the one he always ended his 'discussion' with. "You like the sex," he'd say. *Yeah, right.*

Linda was working herself up into a twit, and here was Bull walking along beside her not knowing her anger. How could he be so dense? And why couldn't she tell him how she felt? She'd tried a couple of weeks ago to tell her mother about it. Super Woman if there ever was one. How could she compete with that? You'd think her own mother would listen and sympathize. Oh no, she had to get on her high horse and give Linda a lecture about sticking with your man. You made your bed; you have to lie in it. The sanctity of marriage–that was a laugh. What other tired cliché had she come up with? Oh yes, how could she forget? Til death do us part.

And one thing she'd said hadn't made any sense to Linda at all. "Stay with him for another three weeks, and see if you don't change your mind." What kind of difference could three weeks make?

I'm going to finish this walk, thought Linda, and then I'm going to tell him it's over. This time I mean it. He can move out next week. The kids are gone now, and I've got enough casseroles in the freezer to last him a good long time. He can take them with him. Or come back once a week and check some out, sort of like a casserole library. No, that wouldn't do. Once he was gone, she wanted him to stay out of her life.

There wasn't much of a moon that night, at least not one that showed through all the clouds.

* * * * * *

I know that jogging is a good thing. It keeps the muscles active. It keeps the blood flowing. When you are used to jogging, the rhythm gets into your mind and shuts out all the hurt and the pain. The pain of your body pays you for the hurt of living. Of having lived. The pumping of the blood makes a sound that drowns out the voices in your head.

It is time to leave. Tonight it is important to hurry. Put on the black pants and the big black sweatshirt to cover my arms. The black shoes are not comfortable to run in, but they will not show up in the dark. It will not matter if they hear me running up close to them. There are always joggers on the River Walk, but not at this time of night. The other joggers do not wear stockings on their heads.

The wide-mouthed jar is ready, sitting in the sink. I have cleaned it of any smudges. I turn out all my lights and step outside my kitchen door to retrieve the water-filled can. The can is nothing special. It came from a department store. The same one where I bought the wide-mouthed jar. I have been saving this water for months. I did not know that I would ever use it for this. It has been good to know that I have held a can of death near my door all this time. I pour the liquid into the jar with care. There are no spills. I am wearing rubber gloves. I rinse the sink. I screw the lid gently onto the jar. It must be easy to open while I am running.

I leave by the back door, standing a moment to be sure my eyes, through the holes in the stocking, are adjusted to the night. It is a simple matter to slip through the hedge, across the neighbor's back yard, avoiding the light from the back porch, and into the park. From the park I pass near the hotel and see two cars still in the parking lot. I begin to increase my stride.

They must have taken a long walk. I see them now. I am sure from their clothing and their relative heights that they are the ones I am looking for. The grip of the rubber gloves is sure. I begin to loosen the jar lid. They are not looking at me. They are walking with their heads down. The man raises his head as I get closer. He is looking at me, but my face is dark as I hold my eyes half-shut. I make the final twist of the lid, pull it from the jar, and fling the liquid onto the man's face. He flinches, but he is too slow.

The woman is faster than I expect. She grabs at my shirt. I drop the jar and twist around. I hit her in the face. As she falls, I run into the shadows. I turn left into the park and lose myself in the trees. There is no sound behind me. I run until I can make my way behind the neighbor's yard to the hedge that borders my yard. I walk unseen into my kitchen. Some of the liquid splashed on my sweatshirt. I take it off with great care. I place the gloves in my trash. It will be collected tomorrow morning.

I put on another pair of gloves and take off the stocking and the pants. I place the sweatshirt and the pants in the washer. I add extra detergent. I light the gas logs in the fireplace and feed the stocking to the flames. I wash off these gloves and put them beneath my sink. I clean myself in a long shower. Now I am safe. Now, I am safe.

* * * * * *

The phone was entirely too loud for its own good. Millie Cappell supposed she would have to face it–a late night phone call always meant an emergency at the River Landing. She briefly considered throwing the phone against the wall, but thought better of it and answered it instead.

"Ms. Cappell, I'm so sorry to wake you up, but there's a big disturbance here at the Landing. I think you'd better come quick."

"What's going on, Sally? What kind of disturbance?"

"One of our guests, Mrs. Sheffield, said she couldn't sleep, and she went out on her balcony for some fresh air. She said she heard a woman screaming down on the Walk, so she called me. I stepped out the back door, and I could hear it too, so I called the police."

"The police? Are they there?"

"Not yet. But the people who heard the scream ran out to see if they could help, and now there are five or six people in the lobby wondering what's going on. Could you possibly come over here?"

There had been many times when Millie regretted her decision to live in the little cottage provided by the hotel. It was convenient, of course, to be able to hop over to the Landing on a moment's notice, although she had needed to impress on the staff that their idea of an emergency was probably altogether different than hers. "Don't

call me," she had told them with great emphasis, "until you've exhausted your own resources." Some of them had more resources than
others.

"Give me a minute or two. I need to splash some water on my
face and get some clothes on. I'll be there as soon as I can."

As she left her house, she noticed lights in two other houses on
her side of the street.

* * * * * *

Colly Sloan and Brando Williston were the closest unit. As
Brando drove up to the Landing, a man wearing jeans and a striped
pajama top ran around the corner of the hotel yelling, "Get an ambulance! Get an ambulance!"

Colly stepped out of the cruiser, and Ms. Cappell ran up as the
man hollered out, "A jogger. A jogger. He attacked some people on
the River Walk!"

Colly put on her best soothing-but-firm voice and tried to make
some sense out of the man's ravings. "Now, try to calm down a little.
How do you know about this?"

"I heard a commotion in the hall and called the front desk. She
said somebody was screaming, so I woke up my brother-in-law in
the next room and we dashed out to see what was going on." He kept
talking as he motioned the cops to follow him. "They were a little
ways down this walk. The woman was holding her jaw—she said a
jogger threw some stuff on her husband and then hit her. Knocked
her out. When she came to, he was groaning and she screamed for
help. That was when we all heard her. There's a man doing mouth-
to-mouth 'cause the guy's having trouble breathing. He said we
shouldn't try to move the guy, so I ran back to call for an ambulance,
and then you showed up."

Colly and Brando followed the pajama-topped man around behind the Landing, where a woman knelt over the inert body of a
man. Brando started to run. As Colly got closer, she recognized the
woman as his sister-in-law, Linda, the short woman in the restaurant. She was Diane Williston's sister. One of the bystanders was
leaning over the wall, vomiting into the river. He turned around at
the sound of the officers' voices, said "I don't feel too good," and
crumpled into a heap at the foot of the wall. Some woman—probably
his wife—grabbed him as he fell. Colly and Brando pretty much ignored him. Obviously a case of the shakes over seeing a guy who

appeared to be dying. Despite what the pajama-clad man had said, Colly didn't see anyone trying to resuscitate Bull.

By the time the ambulance crew arrived, the carpenter was clearly dead, although, of course, Colly said nothing about that to the stunned wife. One of the crew checked the bump on Linda's jaw and suggested she come in to have an X-ray. They declined to let her ride in the ambulance. With gloved hands, the ambulance crew started to lift the body onto a stretcher.

As they did so, the woman who had grabbed the falling man came over to insist that her husband be taken in the ambulance, too. "My husband tried to give the man mouth-to-mouth resuscitation," she said. "But then he started shaking and wanting to throw up. Something is dreadfully wrong with him. Please help." After a quick look, the medics agreed. The nausea that Colly had attributed to seeing someone die, kept on going, getting worse as each bout of retching shook his body.

Colly wrote down the man's name as a matter of course. Robert Sheffield. The pajama-clad bystander offered to drive the two wives to the emergency room. Linda Finney, still holding her jaw, climbed into the front seat, and Robert Sheffield's wife got in the back.

From the personal notebook of Colly Sloan:

i'm glad it's brando's turn to drive. need to sort out these ideas. writin helps.

jar must have had some kind of poison in it. pretty clear, but lab will verify. thank goodness for gloves. that sheffield guy who tried to resuscitate – hope he's not too sick.

just questioned linda finney at emergency room. she's ok big bump w/ bruise on jaw. doesn't look self-inflicted. said jogger was tall and didn't have a face. stockin maybe? or ski mask? said he was tall, dressed all in black.

note: tall is relative. linda f couldn't be much over 5' herself

brando questioned millie cappell. said she told him she's seen two women hanging around the hotel lately. One always wears black and carries a tape recorder. The other one is real skinny. she noticed them on the river walk this evenin. who are these people? is one of them my murderer? i've been assumin a man – dumb to do that. could have been a woman, i suppose.

millie also said she saw linda and bull start down the river walk–
wasn't sure of the time. doesn't anyone ever look at a watch?

is there a chance jogger got some of poison too? linda finney
said lots of splashin. check emergency clinics.

Chapter 15

Tuesday April 30, 1996 - 10:00am

I've always thought of myself as being able to sit patiently through anything, but this was wearing mighty thin. I've sat through an awful lot so far. Being questioned at 4:30 in the morning by Officer Sloan. Freezing in a bathrobe until I got some real clothes. Spending all last night in the waiting room chair. This is ridiculous. I need something to take my mind off this. Bob will be fine. He will. Why didn't I think to bring my knitting? No, that's more for winter evenings. Wait a minute. This is my honeymoon. The last thing I need to be doing is knitting on my honeymoon. This is my honeymoon, and here I sit in a hospital not knowing if my husband of two and a half days will ever wake up again.

Do not worry. Worry does not help.

No, no, no. I refuse to give in to that kind of thinking. I refuse to think he might be like this the rest of his life. Cancel that thought. I refuse to think–even for a moment–that he might die.

Do not worry, Widelap.

I refuse to think that any moment a nurse could come in here and look at me with a sad face and tell me that it's all over. I refuse to think about that. I won't think about her walking up to me and touching my shoulder and . . . "Yikes!"

The nurse who had walked quietly up beside me was almost as shocked as I was. "Ms. McKee? I'm so sorry I startled you."

"That's okay. You just saved me from horrible thoughts. Oh my gosh, is he . . . ?"

"Don't worry. He's still holding his own. There hasn't been any change. It's time for you to come in and see him for a little while. The doc said we could increase the visits to ten minutes."

I followed her through the automatic doors and around to the right. I swear I was wearing a path in the linoleum. At the door I paused, as I usually did for some reason. I noticed the regular rhythm of his breathing as his chest rose and fell. I was going to have to teach him yoga breathing. No sense in not using the full power of the lungs. If he ever woke up. Once he woke up. When he woke up.

I stood there willing him to open his eyes, to open them and gaze at me with love and say 'Biscuit McKee, I love you more than anything. I feel like I've been dreaming, but all the dreams have been about you and our long and happy life together.' Those would be the sweetest words I ever heard.

His eyes did not open, even though I watched and willed them to for ten whole minutes.

When I walked back into the waiting room, which had several other people in it–I was glad I finally had real clothes on–the phone on the volunteer's desk was ringing. It was Glaze again. Bless her heart. She felt like a lifeline to me. Christina Rossetti wrote a poem a long time ago that started, "There is no friend like a sister." Yes. She was right. I like memorizing poetry. It comes back at odd moments to comfort.

"Do they know what the liquid was?" she asked me.

"I haven't heard. I guess I assumed it was battery acid or something like that."

"What a horrible way to die. And for his poor wife to see it all happening." Glaze was quiet for a moment. "It couldn't have been acid," she said. "Bob would have known right away because it would have burned. No, it must have been some kind of poison, don't you think?"

That wasn't much consolation. Bob's a cop. He should have known better than to touch someone who'd been splashed with something. If Bob hadn't been so ready to step in and save the guy, he'd be all right now. Why did I ever marry a guy who thought he could fix anything? This was getting me nowhere except to the land of high blood pressure, so I changed the subject.

"Has Marmalade been up to any more theft lately? Any more azaleas or cigarettes?"

No.

"You mean cigars," said Glaze. "No. She hasn't stolen anything lately. At least not that I'm aware of. And Larry hasn't shown up on my doorstep."

At the mention of Larry, I couldn't help frowning. I was sorry that Glaze was having to deal with him alone. I wanted to go home. I wanted to go home with Bob.

As I was thinking all this, and only peripherally listening to what Glaze was saying about Larry and Marmalade and Martinsville and Philadelphia, I noticed a movement at the door. I looked up to see Millie standing there, looking at me. She must not have wanted to interrupt my conversation, because she turned and left. That was pretty thoughtful of her.

What Glaze was saying began to get through to my ears. "You what? What did you just say?" I asked her.

You have not been listening.

"You haven't been listening, have you?"

"No. I'm sorry, sis. Millie Cappell was here . . ."

"Again?"

"Yes. She's quite concerned. It's her hotel, after all. But she left."

"Don't worry, she'll be back. The woman's like a yo-yo."

"Glaze, that's not kind. She brings me clean clothes. Now, what did you say when I wasn't listening?"

"I said I was fired. The day before I left there to drive to here. There's no reason for me to go back to Philly in a hurry except to try to find a new job."

There is no friend like a sister. "Can you move back here?" I asked. "I mean to Martinsville or Braetonburg?"

There was a longish silence on the other end of the phone. Her voice, when she finally spoke, was tentative. "Don't think I haven't thought about it, Biscuit. . . . But it's not that simple now."

"Now? What do you mean *now*? Is something wrong?"

She is unhappy.

Silence.

"Are you still there?"

Yes she is. She is winding the telephone cord around and around her hand. And then she unwinds it.

"Sis, I don't want to have this conversation right now. I'm having a lot of stuff come up right now about Tom. I'm scared of what I'm feeling, and I'd really rather wait until we can sit down with some tea and talk about it."

The woman's forty-four years old. She's never been married. Her last boyfriend was a drug-riddled creep who's in jail now. Then along comes a great, great guy who looks like he could easily fall in love with her. And she's scared. Makes perfect sense.

"Okay, Glaze. We'll talk when I get home."

I hope that is soon.

"I have to go back to Philadelphia," she told me. "Whether it's to find a new job or to pack–either way I have to go back."

A new nurse that I hadn't seen before walked into the waiting room and motioned to me.

"Glaze, the nurse is here again. It's time for me to go in and see Bob. I need to hang up. But I love you. And I appreciate you. And I want to be there for you in whatever way you need."

"Go on. Say hi to Bob for me."

As if he could hear anything.

He can. He can, but you need to talk to him.

* * * * * *

From the personal notebook of Colly Sloan:

i just love workin around the clock. it makes me so chipper and pleasant.

never in my entire life did i think i'd be happy to see horse munson drunk on a park bench. took a while but he finally said he "saw some guy" wearin black, runnin through the park. he's sure it was monday night because it was right after bunny threw him out. checked with her. yep. she finally did it. he doesn't know what time he saw the runner (of course) but seemed to be pretty sure which direction the guy went. trouble is there are lots of houses over that way. cute little rows with hedges all around the back yards. real private. wonder if patch and I could find a place along there–nice little bungalow so we could have some roses? tired of apartments.

woman at far end of block thinks she saw margaret's car parked on street sunday when she and husband drove past on way to dinner. can't remember which house it was in front of. know what side of street now. gonna catch this brenda. has to be her.

* * * * * *

11:00 a.m.

This process of seeing Bob for ten minutes an hour was wearing thin. The nurse who had collected me drew a chair up next to him so I could sit close. She even patted my shoulder as she left. I just sat and looked at him, at all the tubes that were running like so much undisciplined spaghetti, in and out of him. The place where the IV tube entered his hand was oozing a tiny bit of blood. I knew they changed the site often. He was going to come home looking like he'd had a run-in with a blackberry patch.

My rear end was sore. All I'd been doing all night and all morning was sitting. Sitting. I reached over and touched his hand. It was cool and still. I wondered if the fluids running into him, feeding him, felt cold to him. They were at room temperature, after all. Air conditioned room temperature. Almost thirty degrees cooler than his internal temp.

Think of it, I told myself, as a drink of cool water on a hot day in August. Say it's 98 degrees outside. I've been working in the yard. I come inside and fill a glass of delicious deep-well water at the sink. I hold the glass up to my face for a moment and absorb the refreshing coolness into my cheek. Then I lift the glass and enjoy the feeling of the water as it courses down my throat.

That's a far cry from an IV tube, but right now it's the best he's going to get. It seems such a shame that someone who likes to eat as much as Bob does, should be lying here being fed cold fluids through a tube. Maybe I'm all cried out. Thank goodness for the boxes of tissues liberally sprinkled around the waiting room. I've used about half of them, but there aren't any more tears right now.

I idly picked up his hand and looked at the blue veins that ran in a lumpy pattern next to his knuckles. One day last month he'd been munching on a stalk of celery while I was stirring the soup pot. There was a slant of light from the yellow lamp on the kitchen counter that shadowed his veins as he lifted the celery to his mouth.

He held the little plate out toward me. "Don't you love the crunchy sound?"

I reached for a big fat stalk. "Yes, I do, as a matter of fact." I handed him a shallow dish that held olive oil mixed with herbs from the windowsill garden above the sink. "Would you set this on the table? The soup's ready, and I'm hungry." I cut some wide slices of the dark brown bread I'd made that morning and put both of them on a small blue-ringed plate. Bob took it and tucked it next to the olive oil, in the middle of the little round table by the bay window. I love my kitchen.

For some reason I think it was a Wednesday evening, but the day doesn't matter. We must have spent an hour over our simple meal of fresh cold munchy veggies, warm bread dipped in olive oil, and hot soup. "I don't understand people who eat fast," I told Bob. "They seem to miss so much."

"What do you mean?"

"Did you ever notice how some folks rush through a meal?"

"Sure, all the time in the service. That's the way we had to eat then, but I didn't like it. It's bad for digestion."

"It's not just the digestion, Bob. It's important to enjoy the taste. And the smell of the food." We both took a big breath. The yeasty bread aroma was almost palpable.

Bob broke off another chunk of bread and looked at its grainy surface. "What about the texture? This looks like soft dirt after it's been spattered with a light rain. And it feels like a handful of warm mud."

Only a true gardener would appreciate having her bread compared to dirt, but I knew what he meant. Picking up the last stalk of celery, I crunched into it. "The sound, too. The sound."

Bob ran his bread around the little bowl, sopping up the last of the olive oil. "You realize we've mentioned all the five senses?"

"There's more. What about sheer gratitude for the food?"

He reached across the little table and picked up my hand–the one that wasn't holding the last bite of celery. "And I appreciate the one who cooked it."

I love this man.

I sat a while longer and pictured him well and happy and sitting across from me at the little round table. "Wake up, Bob," I thought. "Please wake up."

* * * * * *

From the personal notebook of Colly Sloan:

nicotine in jogger's jar. lab results. nasty stuff. doc said only reason linda finney survived being splashed is she's a heavy smoker. gave her slight immunity. linda told doc she's quittin cold turkey. wish her luck.

asked linda to let me know if she thinks of somethin that might be pertinent. gave her my card. special investigative unit–sounds good, still don't know if this is goin to work, havin beat cops do investigation.

brando said diane told him linda's been wanting to divorce bull for years. is this a motive?

* * * * * *

11:30 a.m.

Sam and Ernie came up from Margaret's floor to keep me company for a little while. It was good to see some faces from home again.

"How's Margaret doing since they moved her downstairs?" I asked them.

Sam sank onto the flowered chair in the corner. "Bout the same. How's Bob?"

"About the same. They identified the poison. It was nicotine."

"Nicotine? You mean like in cigarettes?"

"That's right. I've known all my gardening life that it's an effective insecticide, so of course it's a poison. I just never thought about it being used as a weapon."

Ernie was still standing. "I think I'll mosey down to the cafeteria. Do you want anything, either of you?"

"Coffee," said Sam.

"Nothing for me, thanks," I told him and watched as he walked past the volunteer's desk and around the corner.

Sam and I sat there for a few minutes, talking about nothing much. It was more to fill the void and keep us from having to think. Not a great way to create stimulating conversation. He mentioned that Officer Sloan had interviewed him and Ernie both. As we were rounding up the weather, having decided that we could use some rain and wanted to avoid thunderstorms, Millie stepped into the waiting room. Didn't that woman ever work at the hotel anymore?

She started to turn around, but I called her over to where we were.

She reached up her left hand to straighten her already straight collar. "I don't want to interrupt you, Biscuit. I was in the area and stopped by to see if you needed anything."

"Come meet Sam Casperson. He's Margaret's husband."

Millie stood for a moment without doing anything, her hand hovering near the top button of her blouse. Then, when Sam held out his hand, Millie switched the paper bag she was holding from her right hand to her left, and reached forward to shake his hand. "Have we met before?" he asked her. "You look familiar."

"Have you ever stayed at the River Landing? I've worked there forever."

"No, this is my first time in Savannah."

"Well," Millie said, "they say middle age is when everyone you meet reminds you of somebody you already know."

Sam didn't appear to me to be too happy at being labeled 'middle-aged'.

Millie hadn't been gone two minutes when Ernie walked back in, balancing two cups of coffee and a plate of bagels with cream cheese. "Sorry it took so long. I was hungry," he said as he handed one of the cups to Sam and offered me a bagel.

"You just missed meeting Millie, the hotel manager," I told him.

"Yeah," Sam spoke up. "She seemed like a real nice lady."

"She is," I said. "She's been stopping by a couple of times a day to check on Bob and Margaret."

"She sure looked familiar," Sam chimed in.

"Well, you know what they say," Ernie said through a bite of bagel. "Middle age is when . . ."

"Oh, hush up, youngster!" Sam interrupted him. "What would you know about it?"

Shortly after that we wandered down to the cafeteria, and over a quick lunch Ernie, who piled his plate full despite the bagels he'd just eaten, entertained us with stories of his new kitten, Puddin Head. And then, bless his heart, he volunteered to take a taxi back to the Landing and drive my car over to the hospital parking lot for me. It hadn't even occurred to me that I'd be needing it at some point. Of course I would need it. When Bob was ready to go home. So I handed him my car keys.

As we walked upstairs I told him of some of Marmalade's recent antics. And then, back in the waiting room, the two men started reminiscing about Margaret. Sam even whipped out a couple of photos he had in his wallet. I could see that they were wrinkled around the edges. They were curved slightly, as if they'd been in there for years. He handed them to me. I had a glimpse of the top photo. Two or three women and a little girl. It looked like one of those square pictures taken by an old Brownie camera. But then the nurse came in and I gave them back quickly.

"Hey, let me take a look at those," Ernie said. "Are you still carrying these? It's a wonder they haven't fallen apart."

"Sure," Sam said. "When you get back, Biscuit, we'll show them to you."

I watched Bob breathe. Again. I kissed his forehead and brushed back his hair with my hand. He needed a haircut. I made my fingers into a makeshift comb and made sure that his part was straight and his wavy hair was tidy. I thought about how he'd wake up soon and look at me and say something sweet like, "My beloved Biscuit, you have filled my dreams. I have felt your presence here beside me." But he didn't wake up, and he didn't say anything, and I sat there beside him shaking my head and wondering why. Why? Why?

By the time I got back to the waiting room, Sam and Ernie were gone. The volunteer looked up as I walked in and said, "One of those two nice men asked me to tell you they had to go back down to the other floor. Somebody called up here right after you went in and said his wife was beginning to respond."

What wonderful news. Why couldn't it be Bob?

* * * * * *

From the personal notebook of Colly Sloan:

i'm thinkin about that interview with ernie robeson, nephew of margaret c.

he told me margaret found a letter about parentage of this elusive cousin brenda. seems she is not the daughter (heir) of peter a holvers the underwear king.

so, three things havin to do with the holvers under-wear money is one (or two) too many. don't believe in coincidences.

first thing is the fact that our dead body, one bull finney has the same name as peter angus holvers with all the money even if he is dead.

then there's that margaret casperson who knew about the letter because she's the one who found it, and probably showed it to her cousin brenda (dumb thing to do)

and brenda holvers with a new last name (some-body must know what it is) who shouldn't be gettin it (the money) but probably poisoned margaret so she would get it. she meanin brenda. but how does that tie in to bull? must be a connection. can't reach mother mildred to find out last name – she's somewhere in europe, doggone it.

number four: two poisons. nicotine and azalea. one by skin absorption and one ingested. connection? has to be a connection. it has to be this brenda person. makes sense that she tried to do in margaret. but why bull?

doesn't make sense to have a jogger and brenda both killin people. why would jogger want to kill bull? is jogger completely unrelated to this holvers stuff? coin-cidence again? no. jogger must be brenda. makes sense but no motive.

brando and I combed the street lookin for our jogger's house. interrupted millie cappell in her rose garden. didn't know she lived along there. nice yard. said she didn't notice margaret's car on Sunday. doesn't anybody ever watch their neighbors around here? now, she did say she saw two lights on when she left home monday night. no idea which houses.

is this brenda invisible?

Noon
* * * * * *

Millie's voice broke into my thoughts. I glanced up to see her looking around as she slipped into the chair beside me. The waiting room was empty again, and I'd been halfway dozing. Not snoring, I hoped. I ran my hand across my chin, trying to make it look like I was just scratching an itch. I was checking to be sure I hadn't been drooling in my sleep.

"Have you felt lonely, here, Biscuit?"

Lonely? No. Desperate, angry, raging, fearful, disbelieving, shocked, full of dread, furious. And a little hopeful, which I had tried to nurture. "No, not too lonely. There've been some other families here off and on, and a couple of sweet volunteers. The chaplain's come by a few times, and of course, the nurses have been great."

"I brought you a little snack." She opened a paper bag and offered it to me. I pulled out a little plastic container, wrapped in a paper napkin. There was a plastic spoon in its own plastic wrap tucked inside the tidy package. She folded up the paper bag. "I didn't have time to make anything fancy, so I whipped up a fruit cup."

It looked like a deli special to me, but I was sure she meant well. "Thanks, Millie. That's sweet of you. I'll eat it after I see Bob. I'm waiting for the next visiting period." I didn't have the heart to tell her that I'd just had a cafeteria meal, and of course, since it hadn't been four hours yet, I couldn't eat any fruit. Even in a hospital waiting room, I was determined to follow the food-combining regimen that Bob and I preferred. "I'll tuck it right here in my bag so it'll be ready when I am."

"Well, you be sure and eat it all up. It's good for you." She patted me on the arm and stood up. "I need to get back to the hotel. Call me if you need anything."

After she left, I realized I'd forgotten to tell her the good news about Margaret.

Ernie stopped by a few minutes before one o'clock with my keys, and said my car was in the fifth row.

2:00 p.m.

Bless Glaze for house-sitting for me, but I knew she wasn't doing any outside work. As I sat there, I thought about how many spring chores there were to be done in the yard. I'd been ignoring the yard for too long, getting ready for the wedding and such, and then there was all that furor before the wedding–had it been only a week ago that we'd felt like we were under siege? And now here was a siege of a different kind. The watching and the waiting. Well, I could at least make a list of everything that needed to be done once Bob and I got back home. I lifted my journal from my purse and started writing.

1. Go through all the flower beds and weed, weed, weed.

2. Prune any winter-killed branches. Run them through the shredder.

3. Rake the yard thoroughly, and haul all that dead thatch to the compost bin.

4. Dig up the hostas once they've grown up a little more. Divide them and replant.

I could rip out the section of lawn that's tucked up under the tree line and put in a shade garden. There were way too many hostas close around the house. They always fade away to nothing in the winter, leaving the flower beds looking bare.

5. Plant something taller between the hostas by the house, something that would fill in–maybe some nice *Daphne* that would bloom in late winter. Or I could get some *Vinca* started there. Of course, the wintergreen would take over, so I'd have to plan on doing a lot of yanking in a couple of years. At least it's not as invasive as ivy. I'll never again plant that stuff.

6. Go back to the old house in Braetonburg and dig up some of my Grandma Martelson's irises to transplant.

They'd look good by the mailbox and on the south side of the house. And the east side. And the west side–heck, iris looks good everywhere. I remember watching my grandmother heading off to tend her iris patch after all the farm chores were done–not that they were ever done, but she managed to work in some time for herself. She spent that time in her iris garden. No wonder I love those plants. They'll grow just about anywhere, they can be taken up and divided, so a few plants will soon fill an entire flower bed. There are always lots of baby ones to give away.

7. Dig up and divide the *Hemerocallis*.

Daylilies are so hard to divide. I always use a sharp shovel to rip them apart. I remember the first time I ever tried to divide a daylily. I carefully dug up around the plant, making sure to treat the roots tenderly. Then I took a little trowel and gently pushed at the tangle of roots, trying to wedge my way into the mess. Hmph. Now I dig up the whole thing, throw it on the ground and attack it with the point of the sharpest shovel I have. I stomp on the shovel, forcing it through the hardened lump of roots, and finally tear my way through. After I make two or three cuts like that, my big hunk of *Hemerocallis* is thoroughly tamed and has become four or five plants of more civilized size. Stick 'em in the holes I've already dug. Water 'em. They perk up soon enough. Instant garden.

We gardeners really are blood-thirsty creatures. We're always digging with sharp implements and cutting and pruning and shredding and hacking. We tear up weeds by the roots and take perfectly happy plants and move them away from their homes into strange parts of the yard, where they might or might not be able to make friends with the other plants that are already there.

I have a friend who grew up in an Air Force family. She must have felt like a transplant every time she moved. Four different high schools. How did she ever do it? I looked down at my list and added one more item.

8. Stand in the middle of my yard and look around and love it all.

"Ms. McKee?"

There must have been a shift change. I recognized the nurse standing there as the one who'd been on duty Monday night when they transferred Bob from the emergency room up here to the ICU. She was the blonde with the square shoulders. The one who had left half-way through her shift. I couldn't recall her name, and her ID tag was twisted around backwards. I hadn't seen her since that first night.

"Ms. McKee?" She seemed strangely hesitant, and my heart tightened up. She must have seen the fear because she shook her head. "It's okay. He's fine. I didn't mean to alarm you. I came to work early so I could thank you."

"Thank me? For what?"

She sank into the chair facing mine and leaned forward with her elbows on her knees. She looked completely bushed. "Your husband was the one who tried to save Bull's life. Bull's wife is Linda, my sister. She told me how kind you were to her before your husband collapsed. We're both grateful to you."

My husband was at least still alive. And this woman had a dead brother-in-law. A murdered brother-in-law. "I saw you leave the floor shortly after Bob was admitted. Was that when you found out Bull was dead?"

"Yes. Linda was sitting down in the emergency room. Just sitting there, and someone who knew us both asked if she wanted me to come down. It was pure luck I was here for the night shift, since I usually work the evenings."

"I'm so sorry for your loss."

"I'm sorry for my sister's loss. Bull and I weren't great friends at all, but I love my sister very much. My elderly mother is the one I'm really worried about. She freaked out when I told her Bull was dead. She's eighty years old and I don't think I've ever seen her cry, but she threw a fit about his murder. Of course, she always did like him. In fact, I think she pushed my sister into marrying him." She flashed me a bright smile, extended her hand, and said, "My name is Diane, by the way. Diane Williston."

"Call me Biscuit. Everybody does." Everybody except my husband, who wasn't talking. And he called me Woman.

2:40 p.m.

Linda Finney stood in her front hallway waving the envelope like a fan. She hadn't thought to check the mail yesterday. The sultry day held a threat of rain, but without any cooler air yet. They hadn't even planned Bull's funeral, and here was a letter from some law firm in Atlanta. She hoped it wasn't some ambulance chaser.

She took the envelope and the rest of the mail into the kitchen, plopping it all down on the table while she poured herself some lemonade. Sorting mail would be something sane and ordinary to do. Linda supposed she ought to feel something, but she'd already removed herself emotionally from Bull years ago. Heck, her mother was more upset about his death than she was. What was the difference? She had wanted out of his life, and now he was out of hers. She didn't want to seem callous, but that was the way it was. Now she had to a funeral to plan.

The lemonade felt cool on its way down. "Do you want some, too?" she asked her mother who had been tidying up the kitchen as if she owned the place. Not that Linda should be surprised. That was what Mother always did. Even at eighty years old, she never sat still.

Estelle turned and looked at the mail on the table. "Yes, thank you. I'd be happy to sort through that mail for you, too."

"No, Mother. I'll do it."

Estelle dried off her hands and picked up the stack of envelopes. Ignoring Linda's raised eyebrows, she shuffled through it, looking at the return addresses. "Open this one," she said, handing the long envelope to her daughter. "Open it right now."

Linda gritted her teeth as she poured another glass of lemonade and handed it to her mother. "Open it? Why?"

"Just do it. It's good news."

Black print on a heavy ivory stock discreetly proclaimed *Scroop Grey & Cambridge LLC* with an address on Peachtree Street in Atlanta. Linda looked down quickly to see who had signed it. Some lawyer. Derry Murphy, Esquire. She'd never heard of him. There was a phone number at the top and an extension under the lawyer's name.

Linda read the first paragraph of legal talk without understanding where it was heading. It was something about Holvers Enterprises, the underwear company her mother used to work for until she retired. What was this all about? She couldn't see it, until she came to:

> *I, Peter Angus Holvers, being of sound mind and body, declare that this addendum to my last will and testament will govern the disposition of the remainder of my estate, held in trust by Scroop Grey & Cambridge LLC.*
>
> *Peter Angus Finney, born to Joan Fredericks in 1944, first named Peter Angus Fredericks and later adopted by Russell Finney, is the only child of my body and my only intended heir. In the event he is deceased on or before May 1, 1996, his share in my estate, with the below-mentioned exception, will revert to the estate proper to be apportioned on May 5, 1996, to the alternate beneficiaries.*

The letter went on for a bit, but Linda didn't read any more. She turned and handed the letter to her mother. "You knew about this, didn't you? Is this why you pushed me into marrying that s.o.b.– is it?"

"Revert to the estate?" Estelle's face, already blotchy with age, turned a mottled shade of red. "That bastard. No! We've got to fight this. We could do so much with that money. What does he mean, five million? That's all? That's pocket change to him! How could he do this to me?"

"Mom, what do you mean to *you*? I'm Bull's heir."

"We could have had it all . . . we could have had it . . . all."

Estelle threw the letter onto the floor and stomped on it for quite a while. When she was all stomped out, she sank down onto her bony knees beside the crumpled paper, holding her arms crossed like a shield against her breast, and moaned.

Linda had never seen her mother so out of control. She scooped up the letter and continued reading where she had left off. Everything, it said, would revert to the estate to be distributed among the alternate heir or heirs. Except for five million dollars to the estate of Peter Angus Finney. Five million dollars. That's what it said. My gosh! It's a fortune! Linda looked down at her mother, cringing and groaning on the floor. She would never, ever understand that woman.

"This is why you talked me out of divorcing him." It wasn't a question.

Her mother raised her head and tried to stand up. Linda reached out to give her a hand. "We can win," Estelle croaked. "You're entitled to that money."

"No, mother. I'm not, and we won't do anything except call this lawyer back and tell him Bull is dead."

"Linda, you don't understand." Estelle was shaking her finger in Linda's face. "This is a fortune. A fortune. I've worked for this for years, and I'm not going to let you throw it away."

Linda's eyes narrowed. "What are you talking about?" She watched in disbelief as her mother's heavy brows began to contract and tears spilled down her face.

"I knew Bull was Peter Holvers' son," she said, sinking onto the chair across the kitchen table from Linda. "Why do you think I made friends with his mother? I was even her matron of honor when she married Russell."

"I thought you'd always known her."

"Why? Because I called her Joanie and she called me Star?"

"But, that was what Grandma called you as a little girl. She told me that." Linda leaned back against the wooden slats of her chair. "You engineered this whole thing, didn't you?"

"I wanted you to be wealthy. I wanted you to have everything I never had."

"No, Mother. You wanted to run my life. You made me marry that man."

"That *man,* as you call him, was meant to be fabulously wealthy." Estelle spit out the words.

Linda remembered eating watermelon with Grandma in the back yard at the old house. They used to spit the seeds out onto the lawn. Every year, there'd be little watermelon vines growing up beside the sidewalk, and Grandma would pull them up and laugh.

"You would have been wealthy, too," Estelle added, in an after-spit.

Estelle, Linda thought, means star-like. Her mother was about as far from being star-like as Linda could imagine. "Mother," she said, stretching the word out as only a daughter can, "it is quite clear from this letter that we could not win. Bull is dead, and he died before May first."

"Only by two days. One and a half, really. There's got to be an exception to this. He wanted Bull to have the money. All we have to do is . . ."

Linda turned her back on her mother's frenzied diatribe and reached for the phone. "No. You're the one who wanted it. All I wanted was a happy marriage. And look at what I got. I will not try to fight this."

A low-pitched, cultured voice with a British accent answered. "Scroop Grey & Cambridge. May I help you?"

"Yes," Linda said, looking at the signature. "May I speak with Derry Murphy, Esquire?"

"I'm sorry, but Ms. Murphy is out of the office until May 2nd. May I connect you with her assistant?"

"No, thanks. I'll call back in a couple of days."

Linda hung up, then lifted the receiver again and dialed another number. She spoke for a few minutes. Estelle sat without moving, even when the front doorbell rang. When Linda opened the door, there was a tall, blond-haired woman who said, "Is Peter Angus Finney here? I have an appointment with him."

From the personal notebook of Colly Sloan:

got it! the connection. linda finney called station. brando took the call. bull finney is heir to holvers fortune or would have been if not dead. perfect motive for murder. who else had a claim to that money? am I lookin at more possible murders or attempts?

this lets linda off the hook. she'd lose big-time if he was dead—no more money.

anyway, she's diane's sister. and she called me about the letter.

linda's mother estelle—hard woman if I ever saw one—wouldn't have killed him cause she wants to get her hands on the money that's pretty clear from what linda said.

that gal with the tape recorder? turns out she's some professor on sabbatical making recordings of bird songs. it takes all kinds.

found the solitary woman linda told me about. same one I saw in the yellow moon at my party. she's not brenda. no connection. just a lady here to rest. recovering from chemo. wish her well.

gotta find this brenda. know she lives in one of those bunga-lows. how to find her? goin back to look some more. have to find her before she kills somebody else.

* * * * * *

My gratitude list for Tuesday
Bob is still alive. That is all that matters.

my gratitude list
all four of my humans
going within
naps
safety
being a cat

5:00 p.m.

Diane was talking with me when the doctor walked into the waiting room holding a patient file in his hands. Diane excused herself and started to walk away, but I saw her back stiffen as she heard the doctor call me "Mrs. Sheffield." I didn't even try to correct him. By this time it didn't matter what I was called, although all the nurses knew my name was McKee. And one of them had told me she'd written a note about it on Bob's chart.

He was explaining it all carefully to me, referring often to his file folder, but I wondered what he was hiding. "So tomorrow, if nothing changes, we're going to move him up onto one of the regular wards."

"Will he be okay?"

He is alive. Be grateful for that.

"He's completely stabilized. His vital signs are within normal limits." He was choosing his words the way I choose potatoes in the grocery store, one at a time. "He is holding his own."

Whatever that means. With only a bit more emphasis, I repeated my question. "Will he be okay?"

He is breathing. Be glad.

"Mrs. Sheffield, you are asking me for an opinion. I have no answer. He will be cared for. He will be monitored. If anything changes, we will notify you immediately."

"But, what . . ." I paused, not even knowing what to ask.

"You might want to go home now and get a good night's sleep. We won't move him until at least 10:00 in the morning."

"Doctor, my home–my real home–is hundreds of miles from here. This is my honeymoon. I don't even know if my husband will live through this. Please tell me something, . . . something good."

Softfoot wants to be well.

"Mrs. Sheffield, your husband is extremely lucky even to be alive. Nicotine poisoning is almost always fatal, particularly if the poison is absorbed through the skin. The woman who was splashed, the deceased man's wife, is alive only because she's a heavy smoker, which gives her a certain amount of protection. It is the only reason I can think of to justify smoking. You told me that your husband has never smoked. That means he was immediately susceptible to the nicotine."

All because he was trying to help, I thought. He should have known better.

"Death usually occurs within five minutes. I cannot explain why your husband even survived. The fact that his vital signs are stable is encouraging, but it does not preclude his remaining in a coma for . . ."

"For what? For what?" Would the man never get to the point?

You are shouting again, Widelap.

"The course of a coma," he went on with unbearable precision, "is always hard to predict. In fact, it's impossible to predict. I cannot give you false hope, but I can tell you that there have been many instances when someone who has been comatose has returned to consciousness."

Just as I began to see a glimmer of joy, he squelched the little flame. "Even if he regains consciousness, he will need what may be an extensive regimen of rehabilitation to reestablish muscular coordination."

He has been lying still for so long, I thought.

"Sometimes," the doctor continued, "the return to consciousness does not include a return to full mental acuity. Someone from our counseling staff will be happy to advise you about nursing homes in the area, since that may need to be an option. Or he could be transferred to a facility nearer your home."

There was a late afternoon sunbeam coming in the window on the side wall. It played across the carpet and touched the leg of the chair where the doctor was sitting. I noticed that the tight weave of the beige carpet contrasted nicely with the dark wood of the chair leg. There was a tiny feather wedged into the weave. Maybe someone had brought a pillow here for comfort and the little bit of down had escaped.

"Mrs. Sheffield?"

"May I go in and see Bob now?"

"Did you understand what I was saying?"

"Yes. . . . Yes. . . . I did. . . . I want to see my husband. . . . Now."

He shrugged as if to divest himself of the responsibility of having destroyed my hope. He didn't have a clue, though. He had not destroyed my peace of mind. I would not even entertain the thought. I would never believe that Bob would be less than the vibrant laughing wonderful man I had come to love so deeply. The man I had married.

He was breathing slowly and steadily. I sat down next to him and held his hand and willed him to wake up and say my name and tell me that he loved me. After my allotted time, I went back down the hall, picked up my purse and the big bag of toiletries that Millie had been adding to on what seemed like an hourly schedule, and walked out the front door. It took me a while to find where Ernie had parked my car. Thank goodness it was fairly near the front.

In the main lobby at the Landing, Millie Cappell saw me walking in the front door. She looked at her watch. "Biscuit, is everything okay? How are you feeling? How is Mr. Sheffield?"

I took a deep breath. "Nothing has changed Millie. I came back to get cleaned up and take a nap . . ." or sleep for the next five days ". . . and then I'm going back. They're moving him tomorrow to a regular ward."

"What does that mean?" Her concern was so touching.

"It means . . . oh, Millie, I don't even want to think about it."

"Well, let's think about something nice. Did you enjoy the fruit cup?" she asked.

I thought about lying, but I'm a lousy liar. Nobody ever believes me because I blush and humph and dither around, so I told her the truth. "Millie, I forgot all about it. I'm sorry. I tucked it in my bag here. It may have started growing bugs by now, so I guess I'll need to throw it out."

"You poor thing." She looked around at the otherwise empty lobby, then reached out and took my bag. "Come on, I'll walk you up to your room."

"You don't have to bother."

She put her free hand beneath my elbow and firmly guided me toward the elevator. "It's no bother at all."

"Well, thanks." I supposed a little company would be welcome for a short time, but then all I wanted was to get a bath and lie down.

We met nobody in the hall. For a highly successful hotel, this one seemed to be unusually quiet. Of course, the weather was so pleasant, maybe all the guests were out having fun. Phooey on them. How dare they, when I wasn't having any fun at all? And neither was Bob.

Once we were in the room, Millie walked over to the balcony door and glanced outside. "Come on over here and get some fresh air," she said. "You look like you've been cooped up in that hospital for way too long."

Don't!

She should know. She'd been bringing me fresh underwear and clean washcloths and a fruit cup that I hadn't eaten.

"You stand out there on the balcony, right by the railing so you can get a big dose of sunshine. I'll start you a tub of hot water and turn your bed down." She gave me a little push, which started me moving out toward the sunshine . . .

Stop!

. . . but for some reason it didn't feel right, so I turned around rather abruptly. Millie wasn't headed toward the bathtub. She was following right behind me.

"What's wrong, Biscuit? Go on out in the sun."

Do not do it!

"No, I don't want to. I . . ."

Millie took my arm and started moving forward. Whatever was going on? What was this all about? But then her head jerked around as we heard a knock on my door. Something propelled me around her. I didn't think I had put on the double lock, but apparently I had. I slid it open, flung the door back, and in walked Ernie.

"I thought I heard your voice over here. Is Bob okay?"

"He's still the same. What are you doing here? I thought you and Sam were at the hospital with Margaret. I heard she woke up. That's wonderful."

"Yeah, she'll be fine. Her voice is still shaky, and they've told her not to try to talk yet, but she should be back to normal soon. Sam's still there with her, but I came back here to take a nap, and I heard you come in. Are you sure Bob's okay?"

"Yes," I said, as I leaned back against the table for support. "He's stable, whatever that means." I turned to Millie, not quite knowing what else to do. "Millie, I'd like you . . ." She was standing awfully still. ". . .to meet Margaret's cousin, Ernie Robeson. Ernie, this is Millie Cappell. She's the general manager here."

"That's funny," he said as he walked past me into the room to shake her hand. "You look an awful lot like my sister. Of course, I've never seen her. She left home before I was even born, and I've only seen some old pictures of her. In fact, let me show you. I've got one right here." He reached up to his shirt pocket and extracted the photographs Sam had been planning to show me. Selecting the grainy photograph I'd seen earlier from the top of the stack, he said, "This one here is my mother, and that's my aunt. Here's my cousin Margaret when she was a little girl. She's the one who's in the hospital now. And this one is my sister Brenda. They're at the zoo. See? You really do look alike, except she's a lot heavier than you."

She might have gotten away with it if she hadn't panicked. Millie–I still thought of her as Millie–hauled off and hit Ernie, grabbed the photo as he was falling, snatched up my bag, and started toward me. I suppose she was planning to run for it. Who knows how far she would have gotten? But something, some little voice inside my head said . . .

Stop her!

. . . so I grabbed the lamp and hit her with it.

11:00 p.m.

It was Diane who woke me from my snooze. I'd been stretched out on one of the couches in the waiting room. I was tired and sore and probably smelly, too. It was a blessing of sorts that my nose seemed to have stopped working, but I knew that all this time without a shower was going to be a problem soon, if it wasn't already. By the time we'd called Officer Sloan to the hotel, and she'd arrested Millie–Brenda, that is–I'd been away from the hospital so long I didn't even bother to shower and change. I just drove back here. I will probably throw out this yellow polo shirt when I get a chance. It has too many awful memories associated with it now.

"Biscuit." Diane called my name softly.

I couldn't stifle the yawn, so I gave in to it and stretched, too, once I saw that she didn't look worried or anguished or anything like that. "Is it morning yet?"

"No. It's eleven. I'm getting ready to go off my shift, and I wanted to wish you and Bob the best. By the time I come back on tomorrow, he'll be on the other ward."

"Thanks." I yawned again and stretched. "Have you heard what's happened?"

"Yes, Linda called me a few hours ago to let me know that Bull's murderer was caught, but we were busy, and I didn't have time to listen to any details. She asked if we could have lunch together tomorrow. She said she has a lot to tell me."

"If you want, I'll fill you in with what I know." So I took a few minutes to tell her about Millie and who she really was. Ernie had told us all about the letter, which explained why Brenda had wanted to kill Margaret. We still had no idea why Millicent Brenda Cappell (formerly Holvers) had killed Bull and tried to kill me, but I thought Officer C. Sloan would probably have figured that out by now.

A few moments later, the phone rang, and the volunteer nodded to me to pick it up. It was the welcome voice of my dear grand-daughter, Verity. What was she doing out of bed at this time of night?

"Grannie, I'm very unhappy. Bob died."

"Grandpa Bob didn't die, honey. He's going to be okay."

"No, Grannie. Bob my goldfish died. Will you come to the funeral?"

I took a deep breath. "Yes, dear. Ask your mommy if you can put Bob in the freezer until I get home."

"Mommy wants to talk to you."

"That's fine, dear. Give her the phone."

"I love you Grannie."

"And I love you, with all my heart. Good night, sweetie."

I listened to the muted noises of a small child directing her mother.

"Mom, I'm so sorry. She woke up and insisted on calling you before she'd go back to bed."

"That's quite all right, Sandra." I said. "I needed a laugh."

"Is he any better?"

"Not yet, but I haven't lost hope. At least he's not getting worse."

"Well, keep us informed."

"I will," I said, and wondered if I should tell her what all had happened in the last few hours. Not at this time of night, I decided. "By the way," I said, through a big yawn, "I told Verity to ask you to put the goldfish in the freezer until I can get there."

"I hope it's soon, Mom."

"So do I," I said. "So do I."

As long as I was awake, I decided to see if I could go into Bob's room again for a few minutes. He lay there as still as ever, and I was flooded with a feeling of relief that he was breathing. I sat and told him about everything that had happened with Millie who was Brenda, and Margaret who was awake.

"And as soon as you wake up," I added, "I want to tell you about what Verity just said." Then I sat and watched him breathe for a while. "I promised to laugh with you every day," I told his quiet face. "Please let that happen. Please."

And then I took his hand in mine and said, "I love you, Bob Sheffield." As I laid my head down on the hospital bed, I almost thought I felt his hand tighten a bit on mine. I looked up just in time to see his eyelids flutter open. And he looked straight at me.

"I'm hungry, woman."

Those were the sweetest words I'd ever heard.

THE END.
Not quite.

Epilogue

Barry Murphy sold the River Landing Hotel to Linda Finney. He is now traveling around the world.

Linda Finney received the prestigious Hotel Owner of the Year Award by the American Association of Small Hotels. She attributed part of the success of her hotel to her hard-working general manager, **Sally Whitehead**. In a recent trade journal interview, Linda said that she "loved the challenge of restoring the Landing to its former level of excellence."

In October of 1996, **Colly and Patch Sloan** moved from their apartment into a small cottage that they bought from the River Landing Hotel. Colly recently won first place for her "Yellow Lady" rose at the County Fair. She is expecting their first child.

When **Brando Williston** retired, his wife **Diane** switched to part-time work at Guildencrantz Memorial Hospital. They are taking ballroom dancing lessons and competing at the regional level.

Bunny Munson divorced Horse. She remarried two years later and recently gave birth to a premature baby girl, whom she named Catherine. Little "Cat" is reported to be gaining weight and doing quite well.

Horse Munson left town and has not been heard from since.

Margaret & Sam Casperson still live in Martinsville. They don't talk much about the additional money that Margaret inherited, as one of the alternate beneficiaries, during the final disposition of the estate of Peter A. Holvers. They do drive the Duesenberg more often, though.

Conrad and Mildred Robeson live in a modest retirement center in Atlanta. Conrad volunteers with the Service Core of Retired Executives, helping small business owners. Mildred is taking yoga lessons. They formed a charitable foundation with the bulk of the fortune Conrad inherited from Peter Holvers. It is managed by **Sandy Holvers**, who will be retiring next year.

Melissa Tarkington continues to run *Azalea House Bed & Breakfast*.

Ernie Robeson has two cats now. He was promoted to general manager of the catalog company last month.

Derry Murphy was just named a junior partner with Scroop Grey & Cambridge.

"Bird Songs of Savannah" is available on tape from the producers of the popular educational television show *Doodle Bugg's Everyday Biology*. These songs were recorded in Savannah, Georgia, in 1996 as part of the doctoral dissertation of Andrea C. Bugg, daughter of the now-famous **Dr. Dolan Bugg.**

The **thin woman** is in remission. Her prognosis is excellent.

Biscuit McKee drove to Martinsville on Saturday, May 4th to take care of some personal affairs, such as attending the funeral of Verity Marie's goldfish. She returned to Savannah on Monday, May 6th and brought **Bob** home four days later. All is well on Beechnut Lane.

The End
Yes. For now.

Questions for your Book Club's discussion of *Yellow as Legal Pads*

1. Journaling and gratitude lists form part of the structure of *Yellow as Legal Pads*. What functions do you feel they serve in the narrative?

2. Fran Stewart has said in various interviews and in the acknowledgments for this book that keeping a gratitude list helped her to change her life. What has been your experience with gratitude lists?

3. The entries from the journal of Colly Sloan give a view of the way she gradually uncovers evidence leading to the discovery of the murderer. What else do they show about her? Why do you think the personal journals rather than her official police notes are used?

4. Biscuit McKee often tends to *think* rather than *talk*. In what ways does this pattern serve her? How does it create a problem? Who are the people in your life who react in that way? What sort of challenges have you experienced as a result?

5. Nonverbal communication is the topic of one of Dr. Bugg's lectures. If Biscuit McKee, Margaret Casperson, and Joan Fredericks had paid attention to non-verbal communication, in what ways could they each have been forewarned? What role has non-verbal communication played in your life?

6. Compare Margaret's view of Brenda to Conrad's view of Peter. How does each perspective help to define the characters involved?

7. When Biscuit talks about the hat veil and the way it was believed that women needed to be instructed in everything in the 1950's, there is a disturbing foreshadowing of Monica's revelation that, although she was raped in 1955, she couldn't talk about it to anyone. What sort of changes have you seen in the intervening years? Are some things still the same?

8.   Peter Holvers was never caught for having hired someone to murder Ernst Wilhelm III. Is it possible for someone to live a vindictive life and not pay for it?

9.   There are people who swear that their animal companions speak to them. What has been your experience in this realm? Is Marmalade an effective character in terms of furthering the action of the story? Are her comments consistent with your view of the cat world?

10. Fran Stewart has described her *Biscuit McKee Mystery* series as metaphysical murder stories. Would you agree or disagree? Why?

The following is an excerpt from the next book in the Biscuit McKee Mystery Series

Green as a Garden Hose

There were three Diane Marie's in Martinsville. One of them I liked. One of them I loved. And one of them I hated. And now one of them was dead. It was 1996, and Atlanta was caught up in the excitement of the Olympics. My twenty-two-year-old son, who had flown home after three years in Alaska, to attend some of the Games and to be here for my wedding–Bob was my second husband, since I'd been widowed six years ago–asked me if I wanted to go on an adventure.

"An adventure?" I asked.

"Yeah. It'll be lots of fun."

"Like the time when you were nine and we went up into the high meadow and looked for snakes?"

"Oh Mom, they weren't poisonous. And you learned a lot of new stuff."

Scott really believed in learning new stuff. In large part, I had to admit, because I'd taught him that people need to learn and grow all their lives. Stretches those brain cells. Keeps them active and vibrant. Me and my big mouth.

"Are you sure this thing will hold me? What if I fall?" I put my hands up against what from a distance had looked like a solid rock wall. This close, though, I could see the knobs and fissures and cracks and dents. Surely a cliff that had been standing here for thousands of years wouldn't collapse on me or break apart in my hands.

"Mom, just trust it, okay?" Scott leaned back against his end of the rope. "You're not even off the ground yet."

"That's easy for you to say. This is scary, Scott."

"Of course it is. So what?"

So what, indeed. I was, after all, the one who had agreed to try rock-climbing. I just had not envisioned such a steep first attempt. Tightening my hold on a projection at about shoulder-height–I'm five foot seven–I looked down so I could place my feet, shod in an extra pair of Scott's climbing shoes, on a likely bump. As I pulled myself up a good three inches, Scott leaned back so the harness I was wearing snugged up, ready to support my weight.

"Great, Mom. Now try a real step. And don't try to pull yourself up with your arms. You'll get exhausted that way. Use your feet. Those shoes grip the rocks. Make them work for you."

Right.

"Go on, Mom. It'll be fun. You'll see."

Fun. Right.

"Mom?" He didn't sound worried as much as puzzled. Even as a baby he'd had no fear. He would climb up anything, over anything, into anything. And always came up laughing. Maybe laughter would help in this case.

"Tell me a joke, Scott, so I'll relax."

"Okay, why did the chicken cross the road?"

"I don't know why. Why *did* the chicken cross the road?"

"To get to the other side."

"Scott, that's not even funny." But I laughed as I said it.

"See, Mom, it worked. A corny old joke and you laughed anyway. Here's one more. What did the prosecuting attorney ask the defendant in Fairbanks?"

"I give up."

"Where were you on the night of October to April?"

Before I had a chance to register that this was an Alaska joke, Scott was ordering me around again. "Take a big step."

So I found a spot for my right foot. There was this crack, and if I wedged my foot into it sideways, I could . . . No, I couldn't.

"Push with your left foot, Mom, and as you do that, shift your weight onto the right foot."

"Oh! Hey, this works!"

"Yep. Now you're about two feet up. Only forty or fifty to go."

"Thank you for your encouragement, kind sir." I looked for another foothold, moved my hands higher, grabbed a likely rock that jutted out from the cliff face, and pushed with my right foot. Yes! What fun! I'm forty-nine years old and I'm rock-climbing!

Before I started this climb, Scott had free climbed–that means without any rope holding him from above–and had tested the bolts that were already in this section of cliff. When we'd given him rock-climbing lessons for his eleventh birthday, this was where he had learned to climb. This huge L-shaped cliff shuts off the end of the little dead-end valley where we live. The Metoochie River runs through a narrow gap in the short arm of the L, and the small town of Martinsville is nestled between the river and the L's long arm. The valley contains six little towns, one of which is the county seat for Keagan County, the smallest county in the state of Georgia. In fact, it's so small, most Georgians don't even know it's here. There's another little town called Enders, just a short way down the river from Martinsville, but a good seventy miles away by road. As my Grandma Martelson always used to say, you can't get there from here. These cliffs extend the whole length of the valley, so anyone who wants to go anywhere has to drive twenty-five miles up past Russell Gap before they can turn west, away from the river. There are a few places where the cliffs give way to gentle upland valleys with lovely meadows. Some of the families along the river maintain farming fields there. Kenaf is the major crop. But there's no terrain above the cliffs that will allow regular roads. There are lots of places for hikers in these hills, though, since paths criss-cross the uplands.

Rock-climbing clubs from the area had their regular spots all along the valley, but this particular cliff was gentler than the others. It looked plenty steep to my novice eyes, though. It was so quiet here today. We hadn't seen another soul. Just the two of us and Marmalade, who had walked here with us and was prowling around at the base of the cliff.

I am investigating the smells.

The climbing bolts in the rock wall had been in place for years but were still holding strong. As Scott climbed, he hooked his rope onto the rings of the bolts using some little doohickies called carabiners. This meant his rope was always connected to a safety spot no more than eight or ten feet below him, which he seemed to think was safe. I knew he was very well-trained. He'd been climbing for years and had always been safety-conscious. It still sounded pretty scary to me. If he slipped, he could fall twenty feet before the rope would grab. Of course, he had me strapped into a harness below him, paying out the rope. Fat chance I could stop him, though, if he fell. He weighed a lot more than I did. Eventually, though, the line went all the way to the top of the cliff. Scott is lithe and muscular. He made it look easy.

I had stepped back far enough from the cliff that I could watch his ascent without putting too much of a crick in my neck. I saw him climb over the rim of the cliff onto the top. He stood up, looked around, then turned and waved down at me. After a moment he started back down–an act of sheer guts as far as his mother was concerned. He was playing out the rope somehow or other so that he had control over the rate of his descent. I was supposed to be helping from my end, but I think he wasn't trusting me too much, since I wasn't completely sure what I was supposed to be doing. His descent looked terrifying and terrific at the same time. How I longed to do that. Heck, I want to learn how to sky-dive, too, but that'll be a long time coming. It's one thing to think about it. It's quite another to jump out of an airplane.

Now, here I was attached to that rope he'd threaded through the rings. And he was attached to the other end, counterbalancing my weight. I weigh about one-thirty-five, and he's a good three inches taller than I, so I shouldn't worry.

"Mom, you're thinking again. Stop it and climb."

"Scott, what if . . ."

"Mom, let go of the rock right now and lean backwards."

"What!?"

"I mean it. Let go and lean out and see what happens."

So I did. And nothing happened except that I was supported by the harness. It felt kind of like flying, so I spread my wings. . . .

Your arms.

As I leaned back in enjoyment, I glanced up toward the top of the cliff. I could see Marmalade, the orange and white tabby cat who adopted me when I moved here last year. She was peering over the edge at me. How had she gotten up there? . . .

There is a steep trail nearby. It is not often traveled.

. . . Just a few minutes ago she was down here with us, watching me get harnessed up. I knew she was a remarkable cat, at least *I* think so, but I didn't know cliff-climbing was in her repertoire.

I have many talents of which you are not aware.

Half-way up the cliff I paused for an even longer breath. I looked upward once more. Marmalade was still there. I could see her little head craning over the edge. This was exhilarating. This was energizing. This was exhausting. It seemed a shame not to keep going, though. It had been quite a while since I'd hollered anything to Scott. I needed my breath for the climbing. These legs and shoulders of mine were going to be pooped tomorrow. To say nothing of my butt muscles. After the first fifteen feet or so, Scott had stopped calling up encouragement to me, since he seemed to understand that I'd gotten the hang of it, although I was climbing very slowly. I had to look at my feet to guide them to the available fissures and bumps. And I still had to watch my hands. But I was beginning to rely more on touch than sight. I was *feeling* my feet and hands.

As I prepared to take my next step, I heard Marmalade above me, hissing and spitting and shrieking. I've never heard her do that before. I couldn't see her anymore. Instead, I saw something very big, and very dark against the bright sky, something that appeared to jump out over the edge of the cliff and then hurtle toward me. I saw a blur of green. Instinctively, and that instinct probably saved my life, I threw myself flat against the rock, banging my nose in the process. The harness pulled me up tight and then dropped me a sickening foot or two, as Scott saw what was happening. He must have been scrambling to get out of the way himself. Something heavy slammed against my shoulder, and the afternoon went into slow motion. I will have a bruise there tomorrow, I thought. Then I thought, I'm glad I saw it coming so I could get mostly out of the way. Then I wondered where the awful screaming was coming from. It sounded very close.

It was me.

Once I quieted down, I could begin to hear Scott calling me.

"Mom? Mom? Are you alright? Can you hear me?"

I nodded. I couldn't trust my voice.

"Mom, you're going to need to climb down now. I can't help you, but I can talk you down. Mom, you have to let go with your hands. You're safe. Let go of the rock. Lean backwards in the harness, away from the cliff face. Just feel with your feet. I'll lower you down very slowly. Just keep putting your feet against the cliff, each time a little lower. Start with your right foot. Your other right foot, Mom. Don't look down here. Whatever you do, Mom, don't look down."

So, of course I looked. From thirty feet up in the air, a dead body looks somewhat unreal, but I recognized her lime-green shirt. It was Diane Marie. She was blond, and the almost fluorescent green of her shirt stood out against the low-growing ground cover and the gray stones littered around the small lawn at the base of the cliff. Scott had moved off to one side. I guess he realized there was nothing he could do for her. There was a lot of blood. I could see it even from this far up.

To be continued........

Yellow as Legal Pads is the second book in the Biscuit McKee Mystery series. Look for *Green as a Garden Hose*, scheduled for release in 2005.

Marmalade, of course, will be offering her comments throughout these adventures.

Orange as Marmalade, the first book in this popular series, is currently available.

V isit our website often for the latest update on the availability of *Green as a Garden Hose* and other upcoming adventures of Biscuit and Marmalade. Each book in the Biscuit McKee Mystery series will add clues to the mystery surrounding the 1745 founding of the town of Martinsville, Georgia. The 200-year-old puzzle will finally be solved in *White as Ice*, the eighth book of the series.

http://www.doggieinthewindow.biz

You may learn more about Fran Stewart through her website at:

http://www.franstewart.com